# THE STAR OF SIMBAKO

The Sam Harris Series

Book 3

# PJ SKINNER

First edition

ISBN 978-1-9996427-1-6

Cover design by Self Publishing Lab

Dedicated to my parents who
have inspired and supported me
all my life

Discover other titles in the Sam Harris Series

Fool's Gold (Book 1)

Hitler's Finger (Book 2)

The Pink Elephants (Book 4)

The Bonita Protocol (Book 5)

Digging Deeper (Book 6)

Coming Soon

Reviews are welcome.

Thank you for your support.

Go to www.PJSkinner.com for more information and to sign up for news and offers

This book is available as an ebook at most online retailers

# Prologue

**The Village of Fona, Simbako, 1980**

Pakuteh ran through the trees. The thin branches of the thorn bushes whipped skin from his arms making him wince. He did not slow down.

Behind him, light flickered from the clapped-out generator in the compound of the Paramount Chief, Joseph Sesay. The rebels were closing in. They were bound to kill the Chief, who had stayed in his home refusing to leave. Pakuteh didn't want to die too.

He patted his stomach, which was full of stew stolen from the kitchen, and pulled the strap of his satchel over his head to make sure he didn't drop it. He stuck his hand in the internal pocket of the bag, just to make sure it was still there, and it was – hard and unyielding, like a piece of glass, its dead weight and cold lustre giving lie to the power that made people kill for it.

The diamond represented their future. *Had he underestimated the Chief?* A man with that much wealth and power rarely proved to be human. Joseph Sesay had thrust the diamond into Pakuteh's hand, saying it was a wedding present. Pakuteh had been too stunned to question it, stuffing it into his bag as he left the Chief to his fate. He had heard about the fabled diamond, the Star of Simbako, but, like everyone else, he had assumed that it was mythical or long gone.

*But how had Sesay found out that Pakuteh had married Adanna, his only daughter? Why hadn't he objected?* Perhaps because, like Pakuteh, Chief Joseph Sesay wanted his daughter to be taken away, far from their suffocating culture of subservience and black magic. He had done well to protect her so far, but she was in danger of being sucked into the world of violence and voodoo.

If they sold the diamond, they could live a normal life as a married couple in any country they wanted. They could leave Simbako with its primitive ways and join a different culture. There would be no more sneaking around or avoiding Tamba, the Chief's dodgy sidekick. The way he stared at Adanna made Pakuteh's skin crawl. Not that he blamed him. Adanna was tall and willowy with a regal bearing and exquisite face. She had a smile that melted icebergs and a stare which could create them.

He slowed as he moved closer to the river. There were voices echoing across from the river terrace. *Who would be out there so late? Maybe they were trying to find something before the rebels arrived.* He had heard there was a pothole in the terrace, caused by a whirlpool in an ancient river which caught diamonds in the current and concentrated them in its depths. The rebels would steal them all if they found out about it. War is expensive and diamonds are small, valuable and easy to smuggle.

He emerged from the trees, being careful to stay in the shadows thrown by the full moon and peered into the gloom. Two dozen men worked on the pit in the terrace. They were refilling it with sand and gravel from mounds on the surface. A small figure stood on top of one of them, directing operations, his belly mirroring the full moon's roundness. He issued instructions in a strangled tone, urging the men to greater effort.

Pakuteh crept closer to hear what they were saying, forgetting he could be seen in the moonlight. A twig snapped behind him. He spun around to confront his stalker, but a heavy blow caught him on the temple. He was dead before he hit the ground.

# Chapter 1

**London 1990**

A car door slammed shut on the street outside. It woke Sam from a deep sleep. She swore under her breath. Disorientated, she scanned the room for landmarks. Weak light leaked though the blinds from the street lamp outside the flat, illuminating the wall opposite the bed. A familiar poster of Marilyn Monroe clung to the wall, her white dress visible in the dim light.

Sam tried to sit up, but her boyfriend's outstretched arm pinned her to the bed. Pushing it off, she swung her legs over the side of the bed and stood up. The wooden floor was cold underfoot. She tried to locate her socks in the dark, probing along the floorboard with her toes, but only finding the corpse of a fly which crunched under her foot, making her jump.

Simon grunted in protest. 'What are you doing? For God's sake stop messing around, I'm trying to sleep.'

But she was wide awake and she needed to go to the bathroom. She switched on the bedside light, provoking another grunt. Then she got down on her hands and knees and poked around under the bed, reaching as far as possible with her free arm. One sock emerged, covered in dust, and she searched around for the other. Her hand closed over another object that did not feel like a sock, but she pulled it out to have a look. It seemed to be a pair of knickers. She squinted in the bad light. What were those red things? None of her underwear had that pattern. Most of it was from M & S – boring, white high-legs she had bought in bulk after reading somewhere that men liked white underwear best. Presumably this didn't apply to greying knickers with dodgy elastic, but at least she had tried.

As she focussed on the alien panties, she saw that the red things were peppers holding hands and dancing in a row. She had seen them before in a duty-free shop in Madrid. They had been an impulse buy for her sister, Hannah. But what were they doing under Simon's bed? She held them under the lamp. They weren't clean. She dropped them, hoping to make them disappear. Was she even awake? A nasty sensation crept up her back.

She picked the panties up again with the tips of her fingers, ignoring the cold floor, and stumbled into the bathroom, pulling the cord for the fluorescent light. Shutting the door behind her, she leaned against it, locking it clumsily, her hands shaking. The bulb over the mirror flickered. His-and-her toothbrushes cosied together in a plastic tooth mug on the basin like a bad joke.

Leaving the underwear in the sink, she sat on the bathroom chair, the cork seat warm under her thighs. Lowering her head into her hands, she took two deep breaths and then raised her head again to look at herself in the mirror. Her face was etched with misery, her mouth a thin line in a shocked white background. It was happening again and this time it was with her sister.

\*\*\*

Two weeks earlier, Sam had called Simon from the airport.

'It's me. I'm back.'

Sam had tried to disguise her nerves with false bonhomie, uncertain of her reception. The last time she had spoken to Simon, it hadn't gone so well. She blamed herself for that. Simon had panicked when she'd informed him she might be pregnant. For him, as a serial womaniser, this news was not just unwelcome, it counted as a catastrophe. He had said something that should have been unforgivable, but she had given him the benefit of the doubt, telling herself off for jumping the gun before she'd known what was really going on.

She had arrived back in London after attending Gloria and Alfredo's wedding in Sierramar on the west coast of South America. She'd wanted to stay longer to avoid the British winter and the inevitable clash with Simon, but eventually she'd understood that pushing it into the future would not solve anything. She needed to get home and speak to him face-to-face before another day passed.

Simon had had a tantrum when she went to Sierramar to help Gloria look for Alfredo, who had disappeared, and Sam's false alarm on the pregnancy front had unsettled them both. They hadn't discussed it yet and she was still sulking, but Simon was special and she didn't want to lose him. Her mind was filled with thoughts of sex with him as her flight crossed the Atlantic. The Kama Sutra was tame compared to Sam's lurid imagination.

'Sam, you're here already. Great!' said Simon, his voice strained. *Not a good start.*

'Can I come over? I need to talk to you.' She tried to keep her own voice light, but was betrayed by its high tone.

'Aren't you tired after your long flight? Don't bother, I'll come to you. Where are you now?'

'In my flat.'

'Give me an hour.'

'Okay, I can't wait to see you. Can you buy a pint of milk on your way? Oh, and some bread and eggs and –'

'I know what you like. Have a snooze and I'll be there soon.'

'Don't forget the chocolate.'

*That went better than expected. Perhaps they just needed some time together to get back on track.*

Originally, she had dropped into her apartment in Fulham, intending to stow her bags and have a quick shower before going to see him, but now she could wait there instead. Home sweet home. It was always good to be back, surrounded by the souvenirs of her travels, the wooden parrots, the cheap paintings bought in markets, the ethnic wall hangings. The cacti had survived her absence, but the tomato plant had wilted and shrivelled to a thin brown stick.

She switched on the immersion heater and emptied her suitcase onto the bed, dividing her clothes into two piles, clean and dirty. *He loves me, he loves me not.* Ignoring the fact that the wrong pile won, she loaded the washing machine with a dark wash and stuffed the rest of the dirty clothes into the laundry basket. By the time she put the clean clothes from her suitcase back into the cupboards, there was enough hot water in the tank for a shower.

As the bubbles from the shampoo rolled down her back, she pondered the coming conversation. There was no need to worry. Despite his arrogant facade, he craved her company. Sometimes, he needed her more than she needed him. They would sort this out.

She dried herself with one towel, made a turban with the other and climbed into bed. He could never resist her straight out of the shower.

*** 

Simon put down the telephone and addressed Hannah's bare back.

'That was Sam. She's here.'

'So you're planning to see her?'

'She's my girlfriend.'

'And what am I?'

'Jesus, Hannah, we talked about this. I'll tell her about us, but not today. She needs time to settle in first.'

'You're going to carry on as if nothing happened?'

'I'll try. She doesn't deserve this and I can't deal with it right now. I broke her heart once already.'

'What about my heart?'

'You're sleeping with your sister's boyfriend and you're worried about your feelings? Do you even have a heart?'

'That's harsh. I'm not the only one who is selfish.'

'No, you're not. And I've loved our time together, but I have priorities and Sam's one of them. I'm sorry, that's how it is.'

'Aren't you happy with me? Didn't you say you had chosen the wrong sister?'

'I'm confused right now. Give me time to sort myself out. I need to see Sam to be sure of my feelings. Can't you understand that?'

*** 

Simon let himself into Sam's flat. The washing machine was spinning noisily in the kitchen and a couple of new balsawood parrots lay on the table.

Dumping the shopping beside them, he crept into her bedroom and found her asleep, her head on a damp pillow. Her hair had escaped from a towel and was plastered all over her face. He smiled and brushed the hair away, revealing her brown skin with its sparse freckles. He broke off a square of chocolate and waved it under her nostrils. The aroma woke her and she reached out and grabbed it, popping it in her mouth without opening her eyes.

'Yum. More please,' said Sam, chocolate on her teeth.

'Can I have a kiss first?'

'As well?'

'Okay.'

His lips searched for hers and she tipped her face up to his to receive them. She stuck her chocolaty tongue into his mouth as he pressed it to hers. His kiss set off a chain reaction which made her flush with desire. She moaned and opened her eyes to find him peering at her.

'Did you miss me?' he said.

'No, I didn't. I was too cross.'

'Are you still cross with me?'

'No, I'm so sorry about the pregnancy thing. I needed your reassurance. That newsflash must have shocked you.'

'Sorry to be such an idiot. I shouldn't have asked who the father was.'

She wanted to ask him what he would have done if the test had been positive, but they were having a moment, and she was loath to disturb the layer of heat and sex that was settling over them.

What had she wanted to say to him?

He pulled her closer.

***

9

'Sam's back today,' said Bill, looking up from his newspaper.

'Oh, God, what are we going to do?' said Matilda. She paced the kitchen, straightening bits of fruit in the bowl and refolding tea towels.

'I don't think it's our place to tell her.'

Matilda sighed, a mixture of exasperation and resignation.

'But we're her parents. Surely that's what we should be doing. It'll be my place to listen when she finds out. I can't believe Hannah has been so cruel and thoughtless.'

'The wicked sister. Are you sure she didn't get swopped at the hospital?' said Bill.

'I wish she had been sometimes. She's so complicated.'

'Complicated? Selfish is a better word.'

'That too. Can Sam recover from such a double blow? It'll be hard on her.'

'Every black cloud has a silver lining though.' Bill put down his newspaper and stood up to face his wife.

'How can you say that? What silver lining?'

'As harsh as it sounds, this may be the final straw as far as Simon is concerned.'

'That's true. But what if he stays with Hannah?'

'At least they'll deserve each other. Sam needs someone kinder and more faithful.'

'If this episode hasn't put her off for life,' said Matilda, brushing a hair off her husband's shoulder.

'It'll be okay, darling. You'll see.' Bill put his arm around her waist and gave her a hug.

\*\*\*

Sam had returned from Sierramar to find the commodities market booming and plenty of geologist roles on the market. The flood of jobs had led to a bunfight between recruiters desperate to earn commissions in these good times. She had sent out new résumés to every possible source of work and already had some great leads. Even so, she hadn't yet had any interviews.

'I'm afraid they want a man,' said one recruiter. 'I know that it's 1990 and not 1890 and I've told them how qualified you are, but that's how it is. If you weren't a woman, I could get you a job tomorrow.'

Sam was well aware of the stumbling block her gender created in the mining industry. She sympathised with anyone trying to place her in that male-dominated environment. At least the recruiter understood what the problem was. Some agents seemed to think that people wouldn't employ her because of her record of short contracts.

Exploration geology was like that – six months here, twelve months there. Sam couldn't help it if the junior exploration companies worked in countries that changed their mining legislation with their governments and ran out of money just as the markets tired of supporting commodities. Jobs in exploration evaporated quicker than rain on a hot roof.

'That's okay. They'll run out of suitable male applicants. They always do. Push me to the front of the line when that happens.'

'Good girl. Keep your pecker up and I'll keep putting you forward. We'll get there.'

*Keep your pecker up! Huh, well that was the problem – lack of a pecker. Someone has to be the first over the top though. I wish it didn't have to be me. But I chose this I can do something else if it doesn't work out. Besides, I'm a good geologist and things will change.*

She was sorting through her field gear, separating the worn from the worn-out when the phone rang.

'Hello, Sam Harris here, who's speaking?'

'Sam? Hello, my name is Alex Simmonds. Have you got time to chat?'

'Sure, no problem. How can I help you, Mr Simmonds?'

'I understand you're an exploration geologist?'

'Yes, that's right.'

'Are you working?'

'No, not right now. Do you have something in mind?'

'Would you like to meet me for a coffee?'

'That would be great.'

***

Alexander Simmonds waited for her in the bar of Brown's Hotel in Mayfair. It was almost empty and the hotel staff bustled around behind the counter, getting ready for the lunch hour rush. When she entered, he came across to greet her. He was nearer to sixty than fifty, short and bald with a large tummy hanging over his trousers. A button had come undone on his shirt and black chest hairs poked out. The same black hairs were springing out from his collar and growing up his neck to his head where they petered out. He had rolled up his sleeves and the same dark forest covered his arms and hands.

Despite his dishevelled appearance, there was something hard and dynamic about him. *Was he ex-army?*

'Sam? A pleasure to meet you.' An iron grip, but not showing off, just natural. *Definitely army.*

'And you, Mr Simmonds.'

'Alex, please call me Alex. Everyone else does.' He beamed at her. 'Let's get down to business. You may wonder why I called you when there are plenty of men available for contracts.'

Sam hesitated. She didn't want to launch into a diatribe about the unfairness of life, no matter how tempting it was, even if he seemed to be inviting it. Alex Simmonds smiled.

'Oh, don't worry, I don't expect you to comment on the status of women in the mining industry. I understand how hard it is out there. I was talking to my wife about it and she pointed out that any woman succeeding in the exploration arena must be exceptional. That made me think. I asked the Earth Science agency if they had a competent female geologist on their books. They recommended you and gave me your number.'

'Gosh, thanks.' Sam was taken aback at this logic.

'Don't thank me, thank my wife. This contract needs some serious soft skills. Most men who work in the field tend to be a little rough around the edges.'

Sam grinned.

'I take it you agree. Anyway, I have a private exploration company which I plan to take public.'

Shades of Mike Morton, the entrepreneur who had persuaded Sam to go to Sierramar for shares 'which will be worth a fortune'. She had stuffed those share certificates in a drawer somewhere, along with all the other things she didn't throw out because they might be worth something later. She tried not to be disappointed, but he read her expression.

'I see you are sceptical. I have a broker and some investors lined up.'

'It's not that. I can't afford to work without a salary.'

'What do you mean? What makes you think you won't get paid?'

'My last job -'

'Oh, no, I'm not a charlatan. I've done this before. Have you heard of Redstone Resources?'

'Yes, Rio Tinto bought them last year. Were you? Oh!'

*Now she remembered.* She blushed. Alex Simmonds was the ex-CEO of Redstone, which he had sold for eighty million dollars the year before. She'd read about it in the newspaper.

'I'm so sorry. I didn't realise you were that Alex Simmonds. Redstone's a great company. No wonder Rio wanted it.'

Now it was Alex's turn to look embarrassed.

'Thank you. I'm glad you think so. Thing is, I'd like to set up a new business and Simbako is the place to go.'

'Simbako? Is it safe now? I didn't realise the civil war was over.'

'Oh, yes. The ceasefire came into effect two years ago. The UN collected the weapons and everyone returned to work. Anyway, most of the trouble came over the border from their neighbours.'

'That's great news. The geology's so prospective. What will you be exploring for?'

'Diamonds, perhaps gold too, in alluvial deposits. And that's where you come in. Despite having a democratic government these days, the country's still run by the Paramount Chiefs. They don't recognise the validity of the mining licences given out by the government. We must pursue delicate negotiations to persuade them to allow mining on their turf.'

'I haven't worked with diamonds before, although I have experience of alluvial deposits in Sierramar.'

'If you go there for me, I'd like you to establish friendly relationships first. You can do geology too, but not enough to scare the horses. We'll take it a step at a time.'

'Where will I live?'

'In Fona, central Simbako, but you'll spend two days in the capital, Njahili, before you go so you can meet the other members of our team, Fergus and Ned.'

'What do they do?'

'Fergus is the general manager, which covers a multitude of sins, and Ned is his assistant or factotum, if you like.'

'Do we have a budget?'

'About fifty thousand dollars for some preliminary pits and mapping. Oh, and your salary. How does a rolling contract of five thousand dollars a month sound?'

Sam's brain was whirring. *Why did Alex Simmonds think she was the one to lead the project? Could she pull this off? Would the average Simbako male be keen on taking orders from a woman? Would her rudimentary knowledge of diamond geology be enough to see her through? But, as to scaring the horses, she was more worried about looking them in the mouth.*

'When do I start?'

***

'Hi Mummy. I've got news.' Sam's voice was an octave higher than usual due to her excitement.

'What's up, sweetheart?' said Matilda, wrestling with the telephone wire which was stuck under a chair leg.

'I've got a contract in Simbako.'

'Africa! Gosh, that's exciting. Maybe you'll meet Tarzan.'

'I've always wanted to visit and now they're paying me to go there. I can't believe it.'

'Who will you be working for?'

'Alex Simmonds. He used to own Redstone Resources.'

'Will he be paying you, or is it shares again?'

'Cash, thank goodness.'

'Did you say Simbako? Wasn't there a civil war there?'

'The U.N. brokered a ceasefire and collected all the weapons two years ago, so it's safe enough.'

'Hmm, I suppose so. Have you told Daddy?'

'No, not yet. I'm going next week though so it's all a rush. Can I visit for a coffee on my way to the airport?'

'Which day is that?'

'Wednesday. My flight leaves in the evening from Heathrow.'

'That'll be lovely. I'll make a nice coffee cake to see you off.'

'Will Daddy be there?'

'It depends on his schedule. Have you told his lordship yet? I doubt another trip abroad will go down well with Simon. Haven't you just made up?'

'Can't be helped. I'll tell him tonight. He's invited me over to his place.'

'Oh? And what's that all about? Anything I should be told?'

'Don't buy a hat yet, Mummy. It's just dinner and a video.'

'Okay, darling, you know best. See you soon.'

*** 

'Again? For God's sake! Why can't you get a normal job like everyone else?'

Fury and incomprehension made Simon's voice quaver. Tufts of hair stuck out over his ears, giving him his trademark look of an indignant owl. Sam was unmoved by this show of resentment, having been through it all before.

'This is my normal job. And soon I'll have enough money to put a deposit on a flat. I'm still rather young to settle down for the rest of my life.'

'You're not that young.'

'Thirty's not old.'

'It's not young either. You need to have children soon or it'll be too late.'

'I need to marry first. Are you offering?'

Simon went a funny colour. He turned his back on her and sighed. 'There's something important I needed to talk to you about.'

'Can it wait until tomorrow? I'm not in the mood right now.'

Sam's tone was light, but she was scared. *Was this it? Would he go down on one knee? Did she even want to marry him?*

The phone rang, making them both jump.

'Hallo? Hang on a minute.' He put his hand over the receiver. 'Sorry, it's business, do you mind?'

Sam minded, but she shook her head and entered the sitting room, shutting the door. Real terror gripped her. The possibility of a proposal had put her in flight mode. She needed time to think before he asked her. A diversion seemed like the best tactic. She drew the curtains and undressed.

\*\*\*

Simon took his hand off the mouthpiece.

'Why are you calling? She's here.'

'Have you told her yet?'

17

'No, I haven't. This is a delicate matter, Hannah, not helped by you calling in the middle of it.'

'Okay, sorry, I'll call you tomorrow. Good luck.'

'Thanks.'

He took a deep breath and returned to the sitting room where Sam had taken off all her clothes and was posing on the sofa. He frowned.

'I thought you weren't in the mood,' he said.

'I didn't get naked for a chat. This is all yours. Acres of pleasure.'

She gestured at her body, running her hands over her breasts. Simon could resist everything except temptation. He unbuttoned his shirt.

# Chapter II

The train journey to the airport featured the usual blur of scruffy back gardens and graffitied walls. Sam sat by herself, hugging her rucksack and trying not to cry, something that took all of her energy. The last few days had been a nightmare, made worse by her inability to cope with her parents' unarticulated sympathy. She didn't blame them. Strong emotions were anathema to their generation. The fact that the culprit was their other daughter made it hard for everyone to deal with.

After finding the knickers in Simon's flat, Sam had crept out without alerting him. She fumbled around and dressed in the dark hallway. Then she grabbed her handbag and exited his flat, pulling the door to without letting the lock snap shut. If any burglars came, it was his look out.

She had managed to flag down a taxi that had just left its client up the street and was heading back to the centre of town. Stuttering out her address, she had slumped in the back seat and responded with monosyllables to the driver's cheery attempts at banter.

They arrived at her flat where she paid him with cash and let herself in, cursing as the key got stuck in the lock. Once inside, she got into bed, disconnected the telephone on the bedside table and pulled the duvet over her head. Her heart had thundered with shock and adrenaline. She wanted to cry, but the sobs stuck in her throat.

She lay there for hours, trying to piece together the clues. *It must have happened while she was away working in Sierramar, but why did he come back to her if he had fallen for her sister? How long had he been seeing her? No wonder she'd behaved oddly on the phone when Sam called her from Calderon.* Hannah could be selfish and cruel.

Sam had already experienced her sister's need to win at all costs. Even though she tolerated this mania all her life, she found it hard to believe that a woman who could have any man she wanted had chosen her sister's boyfriend.

She needed sanctuary, so she packed her bags and moved into her parents' house.

'Did you know?'

Her mother nodded and hung her head.

'I saw them together. I didn't know what to do.'

'It's okay, Mummy. You're in an impossible situation.'

'I hoped it was a one-off and wasn't sure if telling you would help or not.'

'Cinderella, that's me. The Ugly Sister has gone off with my prince.'

'I'm sorry, darling.'

'That's okay. It's my fault for taking him back. I'll never do that again.'

'Maybe it's for the best. He wasn't everyone's idea of Prince Charming. Shall I make you a cup of tea? There's a lemon cake that needs eating.'

A cup of tea. The Harris solution to everything. Nuclear war, plagues, famines, all made better by a cup of tea.

'Yes, that would be lovely.'

The initial shock had dissipated, but when she'd packed her bags for Simbako, the finality of the situation became clear. She would never get back with Simon. Worse than that, she had lost her sister to him. In doing something so unforgivable, Hannah betrayed their bond in a way that seemed irreparable.

Sam could not deal with such strong emotions. She shied away from conflict, but now she couldn't avoid the consequences. She blamed herself for taking him back more than once. *How had she been so stupid? Simon would never change and the only person getting hurt was her.*

She'd pulled herself together and decided to focus one hundred percent on her job in Simbako. *Let Hannah learn about Simon the hard way. They deserved each other.*

\*\*\*

A commotion in the front part of the aircraft attracted her attention as she buckled her seatbelt. The cabin staff were arguing with a man and directing him to the economy section, but he stood his ground. He had an Irish accent like lazy caramel.

'But my secretary booked me a business class ticket,' he said, putting his hands on his hips.

'I'm sorry, sir, but that's not what it says here. You're travelling in economy.'

'But I'm not supposed to be. Can't you do something?'

I'm sorry, sir. Business class is full today. We can't fit you in. You must visit our office in Njahili to investigate the cause of the mix-up.'

'This is ridiculous.'

'I'm afraid there's no choice. Travel economy or travel tomorrow.' The stewardess folded her arms in defiance.

'You've got me there,' he said, 'Okay, where do I go?'

The stewardess showed him to the seat beside Sam, who took all her belongings off it and stuffed them into the seat pocket in front. He huffed in irritation, but that didn't detract much from the fact he resembled Robert Redford and had the build of an ex- rugby player, taut muscles still showing through his clothes. She tried not to stare at the freckles on his muscular forearms, especially the one shaped like a heart. He didn't appear to notice her and put a pair of earplugs in. Covering his eyes with a mask, he had gone to sleep before the plane had even left the ground.

As the plane sped higher after take-off, Sam dragged her attention away from the hunk sitting beside her and wondered about her decision to accept the job. She had never worked in Africa before. *What could she expect?* Her childhood fantasies about being like Tarzan, making friends with a chimp and hanging out with the elephants only highlighted her feelings of ignorance. *How hot would it be? Would she like the food? Could she persuade the Paramount Chief to work with them?* She hoped they spoke English as she had been reluctant to check with Alex Simmonds in case he thought her ignorant. She fell asleep and dreamt about lions.

Her neighbour woke her as he tried to remove her head from his shoulder. Embarrassed, she checked for drool on his jacket, but there was no damp patch. Since they were both awake, she tried to engage him in conversation, but it was like getting the last drop of ketchup out of a bottle.

'These long flights are a pain, aren't they?'

He grunted.

'Are you going to Simbako on business?'

'What? Yes. You?'

Three words. Not promising. Sam ploughed on.

'I have a contract to work for an exploration company.'

His head jerked around.

'Mining? You?' He examined her with a slight sneer on his face. 'Who are you working for?'

People's incomprehension when faced with a female geologist was normal, but his rudeness made her unwilling to disclose anything else.

'Oh, just consultancy work.'

'Another lemming,' he remarked. 'Well, good luck. You'll need it. If you'll excuse me.'

He got out of his seat and walked to the back of the aircraft where he lit up a cigarette. Every woman in economy class watched him walk by. An attractive man for sure, but the packaging hid a nasty interior. She dug out her Walkman and ignored him for the rest of the flight.

\*\*\*

A veteran of long-haul travel to countries with chaotic airports, Sam expected delays on landing, but Njahili competed with the worst. The queue for foreign passport checks was short, but the only immigration desk was occupied by a woman officer who flirted with every male she processed. The half-light of the early morning illuminated the faces of the passengers, grey with fatigue. Some stretched their calves or listened to their Walkman to pass the time.

When she arrived at the front of the line, Sam got a cursory glance and the usual grubby fingering of the pages of her passport with its peeling visas. The official peered at Sam over the top of her glasses.

'Your husband?'

'Sorry?'

'Your husband. Where is he?'

The immigration official glanced at the man behind Sam, who shrunk under the scrutiny and busied himself with his customs form. Having just lost her boyfriend to her sister, Sam did not wish to discuss the wonders of marriage and there was one way to stop aggressive questioning about her private life in its tracks.

'He died,' said Sam, as she sniffed and reached into her bag for a tissue, using it to dab at her eyes.

'Oh, I'm sorry to hear that. Perhaps you will find a nice man in Simbako,' said the immigration officer, chastened.

Sam wanted to mention flying pigs, but she wasn't stupid. The now sympathetic woman stamped her passport and waved her through. Sam managed a brave smile as she disappeared into an old aircraft hangar converted into a makeshift baggage collection hall.

Two carousels, or what remained of them, occupied one end, but their pitiful state showed that maintenance had long ceased. Hundreds of people milled around large heaps of luggage, shouting instructions to the small boys who separated bags from the pile to get themselves a tip. Sam recognised the Irish man standing beside a heap piled high with bags. The luggage carts arrived and the suitcases were flung off into a new pile at dizzying speed. No-one dared to approach whilst the bags were flying.

'There's mine,' shouted someone.

The crowd of onlookers surged forward and pulled at the stack of bags. Sam realised that she didn't stand a chance in the melee and waited until the worst of the pushing and shoving had finished. She stood back and watched the chaos.

Mosquitos filled the air, each one bigger and more voracious than the last. They circled her, buzzing in her ear. She fumbled in her handbag for her insect repellent. As she removed the spray, a large mosquito landed on her arm and she swiped at it, dropping the bottle. It rolled along the ground, stopping between the gnarled feet of a tall old man in a decrepit wheelchair. The man appeared to be asleep and showed no sign of noticing. Sam approached him.

'Excuse me.'

He straightened, looking up at her, his watery eyes searching her face. The tribal scarring on his cheeks gave them the appearance of a ploughed field and tight grey curls covered his head and neck.

'Hello, my dear, do I know you? I'm sure I'd remember someone with such beautiful green eyes.'

'Gosh, um, no, my name is Sam, Sam Harris. My insect repellent has rolled under your feet. Is it okay for me to retrieve it?'

He peered down at his feet, reptilian in their dryness with long uncut nails sticking out of worn sandals.

'Only if I can have some.'

Sam glanced at him to see if it was a joke. He peered at her and she called his bluff.

'It's a deal.'

She bent down and retrieved the bottle, spraying herself from top-to-toe first so the mosquitos wouldn't bother her. They both coughed in the noxious cloud. She held out the bottle, but the old man stretched out his hands, which were already bitten.

'They love me,' he said. 'Can you put it on for me please? Arthritis, you know.'

An odd request, but it seemed genuine and she had nothing better to do. She crouched at his feet and sprayed repellent onto his hands, rubbing it all over the backs and between the fingers. She caressed the cruel arthritic growths on the joints. The old man purred with relief. She looked up and smiled at him. A smile of pure happiness as she revelled in her career and the surprises it entailed. He smiled too. His rheumy eyes seemed to pierce her soul and transfix her.

A loud voice behind her broke her reverie.

'What are you doing? How dare you touch the Paramount Chief?'

'The who? Um, he asked me.'

'Get away from him.'

Sam stood up and turned around. Behind her, a small, round man of indeterminate age had arrived. He had a pencil moustache and piggy eyes and his head was shaved, leaving a dark triangle on his forehead. A snakeskin belt divided his rotund middle into two equally unflattering halves. He didn't appear to be the owner of the loud voice, but no other potential candidates offered themselves. He grabbed her arm and pulled her away.

'Tamba! That's unnecessary. The young woman helped me. Sorry, he's overzealous sometimes.'

Sam shook herself free of Tamba's grasp.

'Oh, that's alright. I didn't realise I shouldn't touch you. You must be very important.'

'A big fish in a small pond, my dear. I'm Joseph Sesay, Paramount Chief of Fona.'

'Fona? That's where I'm going.'

'You are? How splendid. We'll see you there. Won't we, Tamba?'

Tamba had grabbed the handles of the wheelchair and was already pushing it towards the luggage. Sam moved back in front of them and shoved the bottle of repellent into Sesay's hand.

'Here. Take it. I've got lots in my luggage.'

'Are you sure?'

'Yes, you can give it back to me when I get to Fona.'

She was almost run over by the wheelchair as Tamba shoved it towards her. She jumped out of the way. He stared over his shoulder at Sam and mouthed, 'Stay away.'

She stuck out her tongue without thinking.

'You've just insulted his ancestors.'

Sam recognised the dulcet tones of her travelling companion. She spun around ready to defend herself and saw that he was smiling.

'If they're anything like him, they probably deserved it.'

'Only kidding. Did you get your bag yet? There's a terrible scrum over there.'

'No, I'm waiting for it to die down.'

'Good luck with that.' And he launched himself at the pile of bags, grabbing a large suitcase from the top. 'Bye now, don't forget to buy a ticket for the helicopter.'

*Helicopter? What did he mean?* But he was striding out of the hangar without a backward glance.

The hubbub subsided and Sam moved closer. She held her overnight case between her legs and surveyed the remaining bags without spotting her suitcase. She did a circuit of the luggage while it diminished down to zero. When only herself and another cross-looking woman remained, it was obvious that her suitcase had not been on the flight with her. She let out a sigh.

'Oh, God, I can't believe it,' she said to her fellow victim. 'Do you know where we go to report a missing bag?'

'Yes, I do. This isn't the first time.'

'Did you get it back?'

'Yes, it'll be here on tomorrow's flight. They leave luggage in London when there is a lot of cargo. Come on, we need to go upstairs.' She indicated some shabby rooms at the back of the hangar, accessible by shiny metal steps. *Perhaps the old ones had collapsed?*

They climbed the stairs dragging their carry-on bags and pushed through the door which banged behind them. The woman tending the desk of the left luggage office was talking on the telephone and glanced up in irritation as the door slammed. She showed no inclination to attend to them, turning her back and leaning against the counter. From the bits of conversation that Sam picked up, she was fighting with her boyfriend in a circular argument that threatened to continue for hours.

After several minutes, Sam lost her patience and tapped her on the shoulder.

'Excuse me. We need to report lost luggage.'

'You can wait here. I'm busy.'

Sam's companion said something in a local tongue that sounded quite rude. The other woman hissed something into the receiver and almost threw it into the telephone cradle, which already had a crack running through it.

'What's the rush?' she said.

'We need to catch the helicopter,' said Sam's fellow victim.

*The helicopter again. Why take a helicopter to Njahili? Were the taxi's that slow? Perhaps the centre of town had traffic jams?* Sam had seen the town when they landed so it wasn't far away.

The process of registration seemed calculated to test their patience. Forms were completed in triplicate by inserting pieces of ancient carbon paper between the sheets. Each piece of baggage had its own separate form.

The air swarmed with mosquitos. Sam had given her repellent to the Chief, assuming she could use the other bottles she had packed in her luggage. Now she was defenceless. How could she have been so stupid? She would look like an amateur. Not a good start. She sighed. At least she had covered herself before she gave the bottle away. Now that daylight was setting in, the mosquitos should disappear too.

'Come on,' her companion said, 'we must go now if we're going to catch the helicopter.'

'I'm sorry,' said Sam. 'What helicopter are you're talking about?'

An expression of surprise flashed across the woman's face.

'To Njahili. Otherwise, you must take the ferry from Chena. It'll take you all day to get to town.'

'Where do I get a ticket?'

'You don't have one?' Genuine concern showed on her face. 'Run downstairs. The ticket office is beside the foreign exchange desk. Enjoy your trip to Simbako.'

'Thank you.'

Sam grabbed her overnight bag and descended the stairs into the arrivals hall. She noticed a small booth with a picture of a helicopter on it. As she ran towards it, she saw a man leaving it by a side door.

'Hello? Please, don't go yet, I need a ticket.'

'You're too late.'

'But they lost my luggage. I had to go upstairs and fill in some forms.'

'You should have bought a ticket first. I've shut the desk. You must go by ferry.'

'Please, it's my first visit. I didn't realise I had to buy a ticket.'

'That's not my problem. Take the bus from outside the airport to Chena. You can get the ferry there.' He stalked off without a backward glance.

'You'll need local currency,' said a voice.

# Chapter III

The bus was full to bursting. Sam had to squeeze onto the steps beside the entrance where she hung on to the greasy handrail to avoid being bumped out of the open door. *How could Alex have forgotten to tell her that Njahili town and airport were on opposite sides of the river?* At least she could breathe the cool morning air from her precarious perch as the interior of the bus was claustrophobic. People squashed together, sweating and chatting and sitting on suitcases.

The journey to Chena took an hour and a half, by which time the cheery atmosphere in the bus had evaporated. Sam's legs ached with effort and it was a relief to step down from the door and head for the ferry. She was hoping to sit down and rest on the journey across the river, but, as the vessel came into view, it became obvious they would have to stand again. Designed to transport cattle, the ferry had partitions, but no seating.

The passengers from the airport bus walked up the gangway into the hold and crammed in with locals from Chena and the goods they were taking to sell in Njahili. Sam walked aboard and placed herself against the side of the ferry. She leaned her bag against the rusty paint and, half-sitting-half-standing, readied herself for the crossing. The journey was becoming an ordeal. No wonder everyone was so obsessed with taking the helicopter.

The ferry set off across the estuary; its engine belching clouds of diesel smoke which hung over the hold, making Sam feel sick. The tide ebbed at full strength, pulling the boat down river away from their destination. The ferry rode low in the water and waves broke against the sides. Salt water accumulated in the bottom, sloshing around their feet.

Sam stood up and balanced her bag on top of her foot so the water would not seep into it. People murmured and glanced nervously about the boat. Their anxiety was catching. Sam willed the boat through the swell. The vessel might be safe enough, but it felt precarious as it bounced between the waves. She bet herself a million dollars they didn't keep life jackets on board. Would she make it to shore if the boat sank?

The water washed over her shoes and crept up her trouser legs. She lifted the bag higher, her arms tiring with the effort. On her right, a woman pulled out a rosary and started muttering invocations. Sam tightened her grip on the bag, her heart racing. She tried to focus on the shoreline which loomed closer, wooden houses sloping on its banks. The size of the waves increased as they turned upriver to head for the jetty. One large wave broke over the boat, soaking people and their goods. Just when the tension on the ferry became unbearable, the currents diminished as they entered the leeward side of the promontory which sheltered the small harbour.

They docked to a show of great relief, the passengers spilling out onto dry land with shouts of delight. Sam dropped her bag on the quay, her arms aching with effort and her heart thudding.

'How do I get to Njahili?' she asked a well-dressed woman whom she recognised as having been on the bus from the airport with her.

'The bus leaves from the quay to the centre of town, or you can get a taxi,' said the woman. 'Where are you going?'

'The Plane Tree estate.'

'I'm going there myself. Do you want to ride with me? We can share the cost.'

Sam made a quick decision, taking the lady at face value. They were both in the same boat, or had been.

'That would be great. I don't think I can face standing up again.'

'You wait here and I'll get one for us.'

Minutes later, an ancient vehicle pulled up alongside with the lady in the back. The taxi had seen better days. The door and window handles were missing. The windows had been jammed open with newspaper stuffed between the doorframe and glass. The driver had wired the boot shut, so Sam stood uncertainly with her bag on the pavement.

'Get in,' said the driver. 'Put your bag on the front seat.'

He threw open the door, which sagged on its hinges. Sam put her bag inside and shut the door with caution. She tried not to be judgemental about the state of the car, sliding onto the seat beside her companion. The springs in the back seat poked through the cushions and she found it difficult to sit without impaling herself. Her companion passed her an old newspaper without comment. Sam slid it under her bottom and smiled gratefully.

They set out, pottering along the bumpy road. The heat became suffocating as the sun rose in the sky. There wasn't any air-conditioning in the vehicle and her back soon stuck to the plastic seat covers. The drive into Njahili took them past shanty towns of wood and breeze-block houses with corrugated iron roofs built along roads of red earth littered with ruts and potholes. Tall palms lined the route, interspersed with wide mango trees under which local traders had set up rickety tables groaning with fruit. Small children played football and bent over games of marbles in the gutters. Washing lines festooned the streets with old clothes, some no better than rags, like a poor man's Christmas decorations.

As they got into the suburbs, the buildings contained more storeys and some even had balconies, also being used to dry washing. The road surface changed from mud to gravel and patches of tarmac appeared. Instead of speeding up the journey though, the change coincided with an exponential increase in traffic and their taxi struggled to go above walking pace. Added to that, the road also now thronged with people walking in the street because stalls containing fruit and vegetables and clothes and household goods occupied the pavements.

The taxi stopped on a bridge going over an open sewer. About three metres wide, it contained a stream of filthy water snaking through piles of rubbish and discarded plastic bags. Pigs squealed in the putrid soup and, to Sam's horror, several small children played there with the swine. One of them squatted down and defecated where he stood. Nauseous, she turned away, trying not to breathe too deeply as the foul stench filled the taxi.

'It's disgusting, isn't it? Last month, a dead body lay in one of these and no-one would remove it in case they were made to pay for the burial.'

Sam nodded, afraid to open her mouth. She stared upwards at the birds' nests of telephone and electricity lines and tried to trace them through the air. She wondered how anyone survived such an upbringing. The imagined Africa of her childhood was a universe away from the stark realities of life in the slums here in Fona.

Leaving the suburbs, they drove through the centre of town, a mix of faded colonial houses and stark concrete blocks with no cladding, uphill into a leafier, cleaner part of town with a predominance of colonial villas, where the wires became untangled and the sewers were covered. Sam's fellow passenger alighted at the edge of a tree-lined road, waved and hurried away. After the woman disappeared around a corner, Sam realised that she hadn't given the driver any money.

'Excuse me,' she said to him, 'why didn't she pay anything?'

'Oh, she told me you'd pay.'

'But we agree to pay half each.'

'I'm sorry, but that's not what she told me. She fooled you, eh?'

'Fooled me?' Sam blew the air out of her lungs. 'I guess so.' She had not imagined that a well-dressed and educated woman would be so dishonest. For a minute, she considered jumping out of the car and running after her, but the taxi driver might drive off with her bag so she chalked it up to experience.

'Are we nearly there?'

'Yes, madam, five minutes.'

They pulled up alongside a high wall with a metal gateway for vehicles into which someone had cut a smaller door. After paying the driver and getting a receipt, as she hoped Alex would reimburse her fare, Sam pressed the rusty door bell. To her relief, the door opened after a short delay and a tiny old man as shrivelled as a raisin and the same colour beckoned her inside. Sam lifted her bag over the doorframe and stuck out her hand.

'Hello, I'm Sam. Who are you?'

'William, madam.' He took her hand cautiously as if she might be concealing something in it.

'Nice to meet you, William. Please can you take me to see Mr Simmonds?'

'Mr Simmonds isn't in the country. Only Mr Dockrell and Mr Hunter, but they aren't at home. They left to have lunch.'

'Oh?'

'They thought you had missed the flight. Mr Dockrell said he searched for you at the airport but couldn't find you.'

'My luggage went missing and I had to go upstairs to report it. By the time I'd finished, the helicopter ticket office was shut and I had to take the ferry.'

'The ferry?' A look of alarm crossed his features.

'Yes, it wasn't much fun, but I'm here now. Perhaps you will show me to my room instead?'

They entered a typical colonial style villa with shuttered windows and high ceilings. The paint on the walls had peeled in the heat and she had to stop herself reaching out to pull a strip of it off. Her room sat at the back of the house. It had a wooden floor and stained net curtains. There were no mosquito screens on the windows, nor a net over the bed.

'Will you bring me a mosquito net please?' asked Sam.

'The gentlemen don't use them. They say if you have enough whisky in your bloodstream, it will keep them away.'

Sam sighed.

'Is there somewhere that I can buy one tomorrow?'

'I can get one for you when I shop at the market.'

'How much do you think it will cost?'

'Not much. You can pay me back after I buy it.'

'Thank you. Where can I wash? It's been a long trip.'

'Down the hall on the left. No hot water, I'm afraid. If you want to leave your dirty clothes out on the landing, I'll wash them for you.'

'That would be great.'

William backed out of the room, shutting the door behind him.

*Dockrell and Hunter! They sounded like a firm of shifty lawyers. This time, she was her own boss. No-one except Alex could tell her what to do.*

She walked down the hall and found the bathroom. A clean towel sat on the shelf and she found some ferocious smelling soap in the shower. She steeled herself for the cold water and stepped in.

After her shower, she padded back to her room, leaving her clothes on a stool in the landing. She climbed into bed and pulled the sheet over her. Her room was flooded with sunlight and the gecko in the corner revolved its eyes in their sockets as he hunted for prey. Several epic cobwebs hung high from the ceiling, looking like magic cloaks with their coverings of jewelled fly carcasses. Sam drifted off to the sound of people talking in the street outside and the far-off honking of car horns.

She woke at dusk and lifted her overnight bag onto the bed. She had had the foresight to pack several day's clothes and supplies. They should last until her suitcase reappeared.

She snapped open the lock and flipped it open. Her hand flew to her mouth in horror. A pink frilly shirt and some white shorts were the first things she saw, underneath which lay various pink T-shirts and lacy underwear. Hannah's clothes.

The evidence of her weekend away with Simon. Worse still, when she tipped everything out, she found empty condom wrappers in the inner pocket. She had taken the wrong bag. *How on earth had that happened?* But then she knew.

Hannah had arrived at her parents' house as Sam left for the airport and rushed upstairs to hide when she realised that Sam hadn't left yet. Not that Sam had wanted to see her. She wouldn't have been able to think of anything to say to her. Or to Simon either who hadn't bothered to look for her after she had left his flat. The message written in lipstick that Sam left on the bathroom mirror had been clear enough. It said, 'These are not mine' and an arrow pointed to down into the basin where Hannah's knickers lay with their soiled crotch on show. Even Simon was not stupid enough to try to explain away their presence.

Hannah's arrival at her parent's house disoriented Sam who had hoped to leave the country without seeing either Simon or her sister. While her mother had flapped her hands in the background, she only dimly remembered her father carrying her bags to the taxi. He must have picked up Hannah's overnight bag by mistake. It was an easy one to make as they owned the same bag as they had both been given them by their mother for Christmas.

So now she was forced to wear the clothes of her harlot sister, ironically taking the place of the woman who took her place. Some of them even smelt of her. They radiated glamour and were definitely not appropriate for field wear. Oh, God, could the day get any worse?

She opened the door to her room, hoping to retrieve her dirty clothes from outside, but William had spirited them away to the laundry. She considered going downstairs in her towel to see if she might rescue them. Then she heard a voice she recognised, floating up the stairwell.

***

'You're Sam? Jaysus. I'd no idea. I was looking for a man.' It was her fellow passenger, the Irish man from the plane.

'Do I look like a man?' said Sam, her expression indignant.

'I meant I was expecting a man.'

He ran his hands through his sandy hair and wrinkled his freckled face. Still handsome, still horrible. He looked her up and down as if appraising her for market and raised an eyebrow. Sam stood awkwardly at the door. She had dressed in Hannah's frilly shirt and denim shorts and they didn't leave much to the imagination. She tried to be nonchalant, which was hard when she felt so exposed.

'You didn't ask me my name,' she said. 'What's yours?'

'Fergus Dockrell, and this fine man is Ned Hunter.' He indicated his companion, a slim man of average height with thinning hair and piercing grey eyes who wore filthy overalls.

'Alex wants me to go to Fona to start up the diamond project down there.'

'By yourself?' Fergus' face was a picture. 'Anyway, what kept you? I lost you in the airport. I thought you'd be on the helicopter.'

'My suitcase got left behind in London, so I needed to register with the left luggage office at the airport. By the time I'd finished filling in all the forms, it was too late to buy a helicopter ticket.'

'You seem to have found something to wear anyway.' He snorted, joined by Ned.

Sam coloured. 'These are my sister's clothes. It's a long story.'

'Did you come on the ferry?' asked Ned.

'Yes, a scary experience. I won't be doing that again.'

'Those things are lethal. One got swamped recently. It sank, killing most of the people on board.'

'Water washed over the sides –'

'Okay, so you're here anyway. Why don't we all eat something?' said Fergus.

'Have you got repellent I might use? Mine is in my suitcase.'

'Repellent? I don't use that shite. It'll give you cancer. Ned?'

'I'm so hard mosquitos bounce off me.' He laughed at his own joke.

Sam pretended to laugh too. Tempted to ask to borrow trousers to keep the mosquitos away, her pride would not let her. Their cigarette smoke would do the trick. Mozzies hated it almost as much as Sam hated smoking.

She climbed the stairs to get money.

***

'Did you see those shorts she's wearing? Who does she think she is? Daisy Duke? What sort of geologist is she?' said Fergus.

'Your prejudices are showing. Since when have clothes anything to do with brains? If Alex took you at face value, you wouldn't be here either.'

Fergus reached up to his hair and tried to smooth it down. It sprang up in the same wild arrangement as before.

'It's not like my clothes have anything to do with my ability.'

'So how come you think it's alright to criticise her for it? Anyway, didn't she say they're her sister's clothes?'

To tell the truth, Ned agreed with Fergus about Sam's tarty outfit, but he didn't want to say so. She could be a working girl, but not the geology sort, in her miniscule shorts and frilly shirt. In fact, he rather fancied a roll in the hay with her. He imagined ripping that shirt off in double-quick time. Even the cross look on her face and the awkward way she held herself didn't put him off.

'Give her a chance. Alex's not a fool. He must have seen something he liked.'

'I'm not surprised if she wore those shorts.'

\*\*\*

Hannah got back to her flat and threw the overnight bag on her bed. *How typical of her mother not to warn her that Sam would pass by the house before she flew to Simbako.* Hannah had dropped in to see her parents on her way back from a weekend with Simon. When she had spotted Sam's luggage in the hall, she'd run upstairs and hid in the bathroom, emerging after she'd heard the door slam as Sam left to catch the train to

Heathrow. Then she had to put up with her mother's exasperated sighs and her father's puzzled silence. She couldn't leave there fast enough.

She flicked the catches on the bag and flipped it open.

'What on earth?'

She picked up the khaki trousers between her thumb and index finger as if they might contaminate her with their utilitarian nature. Underneath, threadbare T-shirts, greying knickers and some field notebooks made up the contents. A bottle of deodorant rolled off the bed and under the nightstand. She realised with horror that her new shirt and shorts had gone on a trip to Simbako. Purchased with her credit cards, she didn't technically own them yet. Sam would probably wear them in the jungle to get back at her.

'Bugger.'

\*\*\*

Sam ate dinner with Ned and Fergus in a sports bar on a small peninsula that poked out into the Njahili estuary. A stiff breeze blew through the tables, keeping the mosquitos away. They ordered standard expat fare of steak or fish with golden chips. Everyone attacked their meals in silence and watched a game show on the television with half-naked girls and a plump moustachioed host.

'Which football team do you support, Sam?' said Fergus.

'Um, Leeds. I know it's not fashionable.'

'Aren't you from London? How come you don't support Fulham or Arsenal?' said Ned.

'My father is from Yorkshire.'

'And your mother?' said Fergus.

'Cornish.'

'Now that explains a lot,' said Ned, 'we've got a mining pirate in our midst.'

'Steady on now,' said Fergus.

'Do you have much experience working in Africa, Sam?'

'This is my first visit to Simbako.'

'How do you like it so far?' said Ned.

Sam made a face. 'So far, they've lost my bag, forcing me to dress like a hooker, abandoned me in the airport, tried to drown me on the ferry and swindled me in the taxi. I imagine it's par for the course.'

'It won't get better, you know,' said Fergus, with the air of someone who had experience in these matters.

'That's okay. I'm made of tough Yorkshire stock.'

'Why do you have your sister's clothes? I'm guessing she's not a geologist,' said Ned.

'It's a long story. I'll tell you another time.'

She made it through the evening in the restaurant without a single mosquito bite, but several of them bit her on the way back in the car. They hid under the seats and she didn't notice until she got to the door of her room that there were the tell-tale welts on her calves.

She dreaded sleeping unprotected in the villa with its leaky windows. To her relief, she found a brand-new mosquito net set up over her bed, tucked in to prevent invaders. William was a treasure. She made a note to pay him back in the morning and fell into bed just as the generator switched off, reviewing her day in the pitch-black of her room.

The airport debacle hadn't been the best start, but the day had improved once she got to the villa. Her two companions were like chalk and cheese. Fergus, being the general manager of the company, could have cramped her style, but he showed no interested in interfering with her project. 'I've got my priorities.' Whatever they were.

And Ned seemed to be a factotum at Fergus' beck and call, tolerating his job more than he enjoyed it. Despite her first impression, she should fit into Njahili Resources without too much pain. She couldn't guess what awaited her in Fona, but she was ready for anything.

# Chapter IV

Sam woke up early the next morning and opened the shutters. She gazed down at the backyard where dusty chickens pecked the concrete. To her delight, she saw her trousers were hanging on the line and they seemed dry enough to wear. Putting on her sister's shorts and another pink T-shirt from the overnight bag, she bounced down the stairs out into the backyard. Her trousers were flapping in the breeze, pinned to a rope with some homemade clothes pegs. She reached up to remove them.

'Madam, you can't wear them yet. I haven't ironed them,' said William, appearing from an outhouse.

'Oh, you needn't do that. It's a waste of time to iron clothes. I'm desperate to take these shorts off.'

'But I have to iron them.'

'No-one will notice.'

Sam hopped from foot to foot in her impatience. William smiled.

'You will, madam. The tumbu fly will get you.'

'The tumbu fly?'

'Yes, it lays eggs on clothes as they dry on the line. When you wear the clothes, the eggs hatch and the grubs burrow under your skin.'

'Under your skin? How do you get rid of them?'

'They emerge after about three days. Or you can go to the doctor.'

'Ugh, how disgusting!'

'Mr Fergus wouldn't listen and he got one in his arm.' How unsurprising.

'What does the ironing do?'

'It kills the eggs. Please be patient, madam. I'll iron them shortly and give them back to you.'

'Thank you.' She turned to go. 'How much do I owe you for the mosquito net? I'm grateful to you for buying it.'

'I'll put the receipt on your bed with the trousers later this morning, madam.'

Mollified, Sam went back indoors and found the men eating breakfast.

'I'm starving,' she said.

'I wouldn't eat too much if I were you,' said Fergus, 'those shorts are tight already.'

Sam blushed. She loved breakfast, but now she was too embarrassed to eat.

'Don't mind him. Help yourself,' said Ned, sliding over a plate of ham and cheese.

'Don't say I didn't warn you,' said Fergus. 'Oh, yes, the airline called. They have found your suitcase and they put it on today's flight. It'll be at the Grand Hotel this afternoon.'

'I'll take you,' said Ned, 'I've got stuff to pick up in town.'

'That'd be great,' said Sam.

'We need to get you up country as soon as practical. I've a meeting in town tomorrow morning, but we can set out after that,' said Fergus.

'As long as I have my stuff, I'm ready to go when you are,' said Sam.

'Ned, I need you to do the logistics.'

'Leave it with me.'

\*\*\*

The Grand Hotel sat in the colonial district of Njahili, an area clustered with government buildings. The streets contained fewer people and newer cars. U.N. vehicles, big white Toyota four-runners with smoked glass windows, bossed the roads and took up most of the parking spaces. Aid agencies jostled for attention between the government departments, their chrome and glass exteriors contrasting with the faded glory of the colonial offices. A line of enormous palm trees grew along the centre of the road, throwing their shade onto one pavement so people congregated there to stay out of the ferocious heat. Ned parked the car on the sunny side of the street and they crossed the road, avoiding the pools of green slime in the gutters.

They entered the hotel through an ornate entrance. Two stone lions guarded the doorway and a gilded cupola embellished with irises soared over the foyer. Light flooded down from skylights onto a central waiting area bordered by large-leafed plants and a faux Louis XIV chaise longue and matching armchairs. Groups of well-dressed people murmured across tables scattered with the remnants of afternoon tea.

'Wow, this is nice,' said Sam. 'You'd never know from the outside.'

'You can't tell a book by its cover,' said Ned. 'Follow me, the luggage office is under the stairs.'

He gestured at a staircase at the back of the foyer which swirled left and right into the cupola. The carpet had long since worn out and someone had taken it away, leaving only the redundant, brass stair rods as evidence of its former existence. He headed into a corridor behind the staircase which led to a dusty room policed by a man in a purple uniform.

'Good afternoon, sir and madam.'

'Good afternoon. I'm here to collect my suitcase please,' said Sam.

'Which flight did it come on?'

'It's on today's flight from London.'

'Ah, I'm afraid that the flight arrived late. The luggage hasn't arrived from the ferry terminal.'

'When are you expecting it?' asked Ned.

'It should arrive in an hour, sir.'

Ned turned to Sam.

'It'll take us that long to go home and return in the rush hour. Longer. Let's have a drink instead. There's a nice bar here.'

'Yes, please, I hate being stuck in the traffic.'

'Okay then. We'll be back,' he said to the concierge.

'No need, sir. I'll send someone to get you when the suitcase arrives. Can I take your wife's name?'

Ned snorted.

'I'm not his wife,' said Sam, 'but that would be wonderful. My name is Sam Harris.'

'Come on, darling,' said Ned.

'Don't darling me,' said Sam, but she couldn't help laughing. 'If you're my husband, you can buy me a gin and tonic.'

They skirted the foyer and entered an old-fashioned snug with velvet booths and scratched mahogany tables. It smelled of cigars and her shoes stuck to the carpet, but it had an appealing atmosphere. Sam sunk into one of the soft, circular seats lining the booths.

'Lemon and ice?' said Ned.

'Is the ice safe here?' asked Sam.

'Yes, they've a lot of foreign clients, so they can't afford to poison them.'

'Okay, lemon and ice then. Thanks.'

Ned made his way past the tables to the grandiose bar with carved vines and grapes running around the supporting beams and posts. Sam observed him chatting to the barman and noticed how soon the man relaxed under the full beam of Ned's everyman charm. Ned had shaved and changed out of his overalls, presumably due to visiting the hotel. It gave him a younger and more vulnerable appearance. He was not handsome like Fergus, but he was attractive in all sorts of ways that Fergus was not. Fergus mirrored Simon and that was enough to put her off.

Sam tried to imagine the fallout of her departure from England, but it made her tired. Neither Simon nor Hannah had enough empathy in them to worry about how hurt she was. Although difficult to ignore, any time spent thinking about them was better spent getting on with her new job.

'Earth to Sam.'

Ned stood in front of her with the drinks.

'Oh, sorry, miles away. Yum, that looks good.'

Ned had brought a plate of olives and another of pistachios still in their shells.

'Are you alright, Sam? You look sad.'

'I'm fine. Just boyfriend trouble. Well, not trouble, more like extinction.'

'Sorry to hear that. He must be stupid to leave a woman like you.' He hesitated. 'I mean, someone so, so …'

Sam looked at him in amazement.

'What?'

'Nothing. I lost my train of thought there.'

'Are you married, Ned?'

'No, well, yes, no, really.'

'Sorry, I didn't mean to embarrass you.'

'No, I, my Gemma left me for another man. We aren't divorced yet.'

'She must be stupid too,' said Sam, drink making her braver than usual.

'Thanks. Cheers. Here's to being left on the shelf.'

'Cheers.'

They sat in silence for a while, sipping their drinks, immersed in their thoughts.

*** 

Both drunk, they stumbled into the front door of the house in their compound as they giggled and tripped over Sam's heavy suitcase.

'What you got in here? Gold bars?' said Ned.

'Rocks. I'm a geologist, you know.'

'Yes, you mentioned that.'

'Where the fuck have you been?' Fergus was sitting at the table in the dark, an empty glass in front of him.

'Steady on there, old chap. We've been at the Grand Hotel, remember? Getting Sam's suitcase.'

'The plane arrived late. We had to wait for hours in the bar,' added Sam.

'And how was I supposed to know? You might have been in an accident.'

'Sorry, mate. They told us it would be an hour late. I didn't realise it would take so long,' said Ned.

'Why didn't you call me? I waited for ages to go to dinner.'

A self-piteous tone had crept into his voice, like an abandoned child.

'Sorry. We should've called, but we got drunk and forgot.'

They stood together swaying. Fergus stood up and pushed Ned out of his way. Grabbing Sam's suitcase, he lumbered up the stairs, muttering to himself. Sam caught Ned's eye and mouthed, 'Oops'. He raised his eyebrows.

'Night, night,' she said and grabbed the bannister, pulling herself up the stairs. Ned sat down on the bottom step and held his head.

'I don't want to sleep. I'm afraid of waking up with a massive hangover.'

'Too late for remorse,' said Sam.

Fergus had dumped her bag on the landing and stomped off to bed. She hauled it into her room and left it on the floor unopened.

*\*\*\**

The next morning Sam did not greet the sun with her usual glee. Some evil genius had invented a new form of torture while she slept, which involved poking the back of her eyes with a screwdriver. She could remember arriving at the house to a sullen reception from Fergus, who had appeared to take their drunkenness personally.

Her suitcase lay abandoned in the middle of the floor. She couldn't imagine how it got there as she didn't bring it upstairs.

Did Ned put it there? Oh, God, she hadn't invited Ned into her room, had she?

She had wanted to. That was the problem with drink. It made sex seem like an excellent idea. She hadn't thought about Simon though and it was as if he had never existed.

'This extinct boyfriend of yours? Why was he obliterated?' said Ned, at the hotel.

'He took a fancy to my sister.'

'Your sister? What a bastard! Mind you, your sister doesn't come out of this with a halo either.'

'No, and that's the worst thing. Boyfriends are replaceable. Sisters less so.' Her voice had caught at the back of her throat. He'd touched her arm in sympathy, brushing hairs desperate for contact which stretched up to meet his fingers.

'Have you talked to her about it?'

'No, not yet. I couldn't face it and it would've been pointless. She's always got a justification for her behaviour which changes as you argue so you're never right. It's just tiring.' She sighed. 'Truth be told, we were coming to the end of the road anyway, I just didn't realise it. I don't blame Hannah.'

'You planned to break up with him?'

'No, but I got it into my head that he planned to ask me to marry him and, instead of being excited, I panicked. Does that seem weird?'

'No, not weird, sad maybe.'

Sam had hesitated and Ned glanced at her fiddling with a beer mat, twisting it around in her long fingers.

'I loved Gemma,' he'd replied to her unasked question, 'but we shouldn't have got married. We were too young and not suited.'

'How long did your marriage last?'

'Five years. It pottered along just fine until I worked abroad a lot. She didn't last a year with me gone.'

'I'm sorry.'

'Me too. Want another?'

All the hurt surrounding Simon's betrayal with Hannah had seemed to evaporate up into the cupola as she talked about him. She hadn't been sure about their relationship being finished until she'd said it out loud to another person.

She was developing a crush on Ned. Empathy had morphed into attraction by the time the luggage porter came for them. From the way he hung on her every word, the attraction was mutual.

Then she'd remembered it was Fergus who carried the bag up the stairs and not Ned. No chance there. He assumed he was God's gift to women and out of her league. Not that she fancied him. Well, not much anyway. Despite her hangover, she giggled at the idea. He might be nasty, but bad boys always interested her. She had landed in a box of chocolates. So many flavours to choose from. She was on a diet after the Simon fiasco, but no harm in looking if she didn't touch. Professional to the last.

She opened the suitcase with trepidation, but no-one had disturbed the contents. Selecting a pair of khaki trousers and a linen shirt to wear, she sprayed them with repellent. The mosquito bites on her legs were raw with scratching, so she rubbed on antiseptic cream. She decided take everything she owned with her to Fona and leave most of Hannah's gear behind in the house, but she threw the shorts into the big suitcase on a whim. William could store the overnight bag until she got back.

The men were eating breakfast when she came downstairs.

'You're alive then?' she said to Ned.

'I'm not sure yet.'

'Serves you right,' said Fergus.

'Haven't you ever got drunk?' said Sam, finding his assumption of the moral high ground to be irritating.

'Not with the employees.'

'Steady on there. Sam's not an employee.'

'I wasn't talking about Sam.'

There was an icy silence. Sam felt like she had walked in on a private conversation. Fergus had a smug expression on his face. Ned took a step towards him as William came in with a tray.

'Tea, madam?'

\*\*\*

The atmosphere didn't improve much during the day. They didn't speak to each other after breakfast as Fergus attended a meeting and Ned disappeared on one of his errands. Sam hung around the house, hiding from the sunlight and trying not to be sick. When Ned got back, she cornered him.

'Why does Fergus treat you like that?'

'Oh, that's ancient history. Fergus comes from new money. His position in the world is very important to him. It's hard to fit in at a public school when you have an Irish accent.'

'Why does he pick on you?'

'My family are nouveau poor, but we used to own whacking great country estates in Hampshire until the money ran out. Fergus associates me with the bad treatment he got at school, even though I didn't go there with him.'

'So how come you know him?'

'My father, Dick Hunter, ran the racing stable for Fergus' father so they brought me up there. The Dockrells got a lot of mileage from the way the tables had been turned against the old order. They lorded it over us to some extent. My father didn't care, but I used to get teased a lot, especially by Fergus.'

'Where did you go to school?'

'The local grammar. I got a scholarship.'

'Brainy and well-bred, uh? No wonder Fergus is jealous.'

Ned flushed.

'I wouldn't let him hear you say that if I were you.'

'I was only joking.'

But he had impressed her.

\*\*\*

'Hello?'

'Hi Sam. How was your trip?' said Bill. *Her mother must be out as her father hardly ever answered the phone.*

'I got here safely, thank you. There was a slight detour before arriving at the house and my suitcase got left behind, but I've recovered it now.'

'Lucky you had the overnight bag then.' He chuckled.

'I'm not sure Hannah thought it was lucky.'

'I'm in the doghouse. She wasn't pleased at my mix-up.'

'Tell her not to worry. I've stored it in Njahili until I get back.'

'You're too good. I'd have emptied it into the bay.'

'Some of her clothes might come in handy.'

'Ha! Well you know best, darling.'

'We're going to Fona tomorrow, so I doubt I'll be able to call very often. If you don't hear from me, you can always call Alex. Mummy has the number.'

'Look after yourself, sweetheart.'

'I will, Daddy. Love to Mummy. Bye.'

'Bye.'

# Chapter V

Nothing indicated that their transit though the suburbs would be delayed by anything worse than the usual traffic jams. Their car, a black Toyota 4 Runner, crawled along behind minibuses spewing black exhaust fumes. These buses stopped to pick up ever more passengers who disappeared into the back like stars entering a black hole with no apparent limit. Ancient taxis, tied together with electric cable and duct tape, their engines pinking with dirty fuel and firing an ear-splitting cacophony out of exhausts rendered useless with age and damage, weaved their way through the traffic. Every driver in a vehicle with a working horn tried to blast their way to the next junction.

Sam shrank from the noise in the back seat of the car, intimidated by the battle for space on the street. Passers-by peered into the windows and shouted, '*Pomwi*!' at them.

'What does that mean?' Sam asked, startled.

'It's Mende for a white man,' said Fergus.

'Racists,' said Ned. 'Can you imagine what would happen to us if we drove along shouting names at people?'

'Steady on, Neddy,' said Fergus. 'I take your point. We'd get arrested if we shouted the equivalent in England.'

Sam forced herself to stay silent. The rush hour had not improved Fergus' humour and she did not want to be on the end of a tongue lashing from the sarcastic Irishman. They were heading to Fona where she would be independent of Fergus and Ned and doing her own thing. Their business in Fona was a mystery, but she would find out by osmosis, rather than prizing the information out of Fergus. He was far from forthcoming and seemed to have lost all interest in her after she stopped wearing Hannah's shorts.

'Why'd we come this way?' said Fergus. 'Couldn't we have driven over the hills behind the town?'

'It's twice as far,' said Ned. 'I don't think my hangover would've taken all the bouncing about on those gravel roads.'

'And this is twice as slow.' Fergus sighed.

'We'll be out of town soon. I'll drive through Kanta and we'll come out onto the main road to Fona, such as it is.'

'Hurry up then. We only have a couple of hours of daylight left and it's a bad idea to drive at night in the countryside.'

'I'll do my best to avoid the brigands,' said Ned.

'What sort of brigands?' said Sam.

'Oh, the usual, mostly unemployed ex-soldiers or rebels.'

'That sounds dangerous.'

'It'll be fine. Trust me.'

Ned followed a soft drinks lorry which rounded the corner into an open square in Kanta, meeting a sea of people in the road. It drove as far as the centre of the square and then stopped. Ned slammed on the brakes.

Sam almost fell off the back seat and Ned's rucksack slid into the footwell behind Fergus' seat. The driver of the lorry came around the back of the vehicle. He unloaded crates without haste, while his assistant prevented people from stealing bottles from the open container.

The Toyota was trapped behind the lorry in the middle of the crowd who moved closer, surrounding the car and staring at the occupants. A few chanted, '*Pomwi*.' Some of them carried machetes.

A man pulled open the back door of the car. Sam was sitting at the far side and, before she could react, a large arm reached in and grabbed Ned's rucksack. Sam lunged along the seat to rescue it, but it was too late. Instead, she grabbed the door and pulled it shut, almost amputating the fingers of another man who tried to steal her bag too. She scrambled to put the locks on both doors.

Unable to open the doors, the crowd pushed at the car and banged on the bonnet, shouting for money to buy drink. People pulled at the door handles, trying to force them open, making the car rock. Petrified, expecting any moment for someone to drag her out and assault her or worse, Sam's heart beat so fast she was close to fainting.

'Get us out of here,' said Fergus. 'I don't care if you run them over. Just drive.'

Ned gunned the engine, causing the people in front of the car to jump away. He stuck his hand flat on the horn. He pulled out from behind the soft drinks' lorry at a snail's pace, nudging people with the car's front bumper. The crowd parted to let the car through. They complained as the car pushed them out of the way, but they did not stop it leaving. Several people banged on the roof of the car as it went past, demanding money and waving their machetes at Sam in the back, laughing at her terrified face. The Toyota inched out of the square and the crowd became thinner. Ned speeded up and soon they headed out of the suburbs into the countryside.

They drove for about five miles at top speed, the car rattling with effort on the uneven surface. Then Ned pulled the car off the road. No-one spoke. Sam was shaking. She tried to drink some Fanta, but she dropped it into her lap, soaking her trousers in sticky soft drink.

'Shit! I'm covered in Fanta,' she said. 'Can you get out of the car? I have to change.'

This broke the silence and both men jumped out. Sam fumbled in her bag and pulled out Hannah's shorts. It was not exactly what she'd had in mind, but she didn't want to empty everything out looking for her spare trousers which lay at the bottom somewhere. She struggled into the shorts whilst lying along the back seat. The zip got stuck half way, snared in the backing material. She wrenched it free in frustration. Bloody Hannah.

She got out of the car and shuffled over to where the men were standing.

'You can't stay out of those shorts, can you?' said Fergus. 'Whose rucksack did they steal?'

'Mine,' said Ned.

'Anything important in it?'

'Just some old clothes.' His hand flew to his mouth. 'My passport.'

'This is your fault. We should never have driven through town. If you hadn't got so drunk, none of this would have happened.'

'I'm sorry. It's a massive cock-up.' Ned stared at his feet, avoiding Fergus' accusing look.

'You'll have to return to the British Embassy in Njahili and ask them for a replacement.'

'I know. I'm sorry, I'd no idea there was a festival in Kanta.'

'It's your responsibility. You should've checked.'

'What about our meeting with the Paramount Chief?'

'We'll set it up for tomorrow and you can go back to Njahili the next day.'

'Okay.'

Fergus reached inside the car and grabbed his cigarettes, fumbling to remove one from the packet.

'Can I have one too please?' said Sam, her heart still in her mouth.

'Me too,' said Ned.

'But you don't smoke,'

'I do now. Sorry, Sam, that was terrifying.' He touched her forearm and, despite the heat that still lingered in the late afternoon, her hairs stood on end.

*** 

The drive to Fona took four hours. Small villages full of children lined the route, but it became empty as it got dark. Some hamlets looked long deserted, houses with no roofs and blackened shells for walls stood in bleak testament to the passage of the rebels. Clothes hung from the trees like tattered flags.

'Why are those clothes up there like that?' said Sam.

'Those are monkey trees,' said Fergus.

'But what are they for?'

'The human clothes scare the monkeys, preventing them from coming into the village.'

'It didn't work with the rebels,' said Ned.

The subdued group pulled into Fona close to midnight. Still shaken by events at Kanta, Sam pondered the consequences had someone pulled open the door of the car and dragged her out.

'Are you okay, Sam?' said Ned. 'You're very quiet.'

'A bit shaken. I hate to think what could have happened.'

'Doesn't it put you off this sort of work?' said Fergus.

'Not really. The way the day turned from mundane into life-threatening and back to normal again fascinates me,' she said. 'This sort of incident doesn't put me off my work, it makes me feel more alive.'

'Or dead,' said Fergus, but Sam was serious. The thrill of adventure kept her going in a profession that didn't want her. The emotion of unexpected danger overcome and survived. This was something she didn't talk about without sounding pretentious or needy though, so she kept the idea locked inside. Hannah might have Simon, but she had her adventures.

The town of Fona wallowed in almost total darkness. The hum of generators filled the air near the few houses with lighting. Small puddles peppered the surface of the damp mud road, the air redolent with wet wood and rotting vegetation. Choruses of frogs and crickets echoed in the dark night.

'This is it,' said Ned as they pulled into a walled compound behind a thatched bungalow. They got out of the car and unloaded their bags. The air was thick with insects blundering through their rapid life cycles and being swallowed whole by the bats which swooped down amongst the palm trees surrounding the house.

The front door opened and a tall, prodigiously fat woman came out, stooping to avoid the doorframe and blocking out the light with her hugeness. She wore a traditional wax print dress with swirls of orange on a green background and a turban of the same materials tied around her head. Several plaits escaped from her turban and hung in a fringe over her face.

'That lady's our housekeeper. Her name's Fatimata, but she's also known as Auntie Fatou,' said Fergus.

'Why Auntie?' said Sam.

'That's an expression of respect for older ladies. Fatou's short for Fatimata, but don't call her that until you are friends.'

Ned snorted. 'That's a bit unlikely to happen.'

Fatimata approached the car and they all got out to greet her.

'Good evening,' she said.

'Good evening, Auntie Fatou. How are you?' said Ned.

'I am well. And you?'

'I am well too.'

'And Mr Fergus, how are you?'

'Fine, thanks. Are the rooms ready?'

'Yes, sir.' Fatimata fixed Sam with a gimlet stare, looking her up and down with a growing expression of disgust. 'And where is the lady's husband?'

Pulling her T-shirt down to make it longer, Sam searched her brain for a suitable response, but couldn't think of anything polite. Ned came to the rescue.

'The lady is Sam Harris. She is a widow.'

Fatimata appeared to be in a quandary. Her disapproval of Sam's outfit fighting with her natural instinct to welcome a stranger. She sighed.

'I will prepare a room,' she said.

They climbed a flight of stairs at one side of the house which lead onto a veranda which ran the length of it. A striped hammock swung between the rafters and two wooden benches face out into a backyard containing a large mango tree. They entered the house through doors lined with mosquito screens and found themselves in a room divided into two sections. The part of the room at the front of the house contained a plastic covered two-seater sofa and two arm chairs on either side of a battered rug. A battered gateleg table was pushed against the wall under the window. The back part of the room held the dining table and chairs, modern additions of chrome and plastic. A large electric ceiling fan of uncertain vintage hung over this, wobbling with effort as it dispersed a minimal current of air. Several warped cupboards containing an assortment of crockery and glasses lined the walls.

'Sit here. I'll call you when I'm ready,' said Fatimata.

'Thank you,' said Sam, sitting on the sofa and finding it to be lacking both springs and stuffing. She tried to sit back, but found that even more uncomfortable, so she balanced on the edge of the seat, leaning her forearms on her knees. How did people sit on these things?

It seemed like an age before Fatimata came to collect her.

'I'll take you to your room now.'

Sam stood up and grabbed her bag. She followed the enormous, coloured batik expanse that was Fatimata's bottom, unable to prevent herself from wondering how many metres of material would be required to cover the substantial acreage occupied by this woman. Fatimata by name, Fatimata by nature.

'Here it is.'

They had walked the length of the house, passing four doors on their way. Coming to the end of the corridor, Fatimata threw open a door to a miniscule bedroom that appeared to be converted from a cupboard. Not only was it tiny with no window, but also airless with no fan or air-conditioning. Sam didn't dare to complain. The men were already in their rooms and she didn't want to start her stay by whining about her room. Fatimata gave a smug smile at Sam's look of dismay and waddled off down the passage, swinging her gigantic rear from side to side. She knew I wouldn't make a fuss.

Undressing in the cramped space between the single bed and the wall, she sprayed herself from head to foot with repellent. She pulled back the covers on the bed to find that Fatimata had deposited an old stained sheet on the ancient mattress. Praying that none of the stains had appeared since the last wash, she clambered into bed, hitting her head on the backboard as she misjudged its miniscule length. The wafer-thin mattress did not disguise its lumpy base. She considered moving it to the floor, but that only opened her up to invasion by creepy crawlies and lost reptiles. She stayed put and tried to accommodate herself around the bumps.

Outside, the crickets and frogs were still blasting out their greatest hits, but Sam's room had one advantage, it was quiet. She tried to drift off in the stultifying heat, throwing off the covers as her temperature rose. Then she heard a rustling sound from the thatch, only separated from her room by a piece of painted plywood. Something scampered across it, followed by another bounding body. Excited squeaks came through the partition. She stared upwards and coughed to alert them of her presence. Silence reigned for a few seconds and then the noises started again.

More chasing games followed by a thud on the board right over her head.

She jumped out of bed. Sitting on the edge of the bed, she tried to convince herself that these animals couldn't fall through the ceiling and onto her face. Then there was another scampering sound above her head. Sleep wouldn't be possible in here. Maybe if she found another bedroom? Fatimata had put her as far from the men as possible without making her sleep outside in the car. Sam would have preferred the car to a room with an animal circus in full swing.

She put on a pair of trousers and a T-shirt and wandered down the corridor, trying the doors, but the first two were locked. Then she noticed that the door to the bedroom nearest the sitting room was open. She peeped inside, hoping to find an empty bed. She looked straight into the eyes of a wide-awake Ned who sat at a table writing in a journal.

'Sam? Are you okay?'

'Yes, no, I'm not. There are creatures in my bedroom and I can't sleep.'

'What sort of creatures? Are you sure?'

'Pretty sure. I don't want to sleep there.'

'Come on. Let's investigate.'

They walked along the corridor to Sam's room and opened the door.

'Wow! That room is tiny.'

'It's fine, but too small to share with these animals.'

Ned put his finger to his lips. They stood in silence for a minute. Sure enough, there was a scrabbling sound and a fat body bounded across the ceiling. Ned laughed.

'Rats. They are noisy buggers, aren't they?'

'Rats? I can't sleep in a room with rats.'

'No, fair enough. Have you tried the other bedrooms?'

'They are all locked. Fatimata didn't want me in there.'

'Why don't you sleep in my bed?'

'Your bed?'

'Don't worry, I'm not worried by rats. I'll sleep in yours.'

'Really? I'd be so grateful. I don't mind rats on the ground but can't stand the thought of one landing on my head.'

'Sure. I get it. Hop into bed. I'll just finish what I'm doing and I'll go to bed too.'

'Thanks.'

'Oh, that's alright. Just get some sleep.'

'Please don't tell Fergus what a wuss I am.'

'Don't be silly. You're allowed secrets.'

Sam got into bed and pulled up the covers. Almost immediately waves of tiredness lulled her to sleep. She sighed. She could sense him smiling as she drifted off.

# Chapter VI

The next morning, Fatimata opened the door of Ned's room. She brought a cup of tea and came in without knocking. Her bright yellow wax print dress was so bright that a sleep befuddled Sam imagined that the sun had come into the room. She sat up in bed, greeted by a laser-like stare of disapproval.

'Where is Mr Ned?'

'He slept in my room. The rats were keeping me awake, I'm afraid.'

Fatimata snorted and turned on her heel and taking the cup of tea with her, much to Sam's disappointment. She headed for Sam's room, almost bumping into Fergus, who had emerged from his room to ask her a question. He backed into the doorway, alarmed by the look on her face as she swept by with the impetus of a cargo ship and opened the door. Ned, who was standing half in and half out of his underwear, lost his balance and fell backwards onto the bed. Sam pretended she hadn't seen him and turned away.

'Fatimata, you must learn to knock,' he said.

'I found that harlot in your room.'

'Harlot? You mean Sam? How dare you call her that!'

'She dresses like one. This is a Christian household.'

'If you're such a good Christian, why did you put Sam in the maid's room?'

'That woman shouldn't stay here. It's against my principles.'

'Now listen here.' Ned emerged from the tiny room pulling on a shirt. 'Sam is a professional woman with two university degrees. Mr Simmonds has hired her to work with us on the technical side.'

'Why do you defend her? Is she your girlfriend?'

'She's no-one's girlfriend and you've no right to judge her. You will open one of the other bedrooms and make it ready for her.'

Fatimata turned around to face Fergus. 'Do you agree? Do I give that woman a bedroom?'

Fergus snapped at her. 'Yes, you do, and if you don't treat her with respect, you'll be looking for a new position. Is that clear?'

Fatimata sniffed. 'It's clear,' she said and started off down the passageway, wobbling with indignation. As she sailed past on a sea of resentment, Sam knew that there was nothing she could do to improve matters. She would have to hold her tongue and hope that Fatimata didn't hold a grudge. Fergus came out of his room and passed Sam in the corridor.

'Ah, Sam, there you are. We have a meeting with the Paramount Chief in about an hour. Come and have breakfast,' said Fergus.

'Thank you for sticking up for me.'

'It's nothing to do with me. Alex says you hold our key to success out here, so you can thank him. Personally, I think women should be barefoot, pregnant and in the kitchen, preferably in a French maid's outfit.'

'Sorry, I left mine at home. The shorts will have to do.'

Fergus roared with laughter.

'Hoisted with my own petard. What do you say Ned?'

'Never argue with a woman who owns a geological hammer.'

'Fair enough. Let's eat. I'm starving. Fatou! Where are my eggs?'

***

Paramount Chief Joseph Sesay's compound sat on the outskirts of Fona. A traditional stockade surrounded a dozen adobe covered huts with palm leaf roofs in different states of repair. Sam, Fergus and Ned got out of the car and stood on a platform of mud pounded flat by thousands of feet over many years, covered in an array of cracked plastic pots, bottles and flip-flops with broken toe straps. The filth disgusted Sam. Why hadn't someone cleaned up the mess? There were lots of hangers-on living in the compound, as evidenced by clothes drying lines outside every hut, so it would be easy to pick the stuff up and put it in a bin. One pot at her feet was full of rainwater with mosquito larvae swimming in it. She gave it a surreptitious poke with her toe and spilt the contents on the ground. Ned noticed her disgust and shrugged.

The Chief's house was recognisable by its size. It was ringed by a balcony hung with multicoloured hammocks covered in mosquito nets which rippled in the soft morning breeze. Some shaded ones had occupants, their arms or legs hanging outside the material to catch the cooler air. The sun was gathering strength now, ready to beat down on the town.

As they approached the house, a familiar figure appeared at the front door.

'You are welcome back to Fona, Mr Fergus and Mr Ned,' said Tamba. 'And Miss Sam, you've made it.'

'Yes, here I am, thank you.'

'How do you know Sam?' said Ned, astonished.

'I met Tamba at the airport.'

'While she was assaulting the Paramount Chief,' added Fergus.

A smug expression flitted across Tamba's face. Ned turned to Sam who shrugged.

'It's a long story,' she said.

Tamba led them into the central reception room with a plain wooden floor furnished with chairs that screamed discomfort on either side of a square table with short legs. After seating them, he disappeared through a door at the back.

'It's nice and cool in here,' said Sam.

'That's due to the lack of windows,' said Fergus.

The chairs came from the same place as the ones in Auntie Fatou's house. Sam shifted around on hers, unable to get settled.

'What's wrong with the chairs? I can't sit on this,' she said in a whisper.

'It's meant to discourage visitors from staying too long,' said Ned. 'They've a family room in through there with big squashy sofas.'

'Why don't they want their visitors to stay?'

'It depends on whether they have been invited or not. The Chief has a constant stream of people dropping in to discuss minor issues in the Chiefdom. It prevents long visits.'

'What about important visitors?'

'Oh, they arrive at lunchtime so the host's obliged to feed them. It's traditional.'

'What does it make us?'

'Polite.'

The back door opened and Tamba came through it, pushing the Chief's wheelchair. The Chief wore traditional robes in orange, green and black, with a matching fez on his head which was bowed to his chest. Not without difficulty, Tamba manoeuvred the wheelchair close to the table between the two rows of chairs. He was panting as he sat down beside his boss, his eyebrows battling to hold back the rivulets of sweat massing over his eyes. Sam watched them with bated breath. *Would the dam break?*

'Thank you for coming to visit me again,' said Joseph Sesay. 'And ...' He stopped and raised his head a little higher to examine the visitors. His stare dissolved into a delighted smile.

'Miss Harris! You came. She came, Tamba. I told you she would.'

'Yes, sir,' said Tamba, with the air of someone who had lost a bet.

'Come closer and sit by me, Sam.'

Sam stood up and approached, pulling a chair with her. She reached out her hand in greeting.

'Don't touch the Chief,' said Tamba, growling like a terrier.

Sam blushed. Her hand was still extended in greeting.

'Sit down,' hissed Fergus.

'I'm so sorry. I forgot.'

'Ha! She forgot,' said Tamba.

The Chief's scaly hand slid into hers and gave it a squeeze, making her jump.

'Sit down, my dear. Now, how can I help you?'

'Well, as I told you last time sir, we want – '

'I'd rather Sam told me.' Joseph Sesay cut Fergus off in mid-sentence and turned to Sam again. 'What have you got in mind?' A thunderous expression crossed Fergus' face, like the shadow of a rain cloud in summer. He crossed his arms and his legs and almost fell off his chair. Ned hid a smile by scratching his nose.

'Um, Alex, Mr Simmonds, he'd like your permission to explore for diamonds in the river terraces in Fona. We have the license from the government for the mining concession covering the Fona area, but we need your agreement before we do any work. I'd like to start exploration work on the river terraces near the town.'

'What sort of work?'

'Searching for diamond-containing river gravels. After mapping the terraces in the area, we would select the best one where we would dig pits down to the bedrock on a grid system and search for mineral indicators.'

'What if you find something? Who owns it?'

'Alex's company, Njahili Resources. And if we find anything, the government gets 40% of our revenue and first pass at buying the diamonds.'

'And what do I get?'

'Um, we'll use people from Fona and buy local products. Also, the law says the government should spend thirty percent of the tax paid on the revenue in the local area.'

'You don't understand. What do I get? Me.'

Fergus coughed. 'Sam is only a geologist, sir, she doesn't deal with business.'

'No?' Sesay glanced at Sam who shook her head.

'Perhaps we could have a private chat?' said Fergus. 'Ned, can you take Sam and wait for me outside please?'

Sam was about to object when a tall young woman entered with a tray.

'Would you like some lemonade?' she said.

Sesay gazed at her for an instant and then turned to address the others. 'This is my daughter, Adanna, the heir to the Fona Chiefdom.' Ned and Fergus both stood up.

'Nice to meet you, Adanna,' said Sam, 'That's a pretty name. Is it local?'

'It means her father's daughter,' she said and turned to beam at Joseph Sesay.

'Sam's the young woman who helped me in the airport,' Sesay said to her. 'Go and sit on the veranda and find out everything about her.'

Sam noticed Tamba was staring at Adanna with undisguised lust, his hand moving to his groin in harmony with his thoughts. A cocktail of feelings passed through her head, revulsion being the most prominent, but she could sympathise with his obsession. Adanna was exquisite. They followed her outside. She led them to a wicker table surrounded by four rickety looking chairs and gestured for them to sit down. After pouring them all a lemonade, Adanna fixed Sam with a stare she recognised. Like father, like daughter.

'So, you're Sam,' said Adanna, 'you made a big impression on my father. He hasn't stopped talking about you. He told me you saved him at the airport.'

'Not really. He was being attacked by mosquitos, so I gave him my repellent.'

'My father served as an officer in the British army. He says the sign of a leader is someone who looks after others first.'

'I packed more repellent in my luggage, so I wasn't worried but ...'

'But what?'

'Oh, my luggage got delayed and the little fiends got me. It was only a few bites. I'm sure I'll be fine.'

'Is this your first visit to Africa?'

'Yes. I've always wanted to come.'

'Simbako takes some getting used to,' said Adanna. 'How do you like it so far?'

Sam smiled back. She didn't want to tell Adanna about the incident at Kanta. 'Every day's different, but that's the best thing about my work.'

'I'm sure my father will let you work in our Chiefdom.'

'Fergus will sort that out.'

'And how are you, Ned? Still under the iron rule of Auntie Fatou?'

'Yes, she's the real boss. We can't do anything without her permission.'

'I got off on the wrong foot with her,' said Sam.

'What did you do?'

'I wore the wrong clothes and I don't have a husband. A single woman is persona non grata in her house.'

'Be careful. She uses voodoo to get her own way,' said Adanna.

'Voodoo? Isn't Simbako a Christian country?'

'In theory it is, but voodoo was the original religion here and it hasn't died out yet. Most problems are still solved using voodoo spells and fetishes.'

'I'll keep that in mind.'

'Excuse me a minute,' said Adanna and she took the tray back inside.

'What's Fergus' private chat about?' said Sam, who already knew.

'The Chief has requirements.'

'Meaning we have to bribe him?'

'I wouldn't call it a bribe.'

'What would you call it?'

Ned shifted in his seat. Unwilling to alienate him, Sam changed the subject.

'Is Adanna the Chief's only child?'

'Yes, she's the heir to the kingdom.'

'Isn't that unusual? I understood it was customary to have many wives and lots of children?'

'Joseph married his childhood sweetheart when he got back here after his military service.'

'Where did he serve?'

'In Northern Ireland – that's where he met Alex.'

'Where's her mother now?'

'She died giving birth to Adanna. The loss devastated him and he never married again.'

'What do the tribal elders think?'

'About him marrying only once?'

'About him only having one heir.'

'There are complications.'

'Because she's a woman?'

Adanna came back outside. Ned shook his head and put his finger to his lips. Sam experienced both frustration and fascination. There was more to this story.

'Please come back inside,' said Adanna.

*\*\**

After the visitors had left, Tamba sulked and muttered. The Chief was used to his ways, but still found them irritating.

'What now?' he said.

'I don't like it. Why are you letting them mine for diamonds in your kingdom? Colonial days are long gone.'

'Alex is a good friend of mine. He saved my life when we were in the army. He has my trust.'

'But why give them that terrace? We already know it contains diamonds. Why not give them one that hasn't been tested?'

'I have my reasons.'

'I don't agree.'

'Tamba, it is not your place to decide. I know you've had a rough time, but you might learn something from Sam.'

'She's a woman. What could she know about mining?'

'Is there some reason you don't want them mining there? You haven't been digging by yourself again, have you?'

'No, sir.'

'Buck up and stop being a pain. I need your eyes and ears on this project.'

'Sorry, Chief. I'll do your bidding.'

'Good man. Tell the cook to prepare me something to eat.'

*** 

Later that evening, Sam lay in a hammock outside on the veranda, swinging by pushing off against a post with her foot. She listened to her Walkman and was singing along in her head to some Latino music given to her by Gloria when she left Sierramar. The sky was bright with starlight, dazzling constellations twinkling in the black night. Sam frowned as she tried to remember which of them corresponded to the names in her head. As she always did, she vowed to look them up and remember them for next time.

She was thinking back to the meeting at the Chief's house. She had a great deal in common with Adanna as they were both women trying to get along in men's worlds. She planned to get time alone with her to talk about their mutual struggles. Fergus was ploughing his own furrow for Alex Simmonds and was not interested in her projects. Ned came outside and stood with his hands in his pockets, gazing at the sky.

'Penny for your thoughts,' said Sam.

Ned jumped. 'I didn't see you there. You gave me a fright.'

'Any result from Fergus' chat with the Chief?'

'The Chief has agreed to let us explore a terrace on the outside of town. He'll send a team of men there tomorrow to clear it for you.'

Sam sighed. Ned moved nearer.

'What's up? Isn't that good news?'

'To tell you the truth, Ned, I'm pissed off. Geology is a science. I would've liked to explore the river and chosen the best terrace myself, not have a random terrace assigned by people who know nothing about mining.'

'It's not that bad. I guarantee they understand a lot more than you imagine. If you discover diamonds, everyone will be happy. You can do scouting for another terrace meanwhile, in case you don't.'

'I suppose so, but I don't want to disappoint Alex. He is paying me.'

'Don't you worry about him. He isn't worried about small scale production, he is going after bigger prey.'

'How so?'

Ned shifted on his feet. Sam got the impression he had said more than he intended. She waited. He stalled.

'What are you listening to?' he said, changing the subject.

'Music from Latin America - salsa and merengue.'

'Can I listen?' He gesticulated at the hammock. 'Budge up.'

Sam swung her legs aside and he plonked himself down beside her. The ropes holding the hammock up squeaked in protest as they bounced together. She handed him one of the earphones and they lay back against the rough material. Sam could feel a hot flush creeping up her side as she absorbed the heat from Ned's body. She bit her lip to distract herself. They swung back and forwards in the still night, pretending to listen to the music. Sam turned her head towards him and opened her eyes. She found him gazing at her and she held his look, trying to peer into his soul. He stared down at her mouth. It was clear what he wanted.

'Oh, this is cosy,' said Fergus, sarcasm filling the air.

How long had he been standing there? Sam was furious and embarrassed. Ned rolled away, yanking the earphone out of his ear and pulled himself up using the balcony fencing.

'Sam's got great music,' said Ned.

'Can you drag yourself away for a minute? I need to talk to you.'

'Okay.'

He followed Fergus inside. Sam couldn't comprehend what had just happened, or rather, failed to happen. Ned had infected her with a virus. No amount of rationalisation would cure it. Not even thoughts of Simon could ease this strange affliction. Trust Fergus to arrive when things were coming to a head, or mouth even. She strained to hear what they were saying. It wasn't difficult, Fergus had a voice like a foghorn and discretion was not his strong point. She soon regretted it.

'I want you to go to Njahili tomorrow to get your new passport.'

'Okay. Do you need anything while I'm there?'

'No, and keep your hands off Sam. You are being unprofessional.'

'Come on. I'm only having fun. It's not like I'm serious about her. Don't be such a killjoy.'

'I mean it Ned. Cut it out now.'

Blood flooded to her cheeks. She waited until she heard them go into their rooms. When the doors slammed, she stood up too quickly and almost fainted. Steadying herself, she headed for the room that Fatou had prepared for her. As she passed Ned's room, he emerged and grabbed her arm. She glared at him.

'Well, you can fuck off for a start,' she hissed.

'Sam, don't be like that.'

'Like what? I heard what you said.'

'For heaven's sake! Do you imagine I'd tell Fergus the truth?'

'The truth? And what's that?'

'I'm falling for you.'

Sam was stunned into silence. Life had taken an unexpected turn.

Fergus poked his head out of his bedroom door. He showed no sign of having heard their conversation.

'Ah, there you are, Sam. Be ready to go at seven tomorrow morning. We'll investigate the terrace the

Chief has given us. Do you need anything from Njahili? Ned's going.'

'Um, no thank you. I'll be ready. I can't wait.'

She stumbled to the next door and let herself in. The room was bare and clean. Fatou had made up the bed and her bag stood against the wall. She went over to the bed and sat on the mattress without moving for about ten minutes, trying to process this revelation while her heart hammered. This was a new sensation for her. She had been with Simon for so long she had forgotten the thrill of a new attraction, the brush of bare arms in a passageway, the frisson of a shared smile. It made her dizzy with longing and she wished he wasn't going in the morning just when they needed to be together to explore these new feelings.

After she had calmed down, she pulled back the covers to make sure the sheets were clean. One pillow fell onto the floor. As she bent to put it back on the bed, she noticed a tiny bag made of sisal had fallen out of the cover. She picked it up and squeezed it between her fingers. It was crunchy as if it contained grains of sand or sugar. She tugged at the string tied at the top. Some white crystals fell out onto the sheets mixed with a black powder and small grains of something that resembled pepper. She wet her finger, picked up one crystal and licked it. Salt. The black powder was a mystery. She sniffed it, but she couldn't smell anything.

Shrugging, she retied the bag and crossed the room to put it in a pocket of her work rucksack. Adanna would know what it was. It would be a good excuse to chat about the customs of Simbako and how involved she needed to be as the daughter of the Paramount Chief.

# Chapter VII

The next morning, Ned left for the capital before Sam got to the breakfast table. Fergus noticed her glancing around and sniffed.

'He's gone to Njahili to get a new passport.'

'I was wondering how you get a cup of tea around here.'

'You don't fool me. I saw you spooning in the hammock.'

'We weren't spooning! We were listening to music.'

'So that's what they call it these days? Anyway, don't waste your time there, he's still trying to get back with his wife. Unless you'd like to be a diversion?'

'It's none of your business what I feel about Ned,' said Sam, but she suspected there was at least a grain of truth in what Fergus said. 'Pass me the bread.'

He raised an eyebrow and pushed the rolls over to her. Sam wanted a change of subject.

'How are we getting to the terrace today?' she said, before Fergus mentioned Ned again.

'I've hired an ancient vehicle we've used before. It's not much to look at, but it works fine. Can you drive?'

'Yes, but rarely because I live in London and I don't have a car.'

'Okay, you can drive home once you learn the route. It'll be good practice for you.'

'I'm not sure about this terrace. Is it any good?'

'Isn't that your job?'

'Well, yes, but normally –'

'Forget normal. We're in Africa. Just go with the flow. You're a bright girl, I'm sure you'll think of something.'

\*\*\*

After breakfast, they stood outside on the veranda waiting for the car. The sound of flightless wings being flapped broke the silence and a large grey parrot came scuttling around the corner, its beak open, furious squawking sounds emitting from its throat. Fergus' eyes widened and he jumped indoors, shutting Sam outside at the mercy of this hysterical creature. The parrot came to a halt right in front of her, his attack stalled due to a fit of coughing.

The show of fury did not faze her though, having dealt with parrots before. Her maternal grandmother had a pair of vicious old brutes who stalked the corridors of her country cottage terrorising the dogs and any small children who ventured indoors. She reached into her rucksack and extracted a cashew from her lunch bag which she dropped on the floor in front of her. She waited. The parrot poked at it with his purple tongue and almost squeaked with excitement. The cashew disappeared.

Before Sam could extract another nut from her bag, Fatou emerged from the house and aimed a kick at the bird which turned tail and removed itself from the range of her large flip-flops.

'That parrot will have your finger. He doesn't like anybody, not even Mr Fergus,' as if that proved its nasty character. The bird was more discerning than it looked. Sam liked a project. She would get on its good side by hook or by crook, or by cashew. No snack for her then. She considered grabbing something else.

'What's he called?' she said.

'Dembo, but he doesn't answer to that. He just bites people.'

Just then, an ancient jalopy shuddered into the yard, driven by a cheerful-looking young man who seemed to wrestle with the steering wheel. He pulled to a halt in front of the house and leaned out of the window.

'Mr Fergus! Let's go!' he shouted. Fergus poked his head through the door, checking left and right. He tiptoed over the veranda, looking absurd and vulnerable. Sam tried not to laugh.

'You need to watch that parrot. Fatimata teases it with food all the time. It's vicious. Come on then,' he said to Sam. 'Your carriage awaits. This is Sahr.'

'Nice to meet you,' said Sam.

They both got into the Toyota jeep, Fergus took the front seat and Sam sat in the back. She would have liked to go in front to view the town better, but she didn't want to ask. There would be opportunities on other days. Also, Fergus acted as if he was coming with her. She hoped he didn't intend to supervise her. Maybe only on the first day.

They lurched out of the yard and turned left onto the main street through town. The shock absorber under Sam's bottom had expired and each bump and pothole resulted in the body of the car hitting the chassis and reverberating through her frame. She hoped the terrace was close.

Passing the Chief's compound, they drove on for another kilometre until they emerged from the town straight into the bush. The heat was already building and the ground became dust under the sun.

They approached a ribbon of vegetation which grew on the banks of a chocolate-coloured river and emerged onto a flat plain. On the other side of the river, Sam could see terracing containing banded strata of differing stone sizes standing out in the morning sunlight. Anticipation flooded her system with adrenaline. Leaving the car, they walked down a steep path to the river through the cool shade of the trees growing in the rich soil. The high watermarks on their trunks were up to two metres above the ground.

A group of men stood around smoking and coughing at the edge of the glade. They raised their heads as Sam came towards them, carnal interest rising at the approach of an athletic young woman. Among them sat Tamba. He had a smug look on his face that telegraphed his intentions. Sam's heart dropped. She had hoped to do more regional geology in the area to investigate if their terrace was typical of the area, but the Chief must have sent Tamba to monitor her work. He wouldn't let her roam around the territory without permission, but, as always, the best form of defence was attack. She stuck out her hand and approached him, beaming.

'Ah, Tamba! I'm so glad you're here. That'll make my job so much easier. Your local knowledge will be key.'

Tamba hesitated, surprised, embarrassed even, and took her hand as if it might conceal a trap. 'I'll do my best,' he muttered.

Sam caught Fergus' eye. He winked at her, complicit, admiration sneaking onto his face.

'I'll leave you to it then,' he said, 'If you've got Tamba, you don't need me. I'll send the driver to pick you up at five.'

'That'll be great thanks. Let's go then,' said Sam, desperate to explore.

Tamba did not move. 'We can't start work yet. The libation ceremony has not taken place,' he said.

'Jesus, Tamba, why didn't you mention this before?' said Fergus.

'Everyone knows about this,' said Tamba. 'We must perform the ritual to placate the spirits.'

'Get on with it then,' said Fergus.

'I need a bottle of alcohol.'

'I don't have one. Can't we do this later? I can bring one when I come to pick up Sam.'

'The men won't work if we haven't communed with the ancestors.'

Fergus sighed. He stood for a moment searching for a comeback, but, finding none, he returned to the car shaking his head. Tamba's smug expression had returned and he bathed in self-satisfaction. Sam sat down on her poncho and pretended to be relaxed about the delay, determined not to get drawn into his games.

Fergus' trip into town took longer than Sam had expected. By the time he appeared in the clearing carrying a bottle of palm wine, ants had invaded her poncho and bitten her exposed skin. Only vigorous shaking persuaded them to leave. The men dozed and chatted, content to get paid for sitting in the shade. The appearance of alcohol reanimated them and they stood up in anticipation.

Tamba took the bottle and approached a large tree, beckoning the team to draw close to him. He unscrewed the top and poured liquid into it. Wine splashed onto his feet in their ancient sandals and they gleamed black. Muttering incantations in Krio, he tipped the contents of the lid into the roots of the tree. Several of the workers joined in, appearing to be chatting to a mysterious third party. He filled the bottle top with wine over and over and gave it to individual workers and poured it on the ground until the bottle was empty.

'The ancestors are satisfied,' said Tamba. 'We can start work now.'

'Right, I'm off,' said Fergus. 'See you later.'

'You're not staying?' said Tamba.

'Sam's got the matter under control. I've got things to do.' And with that he was gone.

Tamba had the air of a child being deprived of his favourite toy. Sam took a deep breath.

'Please can you tell me why you poured alcohol on the ground?'

'This ceremony creates harmony between man and spirits by awakening the ancestors,' said Tamba. 'We need to build a relationship between them and us before we start work or we might bring bad juju on the project.'

Was he teasing her or not? To her, it seemed inconceivable that people would still believe this in 1990, but he seemed sincere. She played the dumb foreigner.

'We wouldn't want that. Well done, Tamba. Let's get started then.'

\*\*\*

To Sam's surprise, they accomplished a lot on the first day, despite the late start and having a limited supply of ancient equipment.

'Where did you get all this stuff, Tamba?' said Sam, removing a rusty open-reel tape measure from a rotting cardboard box and tugging the fibreglass tape to release it. 'Have you been moonlighting in the diamond fields?'

Tamba fiddled with a bottle top, twisting it around in his fingers. She had struck a nerve. They would have a battle of wills, but she would triumph. There must have been mining in the area, legal or otherwise, due to its prime position in the centre of the diamond fields. It was essential to winkle it out of him if she wanted to find an economic terrace. He ignored the question.

'What shall we do first?'

'We should measure out a grid and pit the terrace at regular intervals. We can set out one set of the grid lines parallel to the river and another at right angles to them, running from the trees to the river bank.'

'I'll get the men to cut branches to use as marker pegs for the pits.'

'Excellent. Meanwhile, I'll have a look at the geology from river level. Do you want to come with me?'

'I'm not sure that's a good idea.'

'Why not?'

'There are snakes down there.'

'Are you afraid of snakes?'

'Of course not!'

'Bring a machete. We will need to cut vegetation anyway and you can chop the heads of any snakes that attack us.'

Tamba's shoulders slumped. He gesticulated at one man to accompany them and they made their way down the slippery bank to the river's edge. Vegetation covered the edge of the terrace which seemed to have collapsed into a mixture of pebbles and mud. None of the original structures or layering present in the terrace across the river remained. It would not tell them anything about the geology of the ground where they worked and Sam suspected that the terrace was not virgin. But it made little sense. *Why would the Chief send her to a terrace they had already exploited?* Perhaps they had only worked on that section. She would inspect the terrace across the river so she could relate the geology to the one they had been assigned. She turned to Tamba.

'Fancy a swim?' she said.

'I can't swim and, anyway, we can't cross, there is a strong current in the centre. Also, crocodiles live in that river.'

She looked him straight in the eye, but if he was lying, she couldn't tell.

'How do we get across?'

'We must drive around.'

She would have crossed the river without hesitation in most places. It was wide and shallow, except for a channel in the middle. It was darker than the rest and might be too deep. *Crocodiles were notorious for taking people in shallow water, but would there be any in this river close to a town, lacking any obvious prey?* Tamba waited.

'Okay, I'll speak to Fergus about it.'

'You must get permission from the Chief first.'

'Understood.'

Tamba's smug expression returned. She had been played. Round one to Tamba.

'Okay, let's get those pits marked out.'

\*\*\*

By the time Fergus and Sahr arrived to pick Sam up, they had marked out the positions of the pits on the ground and the team got ready to leave. The sun was low on the horizon and the mosquitos hovered in the warm early evening air.

'See you tomorrow,' said Sam.

'God willing,' said Tamba.

Sam sank into the back seat of the car and yawned.

'It's only day one,' said Fergus, 'Are you tired out already?'

'I'm hungry,' she said. 'I'm not tired.'

But she was. The hot sun had sapped all her strength. She marvelled at the energy of the workers who laughed and joked all day in the hot sun and didn't appear to tire at all. The palm wine had put them all in good spirits.

And Tamba? He sat there all day in the shade of a large black umbrella as inscrutable as a buddha. It amazed her he didn't burst with all the secrets he kept. He would try her patience to its limit if she were to achieve anything. And she was being sold a pup as far as the terrace was concerned. *What motive could the Chief have for making them explore a mined terrace?*

They pulled into the compound and descended from the jeep.

'Same time tomorrow, Sahr.'

'See you then, sir.'

When he had driven off waving, Sam said, 'Why did you call him 'sir'?'

'Sahr, not sir. It means first-born son in Krio, or is it Mende? I can't remember.'

Fergus pretended to be a heathen, but he was more familiar with Simbako's custom than he let on.

'How come you knew that, but not about libation?'

'Oh, I knew, but I was just chancing it.'

'How is it you've learned so much about the culture here?'

'Don't tell Tamba, but I was born in Simbako.' He winked at her. 'My father worked here when it was still a colony. I understand Krio and some Mende, but I pretend to be an ignorant Irishman. It works for me.'

Sam wasn't sure how to take this revelation. There was more to Fergus than she had imagined.

'And why are you here now?'

'I'm on the trail of a diamond, an enormous one – the Star of Simbako.'

'Alex is funding you?'

'In a nutshell. I'll get a cut of the eventual selling price, if I find it.'

'Are you even sure it exists?'

'My father came across the diamond here in Fona. He told me all about it, but it's been missing for years.'

'What makes you believe it's still here?'

'It never reached the open market and the government have no record of it. If they had sold the diamond, it would have made headlines. Most people imagine it's a myth. In a way, that's ensured it is still missing.'

'So why am I about to dig holes in a terrace which looks like someone had already mined it?'

'For good relations. We need the Chief on our side. When you helped him in the airport, I presumed you knew already. I didn't realise you were just being nice.'

Sam couldn't help laughing. 'What a shocking revelation for you! Someone being kind without being paid for it.'

'Don't be cheeky or I'll make you wear those shorts again.'

They both roared with laughter just as Fatima came out to call them in for supper. On hearing their merriment, she deflated on the spot as if she had been slapped. Sam wondered if she had a crush on Fergus.

'Thank you. Just give us a minute to wash our hands,' he said.

***

Fatimata stood in the kitchen, gripping the sideboard in fury and gulping back tears of jealousy. White slut! First, she found Sam in Mr Ned's bedroom and now she was trying to seduce Mr Fergus, her Fergus. Fatimata had imagined it was only a matter of time before he succumbed to her. He must have noticed that he always got the best cuts of meat, the most carefully ironed shirts, the most ardent glances. But now her plans were in tatters. That woman in her tarty shorts had ruined everything. How could he find such a skinny woman attractive?

But Fatimata fought dirty. She bought a powerful juju from the witch doctor and he had promised her Sam would die. It had been expensive, but it would be worth it. The witchdoctor told her to have patience. Sam would pay and soon. She took a deep breath and rearranged her facial expression to neutral before putting the supper on the table.

# Chapter VIII

After a hearty breakfast, Sam circled the porch to the back of the house in search of Dembo, the grumpy parrot. Cashews nestled in her pocket, taken from the Tupperware box in her suitcase where she kept her emergency rations. On a table beside the back steps sat a large, ornate and rusty cage. Inside it, the African Grey used a clawed foot to clean his head feathers. On hearing Sam approach, he fixed her with a beady eye, his toes suspended in mid-air between brush strokes. She made sure he was watching as she pulled a cashew out of her pocket, placing it carefully through the bars of the cage so it fell into a white ceramic bowl at the bottom.

The cashew sat in the centre of the bowl in plain sight. The parrot took a moment to register its presence and then moved down from the perch by using its claws and beak to navigate the bars. It picked up the nut with a claw and examined it with the air of a connoisseur before popping it into its mouth, the purple tongue wrapping over it. Sam let out the breath she had been holding and dropped another nut into the bowl.

As she did, she said, 'Sam's the boss.' The parrot fixed her with a beady stare, cocking his head on one side. 'Sam's the boss,' she said again and dropped a second cashew into the cage.

She waited on the veranda for Sahr to arrive and take her to the terrace. A big smile lit up her face as he drove into the compound. Working in Africa had infected her with joy.

'Why are you smiling?' he asked her. 'Are you happy, madam?'

'Yes, I am.'

Sahr drove to the terrace, smiling in unison with Sam, his sunny good humour improved by having someone happy to drive about. Instead of going straight there, they stopped in town to buy two large sieves for washing the gravel from the pits. That they were on open sale and relatively cheap confirmed Sam's suspicions about the abundance of diamonds in the area. In her experience, artisanal mining signified good news for the grade of minerals in alluvial deposits. A classic sign of rich pickings was local people who could afford to mine small amounts by hand.

Tamba was waiting when they pulled up beside the river, hopping from foot to foot in agitation. She had not told him about buying the sieves.

'Sorry, I'm late, Tamba. I bought some nice new sieves for us to use.'

'We are all late. Someone has been here before us.'

'What are you talking about?'

'Come with me,' he said and headed towards the terrace.

Sahr followed them through the trees to where the workers stood. They stared at the ground as if afraid to catch Sam's eye.

'Good morning,' she said and received a subdued reply from the men so enthusiastic the day before. She was about to question Tamba, but a glance at the terrace told her the whole story.

Broken stakes littered the ground and the grid, so carefully laid down the day before, had been destroyed. The perpetrators had also damaged the tapes, pulling them out from the reels and cutting them to pieces.

'I'm sorry, Sam,' said Tamba, who did not sound at all contrite. 'Someone has destroyed our work. Maybe we should try somewhere else?'

His tone sounded wrong. He did not seem that concerned about the situation and there was something smug about the way he waited her answer. She refused to admit defeat. If the person who had done this formed part of their group, she wanted him to feel impotent against her will.

'Don't worry, Tamba. It's not your fault. Perhaps some cattle got onto the terrace. It won't take us long to redo it. Can you organise a guard for tonight to prevent it happening again?'

Irritation flashed across Tamba's features. It should have been obvious to everyone that cows could not cut measuring tapes into pieces, but the rest of the crew seized on her explanation with relief and they all nodded and repeated it to each other.

'You're right. We'll leave someone tonight. Let's cut more stakes and start again.'

'Sahr, can you take me back into town?' said Sam, ignoring Tamba. 'We need to buy a thirty-metre tape.'

\*\*\*

By the time she returned, the workers had cut new stakes for the grid. They laid them out on the grass. She handed the tape to Tamba and sat in the shade while they set out the grid again. A pile of rocks rested under a big mango tree and she chose one that the abrasion of the river had smoothed into the shape of a lopsided armchair. She took out her notebook, but what could she write? The morning's events preyed on her mind.

Why would someone remove the stakes? Who tried to slow the work down? Or perhaps they didn't want foreigners working in their village? It was not unusual to encounter resistance from the authorities in the area being against the work and organising protests or fomenting resistance in community meetings. It was odd that someone should go against the orders of the Paramount Chief. Who could be that powerful?

The cracking of a twig behind her disturbed her train of thought. Adanna stepped out of the shadows, illuminating the grove in her bright wax-print dress. She had plaited the same material into her hair and drawn it together in a topknot. Not a single hair had the temerity to escape. Was Adanna as controlled as her coiffeur? Sam wanted to penetrate her regal exterior and find out who hid in that shell.

'Hello,' she said, 'what are you doing down here?'

Adanna gasped. Sam realised that Adanna's eyes had not adjusted to the light and that she had not seen her sitting on the stones.

'Gosh, I didn't see you there,' said Adanna, recovering, but not so fast that Sam missed the real fear that crossed the mask-like calm of her face. 'I thought you'd have finished for the day.' A lie and not a great one. Sam decided not to push her.

'We are only getting started. Some cattle got onto the terrace and knocked over the stakes, but it shouldn't take us long to reset the grid.'

'You are sitting in my chair.'

'I am?'

'Well, not my chair, it belonged to my husband and now it's mine.'

'Your husband? I didn't realise you're married.'

'I'm not. He's dead, I think.'

Sam frowned.

'Don't you know for sure?'

'It's none of your business.'

Anger flooded Adanna's features and she turned to leave. Sam jumped up and grabbed her arm.

'Don't go. I'm sorry. I suffer from foot-in-mouth disease. It must be weird not to know something so important.'

'That's okay. It's a long story.'

'Why don't you sit down?' said Sam. 'And I'll get you some juice.'

\*\*\*

Back at the house that evening, Sam lay in the hammock after supper, thinking about the conversation she had with Adanna.

'Tell me about your husband. You must miss him.'

'There's not much to tell. We only married for a short time and we never lived together.'

'What's so special about this rock?'

'Oh, we used to come here so we could be alone together and Pakuteh used to sit alone in the dark when he needed to think. There's no privacy in the compound. Everyone lives on top of everyone else.'

'When was this?'

'About ten years ago.' She smiled at the look on Sam's face. 'We were young. I was sixteen and he was only a year older.'

'Did your father know?'

'Oh, no, he wouldn't have approved of me marrying so young. He got a lot of his ideas from being in the British army. It's hard for me to fit in here because of it.'

'What sort of ideas?'

'Modern ones, not ideas that go down well here, but it led me to marry Pakuteh without telling my father. I don't think it's related to his disappearance.'

'When did he disappear?'

'The night the rebels came to Fona.'

'The rebels came here? But ...' Sam remembered the villages they had driven through. Fona appeared intact. There was no outward sign of any looting or burning of houses.

Adanna's eyes searched for escape, as if in panic. Sam decided that the rebels could wait for another day.

'Do you think he's still alive?' said Sam.

'No, they must have killed him. He wouldn't have left me.'

'I'm so sorry. Are you still single?'

'Yes, no one will marry me now.'

Sam's ignorance of the customs in Simbako prevented her asking more questions. She guessed that it had something to do with virginity, but she was not indiscreet enough to ask such an intimate question. She stored the knowledge for further investigation.

'They must be mad. Most men dream of marrying a princess.'

Adanna changed the subject. 'Why are they digging here?'

'Your father gave us this terrace to do exploration.'

'My father? But ...' An expression of bewilderment crossed her face and she seemed about to speak. But she changed her mind, leaving Sam frustrated. 'I've got to go now.' She stood up. 'We'll talk again,' she said and walked away.

Sam waved at her departing back. She realised the more she knew the less she understood the world and the weird customs people had. That Adanna had sabotaged the grid seemed unlikely.

Ah! She had forgotten to ask Adanna about the little bag of salt she found hidden in her pillowcase. She would find out what it meant later.

\*\*\*

The next morning, Sam experienced déjà vu. The overall damage was limited, except for a bump on the guard's head, as she had taken the precaution of transporting the tape and other equipment home from the terrace in the jeep. However, the work could not progress if this campaign of disruption continued, so she told Tamba to send the men home. She returned to the compound to ask Fergus to set up a meeting with the Chief.

'Why didn't you tell me yesterday?' said Fergus.

'You were busy and I thought it might be a one off, so I didn't bother,' said Sam.

'I'm not sure what the craic is. Someone doesn't want us to dig here.'

'Maybe the Chief can tell us.'

'Oh, I'm sure he can, but whether he will is another question all together.'

'I'll be ready in a minute. Tell Sahr to wait.'

Sam saw a glimpse of feathers at the corner of the house and realised that Dembo was lurking in hope of getting a cashew.

She obliged and said, 'Sam's the boss,' as she dropped a few on the floor in sight of the bird, before withdrawing to the front of the house.

'Get a move on.' Fergus must have been waiting about ten seconds, so patience was certainly not a virtue for him. Sam didn't mind. He was rude to everyone. She liked to feel included. The Chief might tell them more though if she was the one who asked.

\*\*\*

They pulled into the compound at about two o'clock in the afternoon, almost running over some chickens who were enjoying a dust bath in a dry puddle. The main house shimmered in the heat. No-one ventured out into the sun, except for a small child who was dispatched to ask Tamba for permission to visit the Chief. He was snoozing in his hammock when they arrived and nothing would persuade him to arouse Chief Sesay from his slumbers.

'What'll we do now?' said Sam. 'We need to go back to the house and wait an hour or two.'

'Do you fancy a quick field trip?' said Fergus.

Sam couldn't believe her ears. She almost jumped with joy.

'Okay. I'm game. Where to?'

'There are old diamond fields a few kilometres away, if you are interested.'

'That would be great. Let's go now.'

Fergus grinned at her enthusiasm.

The diggings at Mano were nearby, but the state of the roads verged on atrocious due to the heavy rains. Sahr had a tough time keeping the jeep on the road. It juddered and slid the ten kilometres north, stopping finally on the top of a small knoll overlooking a vast plain covered in piles of gravel with water-filled pits stretching to the horizon. Hundreds of muddy workers toiled in the heat. Rusty machinery littered the roads that led to an abandoned washing plant, its girders skeletal against the blue sky. Sam stood in silence, staring at the ant-like activity below.

'That's why we're here,' said Fergus.

'I don't understand what all those people are doing. Hasn't this ground already been mined?' Sam said.

'Many times. But the methods used in the past were rudimentary. These alluvials had bonanza grades. The companies wanted to obtain the maximum price they could per carat and the maximum number of stones over half a carat. Plant design meant that the largest and smallest diamonds got ejected in the waste and put on the spoil heaps.'

'So, there could still be large diamonds in the material?'

'Bound to be. But some heaps have been processed many times and others not at all. Can you tell the difference?'

'I'd need a set of sieves to look at the size fractions.'

'These people have nothing, but willpower and hope.'

They stood for a while, watching the miners struggling to excavate gravel from the pits. Sam took photographs using her telephoto lens, trying to capture the essence of the place.

'Seen enough?' said Fergus.

She nodded. 'I'd like to come back another time and investigate which materials they are processing. Do you think they'd let me watch them work?'

'I don't see why not. They mine without a licence, so they aren't entitled to privacy. If we approach without fuss, they shouldn't object.'

They got back into the car and left for Fona.

'I'd like to see the terrace we are working on from the other side of the river. Do you think we could drop in there before we visit the Chief? I only need five minutes.'

'Sure. Let's have a look.'

'The thing is, I'm not sure we're allowed there,' said Sam.

'No bother. We won't take anything, will we?'

'No, just look across the river.'

'I'm sure that's fine. Come on.'

Sahr had memorised every road in the district and taking what seemed to Sam to be a tortuous route, he stopped at the edge of a meadow bordering the river. He pointed out the opposite bank.

'That's where you are working, Sam.'

Sam and Fergus walked down to the riverbank along a small path which cut through the terrace. Sam looked across the river at the terrace where they excavated the pits. From where they were standing, it appeared to be a well-formed terrace with defined strata of different sized pebbles in their sandy matrix. The directions of ancient currents were preserved in the imbrications of their smooth forms, worn down by millennia spent in the river. The layers disappeared in the downriver portion of the terrace where the strata dipped down and thickened into the bank.

A lightbulb illuminated in Sam's head. They had explored the wrong part of the terrace. There was no point blaming Tamba. He had affected ignorance of mining for diamonds and, by going along with his suggestions, she had created the beginnings of a fragile trust between them. If they kept working, they would test the best part of the terrace in a few weeks anyway.

She turned her back on the terrace and examined the material in the riverbank. It was similar or identical to that of the terrace on which they worked – bands of imbricated pebbles divided by layers of red sand. She bent down to examine the pebbles on the beach. Some had concentric patterns. She collected a few of the most unusual ones to take home.

'What you got there, Sam?' said Fergus.

'Just pretty pebbles. Chalcedony. Look.' She spat on one and held it out to him.

'Yuck! I'm not taking that.'

'Oh, go on, don't be such a fusspot!'

He took the pebble from her and gazed at it in genuine wonder. 'Wow! These are brilliant! My mam would like one of these. She collects stuff like this.' He reached out to grab one from the bank.

In a flash, something shot out from a hole in the bank, grazing his hand which he whipped away. The viper slithered onto on the sand, casting a resentful backward glance at them. Fergus wiped his hand.

'Jaysus, that was close,' he said.

'Did it get you?' said Sam.

'Only a scratch.'

'Thanks to your reactions. Did you play cricket?'

'I did. Fast bowler. Have you seen what you wanted to?'

Sam gazed across to the other bank with its lumpy surface and a thick wedge of strata. She took photographs for comparison.

'Yes, thank you. This was useful. Sorry about your hand.'

'It's nothing. Just another war wound to add to the collection.'

Sam rolled her eyes and made for the car.

***

After a warm fizzy drink in town, they returned to the Chief's compound to see if he could receive them. Tamba lay slumped in a hammock outside on the balcony, his tummy like a stranded beach ball in a fishing net. A plump boy whisked flies away with a large fan.

'Hi Tamba. We're back. Can you get us in to speak to the boss?' said Fergus.

Tamba looked up with a mixture of irritation and concern.

'What's so important?' he said. 'The Chief doesn't like to be disturbed in the afternoon.'

'I don't think he'll mind this time,' said Fergus. 'We've come about the terrace.'

'Ah, yes, the terrace. Wait here.'

With a mammoth effort, he swung his legs out of the hammock, creating enough momentum to take his stomach with them. The child caught his outstretched hand, braced his short legs and pulled him up in one swift movement before he could fall backwards again.

'That's a neat trick,' said Fergus.

'They've done that before,' said Sam.

Tamba disappeared inside, huffing. Sam kicked over a couple more of the mosquito breeding pots in the yard. Fergus shook his head at her. She spread her hands to question him, but he said nothing. She shuffled her feet in frustration, making scars in the red dust.

Moments later, Tamba reappeared and signalled for them to follow him. To her surprise, he showed them into the family sitting room with the fabled comfy chairs. The Chief sat in one with a thin child on his knee.

'Sam. Come in,' he said, ignoring Fergus.

They sat opposite him, sinking into the soft cushions that felt as if they belonged to a carnivorous plant that might swallow them at any moment.

'How can I help you?' said the Chief, depositing the child on the floor where he was swept up by a harassed-looking young woman.

'It's a delicate manner,' said Fergus.

'Isn't it always?' said the Chief.

'We have a saboteur, sir.'

The Chief blinked. His whole manner changed and he seemed to inflate, his body straightening in the chair. Sam could see the military man inside him straining to escape his useless body.

'What on earth do you mean?' he said, his voice crisp with rage.

'Someone doesn't want us exploring the river terrace. They have twice destroyed the grid and, last night, they knocked out the guard.'

'Is there any reason they might try to stop us?' said Sam before Sesay could answer.

'Reason? No, I don't think so. What reason could they have?'

'I'm sorry if it's upsetting. It's just that we come back to square one every morning and I can't make any progress. If we shouldn't be working there, perhaps we could move across the river. There is a nice terrace there too.'

'Maybe she is right, sir,' said Tamba, 'that terrace is bad luck.'

'Don't contradict me! I'm the Paramount Chief. No-one decides what happens in my territory except me. Do you understand?' He quivered with indignation and Tamba lowered his head as if to avoid imaginary blows.

'Yes, sir, I do. I'm sure Mr Fergus and Miss Sam will carry on the good work with your support.' He didn't look sure though. A sullen look had taken residence on his plump face.

The Chief stood up.

'I will make certain this doesn't happen again. You may go back tomorrow. No-one will disturb your work. Please leave me now. I am tired.'

'Thank you, Chief Sesay. We're sorry we disturbed you,' said Fergus.

Shaken by the Chief's violent reaction to Tamba's interjection, Sam hung back. Her suspicions about the terrace were confirmed. The Chief turned to Sam, seeing her body language and modulated his tone.

'Before you go,' he said, 'I understand you spoke to my daughter yesterday.'

'Yes, sir,' said Sam.

'I would like you to speak to her again. She suffers from a deep sadness and I'm at a loss. She might tell her secret to someone who is not local. I'd be grateful if you could talk to her about it and tell me how it goes.'

Sam had no intention of telling Chief Sesay any of Adanna's secrets. 'I will, although I'm not sure she would confide in me. I'll tell you anything important,' she said, crossing her fingers behind her back.

'Thank you, my dear. I knew I could count on you.'

\*\*\*

'What was that about?' said Fergus at dinner.

'What was what about?' said Sam, blushing. She couldn't lie to save her life.

'Don't act all innocent and rosy-cheeked with me, missy. I'm not stupid and there is something you aren't telling. Am I right or am I right?'

'I've no idea what you're talking about. We discussed girls' stuff, women's problems.'

Fergus blanched. Sam guessed right. He wouldn't pursue that topic.

'You need to tell me if you talk about anything else. It could be important.'

'Pass me the rice please.'

They ate in silence. Fatimata had cooked a goat curry which had so much chilli in it that Sam struggled to eat. Fergus wolfed it down with great gusto, but when he sat back after cleaning his plate, he was sweating.

'Hot, huh?' said Sam. 'I thought you were macho?'

Fergus stared at her as if surprised to find her there. His eyes were unfocused and he got unsteadily to his feet.

'Fergus? Are you alright?'

'I don't feel so good.' He swayed. Sam jumped up and ran around the table in time to steady him.

'Okay,' she said. 'Let's get you to bed.'

He leant on her and she staggered under his bulk as she tried to get him down the passageway. Opening the door with her left hand, she manoeuvred him into the room and left him leaning against the wall. She pulled back the sheets and grabbed him again as he slid down it.

'Come on, you can make it.'

Fergus fell flat on his back in the bed, moaning with fever. Sam noticed his hand. It was red and puffy with a scarlet line of inflammation etched across the back. So, the viper's teeth had been dirty? Fergus flapped out his arm and wrapped it around Sam's waist.

'Are you coming to bed?' he said.

'No, not right now.'

'That's a shame. You have nice boobies.'

Sam giggled to herself. 'Thanks,' she said, 'now go to sleep.'

There were no puncture wounds and a scratch wasn't dangerous. His forehead felt clammy, but he didn't appear to have a high fever and he must be lucid if he could focus on her breasts. She pulled off his shoes, debating taking of his trousers, but as she reached for the belt, she realised she wasn't that brave.

Once she had covered him in a sheet, she went to look for Fatimata to minister to him, but she had vanished. The wound needed cleaning before she let him sleep it off, so she got the first aid box from the kitchen.

She returned to Fergus' bedroom to find him asleep, snoring between the sheets. After wiping the graze clean, she sprayed it with antiseptic and covered it with a plaster, so he couldn't scratch it. Then, closing the door carefully so as not to wake him, she crept down the passage to her bedroom and entered.

She did not see Fatimata watching her from the entrance hall, her face dark with rage.

# Chapter IX

The next morning Fergus was already eating breakfast with his normal gusto when Sam came to the table.

'Morning. You feeling better?' she said.

'Better? Than what? I don't remember what happened, to be honest.'

'You got viper venom in that scratch.'

'Ah, the band aid. I wondered where that came from. Fatimata? Can you bring us more toast please?'

A crashing sound emanated from the kitchen like pots being slammed down or oven doors being shut with force. Fergus shrugged. Fatimata's tantrums were common.

'Are we okay to start again this morning?'

'Tamba didn't seem very enthusiastic yesterday. I can't help feeling he may be involved somehow,' said Sam.

'Tamba? Why would he help us with one hand only to sabotage us with the other?'

'I've no idea. It's just a feeling.'

'And I've a feeling I need more toast. Where is Fatimata?'

The kitchen door opened and she burst into the room carrying a plate loaded with toast which she dropped onto the table before sailing out again like a recalcitrant tanker. The toast was carbonised. Fergus picked up a piece and examined it.

'I like my toast well done, but this is ridiculous,' he said.

'What did you do?' said Sam.

'Who knows? The woman is a complete mystery.'

They finished breakfast in silence. Before they set out for the terrace, Sam visited Dembo, the parrot and gave him a cashew.

'Sam's the boss,' she said holding a cashew just out of reach of the sharp beak. 'Sam's the boss.' The parrot twisted its head to one side as if listening. 'Sam's the boss,' she repeated waving the cashew.

'Where are you, goddamn it? We're leaving.' Fergus' voice. Exasperated. Sam threw several cashews into the cage. Dembo would capitulate soon.

'On my way. I need to use the bathroom first.'

'For God's sake, woman, get a move on. We haven't got all day.'

They did, but Sam did not point this out. Sahr drove them to the terrace where Tamba and the team waited in the shade.

'Hi Tamba!' said Fergus, 'You got a minute?'

Tamba shambled over and the two men stood with their backs to Sam pretending to gaze at the river, but, in reality, they had formed a physical barrier to her presence that said you are not invited to this conversation. Fergus put his hand on Tamba's shoulder and stared straight into his eyes. He spoke to him without smiling and waited. Tamba shook his head. Seemingly convinced by what he read there, Fergus let go, and returned to the car.

'Everything alright?' said Sam.

'Perfect,' said Fergus and jumped into the car beside Sahr.

He stuck his arm out of the window and grabbed onto the roof. The muscles in his forearm and bicep flexed as the car bounced its way back to the road. He glanced back at her and flashed her a big smile with teeth that looked like they would eat her at one sitting. A lion personified. Sam could not pretend to be totally immune to his brand of charm. Annoying and bossy, he was as handsome as a film star on safari. What a pity he knew it.

She wished that Ned would hurry and come back from Njahili. She coped better with them both there. Fergus always lost compared to Ned. She sighed and put her hair in a bun before stuffing it under her floppy hat.

'Okay, then. Let's try again,' said Sam.

Tamba seemed subdued, but he got to work organising everyone. Sam sat in Adanna's chair to watch proceedings from the shade. She emerged to make notes and take photographs. She took handfuls of pebbles to measure and identify. The warm stones lulled her into a state of relaxation and she had nodded off in the humid warmth of the morning when there was a rustle in the trees. She spun around in a panic, imagining a ferocious animal stalking her. Too many Tarzan movies.

Adanna appeared in the shadows, carrying a parcel wrapped in palm leaves.

'A peace offering,' she said, giving it to Sam.

'Gosh, thanks. What is it?'

'Lunch. Do you want to eat together?'

'Isn't it early for lunch?'

'I'm always hungry.'

'Me too.'

Rice, fried plantains, chewy chicken in spicy tomato sauce, all eaten with fingers, licked clean with tongues vibrant with chilli. Sam wiped her mouth with the back of her hand and patted her stomach.

'That tasted delicious, thank you.'

'I'm glad you liked it. I can't cook many recipes. My father has people who prepare his food and they don't like me interfering in the kitchen.'

'Didn't your mother teach you to cook? Mine forced us to learn the basics before we left home.' Sam didn't add, 'so we might find a nice husband.' Ned had already told her that Adanna's mother had died in childbirth, so she was acting dumb to see if she could find out more about the ice princess.

'My mother?' said Adanna. 'No, she died in childbirth.'

'I'm sorry. Nobody told me.' Sam blushed at her bad lie.

'Oh, now I've embarrassed you. You shouldn't worry. My father's done a good job on his own.'

'But he never married again?'

'His heart broke when she died and he's never recovered.'

'Didn't the elders oblige him to produce a male heir for the Chiefdom?'

'Why do you think that? We're not savages. I'm the heir, or at least the first in line. They may choose someone else if there is a better candidate.'

'I apologise. I didn't realise female Paramount Chiefs existed. First-born sons still inherit the throne in England.'

'Yes, you're backward over there.'

Sam caught her expression and saw a laugh danced behind the dark pupils. She smiled.

'We can't help it. I had to cut the chains to escape from my boyfriend. He tried to stop me coming here.'

'I can see why. If you hang around me, you will be li-ber-ated. Big time.'

\*\*\*

Ned drove into the yard of the house at Fona, scattering the palm leaves and almost running over Dembo, who stalked back to his cage, swearing in parrot. He sat in the car for a minute watching the leaves swirl around the yard and trying to slow his heartbeat. He was excited about seeing Sam again. There was something about her that made him want to reach through her guarded exterior and touch her hidden core. Before he left for Njahili, he had decided to start again with her, if she would have him, but the journey to the capital city had confused him and now he didn't know what he wanted.

It started with his call to Alex Simmonds to tell him about the passport.

'Did anyone get hurt? How is Sam?'

'No, only shaken. Sam's fine. She's a trooper. Where did you find her?'

'Blame my wife. She suggested that Sam might have more success charming our Chief Sesay than Fergus.'

'She was right. The Chief almost purrs when she enters the room.' I do too. 'Only Fergus is immune to Sam, she inspires strong emotions. Fatimata is cooking up black magic in the kitchen to get rid of her.'

'Ah, Fatimata. She's dying of unrequited love for the Irish hunk. Sam will prove to be powerful competition for her. Anyway, enough of the soap opera that is Fona. How far have we got?'

'The Chief's agreed to let us explore one terrace near the village. Sam complained that she didn't get to choose a terrace based on geology rather than a royal decree, but she'll get over it. She gets on well with the Chief's daughter, Adanna, who is only slightly younger than her. She's got secrets too.'

'That's encouraging. Fergus seems convinced about the diamond's existence. I hope he's right.'

'Even if we can't find it, it's likely that an area which had one large diamond will yield another. We'll soon find out.'

'I like your logic. Oh, Gemma called me. She needs to speak to you. Can you ring her?'

'My wife? Oh, it must be about the divorce papers. I should have signed them by now, but I admit to avoiding it.'

'You need to do it as soon as you are able, so you can get on with your lives. I only found Sandra after I divorced my first wife.'

'I found it hard to accept that the marriage had finished after such a short time. We seemed to have such a perfect relationship before we married.'

'It happens. Do you remember her number?'

'Yes, thanks.'

'Okay, good luck with the passport. Get back there as soon as possible. I don't fancy Sam's chances alone with Fergus.' Simmonds laughed. Ned forced a bark.

'Sam can look after herself. We'll call soon from there with news.'

'I'll visit before too long. See you in Fona.'

'Bye then.'

'Call Gemma.'

Alex liked to give advice. The divorce from his first wife had been a success due to the mutual loathing they both endured. Neither of them could wait to get away and start again. It was different for Ned. He still loved Gemma, even though she had chosen someone else. The initial hurt and confusion had dissipated, but he still hoped it might be a mistake. Meeting Sam had made things worse though. Now he doubted his original feelings for Gemma. Did their student romance just peter out? Was Sam just light relief? He felt a connection with her that night in the bar, but what if it was it drink and coincidence? He rang Gemma.

'Hello?'

'Hi Gemma. It's me, Ned. Alex told me you wanted to talk.'

'Ned, how are you? I was expecting to hear from you.'

'Sorry about the divorce papers. I promise to sign them the next time I'm in Britain.'

'Oh, I didn't mean about that, although it's something I wanted to discuss.'

'What's the problem? Hadn't we agreed to go fifty-fifty on everything?'

'We had. That's not it. It's just …'

'It's just what?'

'Are you sure you want to go ahead with the divorce?'

'Me? You did this. You didn't give me a choice. It's not me who went shopping for something better.'

'Don't be angry. I'm the one in the wrong. You spent a long time away though. I got lonely.'

'Lonely? What about me?'

'You had plenty to do. It's different.'

'I don't believe it is. You chose someone else. How am I meant to accept that?'

There was a silence. He heard birds in her garden and he imagined the wild roses in the hedgerows, the smell of honeysuckle in the evening. The perfect home for the perfect couple. What a cliché!

'I'm not seeing him anymore.'

Now it was his turn to be speechless. *Was it a trap? Was he on Candid Camera?*

'What happened?' He couldn't risk a longer sentence in case his voice quavered.

'He went back to his wife. She blackmailed him with the children.'

Should he say sorry? Because he wasn't. He felt smug and self-righteous. 'I told you so' hovered in his throat.

'Oh,' he said.

'I don't expect you to sympathise. I made a mistake. You were the love of my life.'

Past tense. 'What am I now?'

'I'm not sure. That's why I wanted to talk to you. To work out if we should try again.'

Ned didn't remember saying anything else. He mumbled something to give himself an excuse to put down the phone. How did he treat this offer? He had longed for her to say this, dreamt about it for months, even though he assumed it was hopeless. And now, out of the blue, it happened. It seemed like redemption. What about Sam though?

A knock on the car window startled him out of his reverie.

'Mr Ned? Are you alright?'

Fatimata loomed across the sun like an eclipse.

'Yes, thank you.'

'You should come indoors. It will rain soon.'

Ned peered through the smeared massacre of insects on the windscreen of the Toyota and saw only a blue sky that stood out like a colour on a paint chart. There was no point arguing with Fatimata, who considered herself to be an authority on the local weather, but his stubborn side won.

'There's not a cloud in the sky. How do you know?'

A dark cloud that passed through Fatimata's face. She didn't like to be contradicted.

'I know a lot of things.'

'So, can you tell me where Sam is?' said Ned, reaching into the back of the car for his bag.

'That woman is digging the terrace with Tamba.'

'I wish you wouldn't call her that. Her name is Miss Harris and she is our guest. You should treat her with respect.'

'Like Mr Fergus does?'

Ned considered his answer. He sensed an ambush, but he shouldn't let her get away with this attitude.

'Yes, just like that.'

'So, are you going to invite her to your room tonight?'

'What are you talking about? How dare you speak to me like that?'

Fatimata gave him a smug glance. 'You told me to treat her like Fergus does. She came out of his room one evening. You should be aware who you are dealing with. That woman is a whore and mine is a Christian household.'

Ned examined her face, trying to discern if she had lied, but he only read a look of triumph. He had walked right into that one.

'I'm not discussing this with you,' he said. 'Make me some tea please, the drive has tired me out.'

Fatimata glided off into the house, her prodigious backside disappearing after the rest of her, leaving Ned winded and shocked.

\*\*\*

116

'Mr Ned is back,' said Sahr as they pulled into the compound and stopped beside the Toyota.

Sam tried to stem the irrational tide of emotion that threatened to make her heart burst out of her chest and bounce into the house under its own steam.

'That was quick. I understood it would take him longer than that to get a new passport.'

'He took a copy of the old one. Maybe that made it easier.'

'Perhaps. Thank you, Sahr. I guess you won't be here in the morning then?'

'I'm not sure. Can you ask Mr Fergus to come and talk to me please?'

That meant that they had a moment alone before Fergus came back in. Sam had been picturing this for days. The last thing Ned had said was that he was falling in love with her. That kind of declaration wasn't common. It happened to other people, in movies, not to Sam. It wasn't easy to put that out of her mind, even with all the shenanigans over the terrace.

She tried to keep a neutral face as she entered the house. Ned and Fergus sat at a table covered in papers held down by dirty cups. Fergus was examining the satellite phone as if he was about to throw it across the room. The fan chugged away on the ceiling, shaking the heavy fitting in a way which suggested it was loosening its moorings and preparing for a death plunge. Sam never switched it on as she was certain it would fall on her head one day.

'That thing's a death trap,' she said to no-one in particular. 'Fergus, Sahr is outside and he wants to discuss his shifts with you. Oh, hi Ned, didn't realise you were back.'

Fergus raised an eyebrow, but he didn't comment. Sam caught his eye and grinned.

'I'd better go outside and ask what he wants,' said Fergus, hamming it up.

Sam glanced to check if Ned joined in with the charade. To her disappointment, he shuffled papers, avoiding her eyes.

'How did your trip go, Ned?' she said.

'Boring. Bureaucratic.'

'You got your passport then?'

'Yes. Are we going to converse about the bleeding obvious?'

Sam jumped back as if he had slapped her. The edge in his voice cut off all romance like a scythe in the grass.

She blushed with shame. What had happened? This was a train wreck. She needed to get out of there.

She whirled around and bumped into Fergus who grabbed her to stop her falling.

'This is cosy,' he said, laughing, trapping her in his arms and missing the distress on her face. She pulled away and ran to her room, trying to keep in the tears which demanded escape.

'What the fuck?' said Fergus. 'What did I do?'

'As if you didn't know,' said Ned, who also headed for his room, his own behaviour having upset him almost as much as it had Sam. He went inside and slammed the door

Fergus stood alone in the dining room, shaking his head. 'Tea, Fatimata! Tea, now for God's sake.'

*** 

Sam did not leave her room again that evening. Fergus and Ned ate in an atmosphere that was far from convivial. Fatimata slammed plates down on the table and had put so much salt in the food that it was inedible. The fan shook bits of plaster onto their plates.

'Sam might be right about the fan,' said Fergus. 'Should we get someone in to fix it?'

'Why don't you ask her?'

'I'm asking you. What on earth happened in Njahili? It must be bad because I've never seen you like this before.'

'It's not about Njahili. Don't act innocent with me. How could you do it? I realise I'm your employee, but I imagined we were friends too, since we've known each other thirty years.'

'Ned, I still don't understand what you're talking about. Did you fight with your wife?'

'I can't believe you're trying to blame Gemma. Did you sleep with her too?'

'Steady on there. There's no need for that,' said Fergus, perplexed. He had never seen Ned like this.

'There is.' Ned stood up, white in the face. 'You had no right. Stand up!'

'Jesus, what the hell's going on? Are you going to hit me?'

'You deserve it. Why did you take her from me? Did you even try to resist it? Hasn't your family humiliated us enough yet?'

'Who, your wife? What are you talking about?' His bewildered expression stopped Ned in his tracks.

'Don't deny it. Fatimata told me.'

'She told you what? Are you crazy?'

'She noticed Sam coming out of your room one night.'

The light dawned. Fergus put his hand on Ned's arm and spoke softly.

'Neddy, listen to me. There's a good reason for it.'

Ned whipped his arm away as if scalded.

'Oh, I bet there is. What was she doing in there?'

'I got bitten by an adder and fainted at dinner. She dragged me to my room and cleaned the wound. Look.'

He proffered his hand which shone pink and inflamed at the edge of the graze. 'I didn't even sense her in my room, but Fatimata must have seen her coming out after she was finished and drawn her own conclusions. That woman is a vicious gossip machine.'

'A snakebite? Do you swear?'

'Come on, Neddy, do you imagine I'd touch your precious Sam? She wouldn't even put the shorts on for me.'

He ducked just in time.

\*\*\*

Later that evening, Ned advanced down the passageway and stood outside Sam's door. He whispered her name, but she didn't answer. It was hard to blame her after the way he'd behaved. She might be asleep. He was too ashamed to find out. It would be easier in the morning. He crept away again.

# Chapter X

Sam got up at dawn determined to get out of the house before Ned surfaced. She packed herself a lunch of fruit and nuts and made a flask of tea and put them in her rucksack, leaving a few cashews out for Dembo the parrot. Then, with some trepidation, she made herself some breakfast in Fatimata's kingdom. Carrying her eggs and toast out of the kitchen, she pulled out a chair and sat at the table. She ate without enjoying her food and sighed several times, unable to keep the disappointment in. She told herself that she was just being stupid and that Fergus had been right in the first place.

Ned had obviously changed his mind while he was in Njahili. Perhaps he had spoken to his wife. Whatever the reason, she was not in the mood to see him and experience the quiet humiliation of the rejected under the scathing gaze of Fergus.

Finishing her toast and gulping down her tea, she went around the back of the house to get some bottled water and feed the parrot. Dembo snoozed in his cage in the early morning sunlight which pierced the bars and warmed his grey feathers. He was having a parrot-themed dream and one of his feet was twitching on the bar.

'Dembo? Dembo!'

The parrot turned to face her and, seeing who it was, he shuffled along the bar until he was almost touching the side of the cage. He opened his mouth, showing her his lovely purple tongue.

'Sam's the boss,' said Sam holding a cashew just out of reach of the bars. 'Sam's the boss.'

Dembo tried to grab the cashew with his lethal beak, but she pulled it back a fraction and waited.

'Sam's the boss,' she said again. Dembo peered at her as if gauging the likelihood of his prize.

'Sam,' he said.

Sam didn't know whether to be delighted or miffed.

Throwing caution to the wind, she offered him a cashew through the bars of the cage and he almost took her finger off. He sat there, looking pleased with himself.

Shaking her hand and holding in the swear words, it occurred to her that they were both trying to get something, both trying to fool each other into doing what the other wanted. Like life really.

Five minutes later, having given him several more nuts without result, she went to get the keys for the car, which were hanging on a nail inside the front door.

She grabbed them and the rucksack and let herself into the jeep, which smelt irritatingly of Ned, reminding her why she was sneaking off early. She tried to concentrate on her triumph with the parrot. Any day now! Revenge was sweet. Imagining Fatimata's face when Dembo finally let rip was some consolation. The next time Fatimata dangled some treat in front of him she would get a nasty shock. And the best thing was that, like Pavlov's dogs, he would still say it long after Sam had left. Revenge was a dish best served cold.

She started the car and turned towards the gate. She hadn't driven for almost two years, but her muscle memory was good as she flicked the car into gear. Putting a cassette into the tape deck, she turned up the volume to drown out her misery. She reversed the car and dragged the steering wheel to the right to turn the jeep. Then she put the car in second gear and crept out of the yard.

As she drove out, she saw Ned come running out of the house, his hair sticking up in the air. He was waving and shouting, but she pretended not to hear or see him. Let him stew, she thought, and swung the jeep into the street almost hitting a cow that was wandering along the road outside the house. She swerved around it and set off down the street.

When she got to the river, she sat in the car listening to the end of the song, singing along with R.E.M. 'That was just a dream, just a dream, dream.'

She gazed across the river, trying not to be upset. The trees were still in the hot air and a haze rose from the ground. Birds were squabbling over their tightly packed territories, squawking and flapping their dusty feathers. She took a couple of deep breaths, letting them out slowly and releasing the tension of the night before. Try as she might, she couldn't fathom Ned's reaction.

She pushed it to the back of her mind. Work came first.

Suddenly, she saw a flash of white between the trunks. Something was moving around in the copse opposite the terrace. Something or someone. Then she saw them. A group of girls sneaking through the trees. Their skin had been painted white. Their strange pale faces contrasted with their dark hair. She got out of the car slowly, but they saw her and withdrew further into the trees, melting into the darkness. Had she really seen them or was she imagining things?

Tamba came bustling over.

'Miss Sam, good morning. We are ready to start again. The men are putting in the grid and we should be ready to start digging after lunch.'

'That's great news, Tamba. Thank you.'

They walked to the river bank and greeted the workers. Sam made her way to her usual spot on the stone seat and was surprised when Tamba came with her. He stood fidgeting like that he wanted to tell her something, but she didn't force the issue.

'Would you like a cup of tea?' she said.

'No, thank you, Miss Sam.' He sat on another one of the rocks, looking out over the terrace and watched the work progressing, but his heart clearly wasn't in it. Sam waited. It was hard for her not to fill the silence with chat, but for once she had the correct instinct.

'Have you heard much about the civil war in Simbako?' said Tamba.

'No, I'm sorry to say that I'm pretty ignorant about it. I know that it finished recently, but I don't know much else.'

'Would you like me to tell you? It might help you understand the way things are around here.'

Sam was not sure to what state of affairs Tamba was referring, but she wasn't going to say so.

'That would be great. I'm all ears.'

'The war was at its height about ten years ago. The rebel soldiers who started the war came not from Simbako, but across the border from Liberia. They were irregular forces hired by warlords who were fighting over Liberian territory containing diamond deposits. When the U.N. entered Liberia, these mercenaries were chased over the border to Simbako by U.N. troops supporting the new government. The rebel forces were not inclined to disband and saw the northern villages of Simbako as easy targets. They followed the trail of the illegal diamonds smuggled out by the Lebanese traders. They were keen to take advantage of the diamond-rich alluvial deposits in east of the country which had no protection from marauding forces with no scruples.

'As you know, river gravels are easily exploited using no more than a shovel and a sieve, and the rich pickings in Simbako were just too tempting. The soldiers were joined by local unemployed youths who wanted to get rich quick. There was little resistance. People who stood in their way were murdered or locked in their houses and burnt to death. Those left alive were used as slaves to dig up the wealth under their feet. Anyone caught stealing a diamond or trying to escape had their hands cut off. The rebels used to ask them if they wanted long sleeves or short sleeves before chopping off their hands at the wrist or elbow with a machete or axe. The women were raped as a matter of course, often by their own soldiers, as well as the rebels. There was no escape from the horror.

'Eventually these soldiers moved into central Simbako. They came to Fona and overran the Chief's compound.'

'They came here? But I didn't see any burnt buildings or destruction. It's impossible to tell that they came this way. Were people killed?'

One of the workers appeared in the shadows to tell them that they were ready to dig the first pit. Tamba jumped up as if relieved.

'I will tell you more later. Can you please come with me and direct the excavations of the first pit? I want you to explain what needs to be measured and how we separate the materials.'

Saved by the bell. Sam frowned. 'I'll be out in just a minute.'

Intensely frustrated, she took a couple of deep breaths before following him to the edge of the trees. She wanted to find out more about the raid on Fona, but she wasn't sure if Tamba would tell her the truth.

And, as if on cue, she saw the painted girls again. They were on the other bank, gesticulating at her. She stood up and they all faded into the blackness again. Standing very still, she waited. One of the girls peeped around a tree and smiled at her, beckoning to her with a white hand with a black palm. Sam smiled back and shook her head. Some of the other girls joined in, making her giggle. The white paint made them look like dappled tree trunks undulating in the wind.

Suddenly, they all disappeared.

Tamba emerged at the edge of the glade, his round silhouette sharp against the light.

'Are you ready? I need your help.'

'Of course.' She peered into the trees, but the girls had gone. 'Did you see them?' she said.

'See who?' said Tamba. 'There is no-one over there.'

'But there were some girls in the trees who had been painted white. At least, I think that's what I saw.'

'The *sowei* are performing their initiation into womanhood.'

'Who are the *sowei*?'

'I think you would call them wise women.'

'But why are they in the forest?'

'It is a sacred place. The *bondo* is hidden from the eyes of men. We are forbidden to enter or look into it.'

'The *bondo*? What is that?'

'I can't tell you. You must ask a *sowei*.'

'But, why …'

'Don't ask me again. I may not speak of it.'

'But I don't know a *sowei*.'

'You live with one. Ask Auntie Fatou to tell you about the *bondo*. She knows everything about it.'

Sam could not imagine that Fatimata would be very forthcoming after recent events. She was not exactly on speaking terms with the living battle cruiser.

'Can I ask Adanna?'

Tamba laughed. A nasty sound that caught in the back of his throat. 'You may ask her, but she can't tell you about it. She's not been to the *bondo*. She is unclean.'

Sam was shocked by this description, but she was completely out of her depth. What did he mean by unclean? It felt like a betrayal to ask Tamba about Adanna. For some reason, he seemed to despise her and Sam was not prepared to feed his wrath by asking him why.

'I will ask Fatimata. Let's go and see this gravel then.'

Tamba shrugged and headed for the terrace. Sam followed him into the sunlight.

*** 

There was no escape once Tamba and the men had gone. Try as she might to drag it out, she had to go home and face the music. She hated conflict of any sort and would normally have done anything to avoid it, but this was different. Work was work and she had to be professional.

Nevertheless, she stopped on the way home for a warm Seven-Up, hoping to delay the inevitable scene. She pulled the car off the road and got out, jumping over the puddles on the mud road onto the wooden boardwalk.

She pushed through the swinging half-doors into the local grocer's shop wearing her metaphorical cowboy hat. She should have tied the car to a hitching post.

Then she saw Ned sitting on a stool at the counter with his back to her. She patted her sides automatically, as if looking for a weapon. Wasn't it Doc Holiday who was shot in the back while having a sarsaparilla at the bar?

She wanted to leave, but she was too slow. Ned glanced back over his shoulder and his face lit up.

'Sam, you're here. Thank goodness.'

She felt as if she had entered a parallel universe. Calamity Sam meet Ned Holiday.

'Oh, hi.' She stood her ground.

'Don't be like that,' he said, getting off his stool and walking towards her.

'Like what? You're the one who treated me like shit on your shoe.'

He stopped. His face fell, he held his hands out helplessly.

'I did. I know. I'm an idiot. I'm so sorry. I'm pond scum. No, it's worse. I'm the mould on pond scum.'

'Enough about you,' said Sam, trying not to laugh. 'What on earth was that all about last night? What did I do to get that reaction?'

'It wasn't you. Fatou told me that you slept in Fergus' room while I was away. It's just the sort of thing he would do to me. I should have known that she was lying. I was jealous.'

'I went to his room once,' said Sam, 'I didn't realise that she had seen me.'

'Fergus told me about the snakebite.'

'So that's what he called it?'

His startled face was a picture.

She burst out laughing.

'I told you I was an idiot,' he said.

'And you were right.'

'It's a pity about Fatou though. She will hate me more than ever now, if she thinks I have been to bed with her crush. I wanted to ask her about something Tamba said.'

'I wouldn't recommend it. She's not talking to anyone. Fergus has had to suck up to her all day just to get us some dinner. Anyway, who cares what Tamba says?'

'Can I have a Seven-Up?'

***

By the time, they went home for supper, they had re-established their connection. Apart from the loud burp that escaped her after the second Seven-Up, it was really pretty romantic sitting in the fading light of the saloon.

Fergus was waiting for them, his body rigid with tension. On seeing them arrive together, both smiling, he beamed and exhaled the breath he had been holding.

'Aha, you're here. Great. I'm starving. Fatou! Please can you serve dinner now?'

Even Fatimata seemed in a better mood, brushing playfully up against Fergus a couple of times and almost knocking him off his chair. And the food was back to normal. Lovely chicken stew with mountains of rice and fried sweet plantains steamed on their plates and up their noses. Sam was so hungry, she almost licked the plate.

'Steady on, girl,' said Fergus, 'leave the pattern on the Delph.'

'What's Delph?' said Ned.

'It's an Irish word for crockery,' said Sam.

'Well, now aren't you the deep one?' said Fergus, 'and how do you know that?'

'Oh, some boyfriend or other.'

'I thought you had some Irish in you,' said Fergus, who got thumped for his trouble.

After eating, Sam went out to sit crossways in the hammock with her feet hanging over the edge. She didn't admit to herself that she was leaving a space for Ned, but it was asking to be filled. Pulling the hammock's material up behind her back, she swung in the night air. The door opened and she held her breath. To her dismay, both men came out.

'Grand,' said Fergus and before she could protest, he fell back into the hammock on Sam's right-hand side.

'Well, this is cosy,' said Ned, and did the same on her left.

Sam examined them both and rolled her eyes. 'Don't even think about a ménage à trois,' she said.

Fergus lit a cigarette for them all to share and they passed it back and forwards as the hammock creaked and groaned.

'Any minute now,' said Sam bracing herself.

'Oh, I think we're all right. Fatou naps here in the afternoons,' said Fergus.

'As long as she doesn't join us,' said Ned.

They all roared with laughter and that proved to be the straw that broke the camel's back. The hammock fell to the floor, depositing them all in an undignified heap, still giggling.

'For fuck's sake!' said Fergus, dusting himself off.

'We need a stronger rope,' said Ned.

'Night, chaps,' said Sam, who floated off to bed without her feet touching the floor.

'Why don't you go after her?' said Fergus. 'You know you want to.'

'Christ! My life is so fucked up,' said Ned.

'You're such a drama queen, Neddy. What on earth could be wrong now? You've made up with Sam and all is right in the world.'

'There's just one problem.'

'What's that then? Don't you like her shorts?'

'Gemma wants to make up. She's coming to Simbako next week.'

'Did you tell Sam?'

\*\*\*

Sam sat in her room beneath the fan. The mosquito net billowed gently in the breeze under her vacant stare. She was rerunning the day in her head. It was hard to be rational about her feelings for Ned. He was all in one minute and all out the next. This, added to her natural insecurity, was not making for smooth running in the relationship, if it even was one.

She was more perturbed by the fact that it was as exciting to have Fergus on one side as it was to have Ned on the other. Her hormones were going berserk with all the testosterone around. And what on earth was going on in the *bondo*? She had no idea what being unclean meant. Simbako was definitely turning out to be a conundrum.

# Chapter XI

The next morning Sam followed her usual ritual with Dembo the parrot, but he refused to repeat her name. She might run out of cashews and patience, but he would capitulate first. Any day now, she thought, and stood up to go to breakfast. She felt dizzy, which she attributed to standing up too fast, but her head also throbbed. How irritating, I'm getting a headache. Sam was prone to headaches. They started in her teenage years and could last for days. She took propranolol to reduce their frequency, but sometimes she forgot.

She returned to her room and took one with two Panadol. The combination killed a headache stone dead if she took them in time. She stuffed the rest of her packet into her rucksack with some fruit and raisins for lunch and then joined the men at the table for breakfast.

Fatimata gave her a plate of scrambled egg and she buttered a piece of toast, but her appetite had gone and she picked at her eggs making no progress.

'Are you okay, Sam?' said Ned, when she pushed away her plate. 'It's not like you to leave your breakfast.'

'I'm okay. Just got a headache and nausea.'

'Are you pregnant?' said Fergus. 'Maybe it's those shorts.'

'Don't be silly, it's just a headache. Can I have the car today?' she said.

'Ah, I forgot to tell you. Ned and I have to talk to the artisanal miners in Mano so we'll need it. The meeting will go on into the night, so we won't be back until tomorrow.'

'Sahr can take you to the terrace and pick you up. You'll be fine here tonight,' said Ned. 'I can ask Fatou to stay if you want.'

'That'll be cosy,' said Fergus.

'Um, not necessary, I'll stay out of her way until you get back,' said Sam. 'Does Sahr know?'

'Yes, I told him yesterday. He'll be here soon.'

As if on cue, a horn sounded outside. Sam glugged down some water and grabbed her rucksack.

'Have a good time. Don't drink too much palm wine. See you tomorrow,' she said.

Fergus grunted and Ned waved and winked, making her blush.

She jumped into the jeep through the door that Sahr held open. A wave of nausea flowed over her and she put her head on her knees.

'Okay, Sam?'

'Yeah, fine, just forgot that I had a headache. It'll go soon. I took some tablets.'

'What sort of tablets?'

'Just headache ones.'

'Can I see?'

'Sure.' Mystified by his interest, she rooted around in her bag looking for the packet which had buried itself in the bottom.

'Can you hold these please?' she said dropping a random selection of stuff on his lap. After further rustling around, she pulled out the packet and showed it to him. He took it and examined it, reading the list of ingredients and nodding.

'Are those from England?' he said.

'Yes, everyone takes them, well, not everyone, they're effective.'

'If you have any remaining when you leave Simbako, can you give them to me?'

'It would be my pleasure. Do you get bad headaches too?'

'Oh, no, they're not for me. They're for my mother. It's hard to get good quality medicine in Fona.'

'Remind me before I go and I'll give them to you. Can you give me back my things?'

Sahr handed her the fruit and raisins, the notebook and camera and patted his legs looking for anything that had escaped. He reached between them to the car seat and pulled out a small bag tied with a piece of string which he dropped as if he had burnt his fingers.

'Oh,' said Sam, 'I'd forgotten all about that.'

The look on Sahr's face, a mixture of fear and horror, was almost comical.

'Where did you get this?' he said, his voice hoarse.

'In my pillowcase. I planned on showing it to Adanna and asking her what it is, but I forgot. Is it something bad?'

'Miss Sam, it is terrible, dangerous juju. Someone is trying to hurt you. That is why you have a headache. We need to purify you. This is an emergency.'

'An emergency? It can't be that bad.'

'Someone wants to kill you. This is a death fetish.' Sahr reached into his pocket and leaned over, pushing the bag into an empty cigarette packet with a pencil.

'A death fetish? Are you serious? Who would do this?'

'Well, someone who bought this from the witch doctor. It must have been expensive. They want you dead, big time.'

Sam laughed. She knew the culprit's identity. Trying not to smile, she rearranged her features into a serious mask. She fancied being treated by a witch doctor. It would be a unique experience. She hadn't realised that Fatimata hated her so much. Perhaps she should talk to her and straighten things out.

If they found common ground, she would ask her about the *bondo* while Ned and Fergus visited Mano. In her experience, women could always bond over the awfulness of men. For a moment, she regretted her indoctrination of Fatou's parrot, but then she remembered that even if she didn't believe in voodoo, Fatimata did, and she had paid a witch doctor for a deadly juju.

'Well, that's terrible,' she said. 'Can you organise a cleaning ceremony?'

'I will, but you must stay here until we can lift the curse. It's dangerous to be outside. The voodoo can work on a snake or a leopard and they might attack you.'

Staying with Fatimata might be far more dangerous, she shook her head. 'No, I'm safe with Tamba and the other men. I'll go to work. You sort out the cleansing ceremony and pick me up later.'

'I don't like it. We should tell Mr Fergus.'

'Oh, no, don't do that. They've an important meeting today and won't be back until tomorrow. We can deal with this by ourselves.'

'Are you sure? We must pay the witch doctor.'

'How much?'

'About fifty dollars.'

'Fifty dollars? Are you sure?'

'Yes, perhaps more.'

'Okay, you sort it out. Let me have the bag.'

'The bag. No!'

'Listen. If what you say is true, you might get cursed too. Give it to me.'

Sahr looked at her with new respect and handed her the cigarette packet which she zipped into an empty side pocket of her khaki trousers.

'You're as brave as a leopard, Miss Sam.'

'Let's go, Tamba will be waiting.'

*** 

During the day, they excavated the first pit down to bedrock and panned and recorded the results from the gravel, finding no diamonds, but plenty of bright red garnets and green chromite grains in the bottom of the pans. This indicated their origin from kimberlite, the rock which transports diamonds from earth's mantle. Sam wrote careful notes of the procedures they followed and placed the contents of the concentrate resulting from each cubic metre of gravel into small plastic bags which she knotted and placed in her rucksack.

Tamba watched her and asked questions about the notes she took as if resigned to his fate and accepting that he was stuck with her. She tried to be gracious despite the thudding in her head. The heat did not help matters. Sweat poured off her in rivers and, no matter how much she drank, her thirst did not diminish. She mixed some dehydration salts into the liquid and stayed in the shade all day so she didn't suffer from sunstroke.

One man, observing her distress, stuck four thin posts into the ground and made a shelter with palm leaves. She sat on a log and waited for them to bring her the samples. Tamba asked her if the men could leave early because they had a festival in the village. He suggested that she sit in the shade on the rock chair and wait for Sahr. It was a relief to stop work and she retired to the relative cool of the glade.

The warm rock comforted her and her eyelids grew heavy. Soon she slept, tossing and turning with fever in the late afternoon. The next thing she knew, twilight was approaching. But where was Sahr? She stood up, soaked with sweat and stumbled to the river. It looked very inviting and she needed to cool down.

What about the crocodiles? There were no prints on the bank and Tamba had his reasons for stopping her from crossing the river. She took off her boots and waded into the river. The cool water almost made her cry with relief.

When the water reached her thighs, she lowered herself into the water and floated out to the central channel. To her horror, the strong current ran through it which grabbed her like a vice and pulled her across and along the river. Panicking, she tried to fight it, but not being a strong swimmer, it was all she could do to stay afloat. She knew if she was swept away by a current, she should try to swim with it, so she did breaststroke in a diagonal line to the other bank. Her wet clothes wrapped themselves around her like mermaids trying to drag her under. She reached the other bank as exhaustion set in.

Recovering on the sandy shore, she realised she couldn't swim back across the river. Her boots sat on the bank far away in the gloom, a testament to her bad decision. She shivered. Now what? There had to be a way out.

Sam claimed to be a glass-half-full sort of girl and she never accepted defeat. She checked her pockets and found only her penknife and Sahr's cigarette packet with its deadly cargo. No wonder she almost drowned! Bloody voodoo. Could there be something to it?

Behind her in the forest she heard a twig crack. She spun in trepidation. Had the leopard sent by the juju crept up on her? But there was nothing there.

Then she remembered. The *bondo*! The women practised their ceremonies there. They would help her get back to the village. With darkness falling like a sledgehammer, it was her only hope. She walked a few steps into the trees and realised that her socks didn't provide protection against the mixture of stones and thorns and twigs lining the forest floor.

Taking her penknife out of her trouser pocket and saying a prayer of thanks for the person who invented zips, she searched for a rotting log. There were many lying around in various stages of deterioration. Some had large growths of white fungi like fallen clouds on them. Others were hollow. She stayed well away from them. Hollow logs often contained nasty surprises.

Not long after, she found a log with some loose bark. Using the short blade, she cut off two pieces of bark and shaped them so they resembled shoe liners. Then she rolled her socks back over themselves forming a tube over her feet into which she inserted the bark.

She tried out her invention. The solution was not ideal with her balance affected by the fever that coursed through her, but it was better than shredding her feet. The *bondo* must be near the river. They would need water for the ceremonies they performed and for the cooking and washing of plates and bodies.

Heading along the shore back in the direction the current had pulled her, she searched the sand for foot prints. She had seen the white painted girls a few times in this area and they would leave a trail.

Just when she doubted herself, she saw it. A faint indentation in the bank left by bare feet, the traces of which led into the trees. The light was fading fast, so she picked up speed as she followed the trail into the forest. It was difficult to stay upright in her improvised shoes, but she could not afford to slow down. Several times, she fell flat on her face and her foot slid out of the bark slippers. Her khaki pants ripped at the knee and blood ran down her leg. Panting with exertion, she stopped to wipe herself down and catch her breath. Her vision blurred. Was it the light or her eyes?

A shriek reached her ears. Pure fear mixed with what? Excitement or anticipation. She couldn't tell.

She headed towards it.

*** 

Sahr reached the terrace about ten minutes after Sam walked into the forest. He had waited for hours to see the witch doctor who had at first refused to reverse the voodoo. Sahr begged and pleaded with him to change his mind. The man demanded one hundred dollars and a large chicken, to placate the gods and cover his services. This large amount scandalised Sahr, but, like most people in Simbako, he was only a Christian on Sundays and the fear of bad juju, witches and malevolent spirits ruled his whole life. You could not argue with the gods. He wondered how anyone would want to harm Sam and his imagination did not stretch to the lovelorn Fatimata protecting her intended from the clutches of the white whore.

He tooted the horn and sat in the car singing along to the radio and waiting for her to emerge from the trees. When she did not come out after five minutes, he realised that something was wrong. On most days, she came out with a big smile, half-walking, half-running, giving him genuine pleasure to see her again.

He switched off the ignition and jumped out of the ancient jeep.

When he got to the terrace, the horizontal sunlight picked out the individual twigs and palm leaves strewn on the ground in a golden silhouette. There was no sign of Sam. He searched the glade and found her rucksack beside the rock armchair and this gave him momentary hope. He called her name, but only birds replied.

Coming back out onto the flat terrace, he walked to the pit they had dug during the day, his heart in his mouth in case she had fallen in and broken her neck in the gloom. There was no sign of her, just tools stored under a tarpaulin.

Then he saw them – a pair of walking boots sitting on the bank above the river. Running towards them, he shouted for her again. 'Sam, where are you?'

The boots sat alone with no clues as to the whereabouts of their owner. He couldn't see any other clothes, but her footprints led into the river. His heart was in his throat. He knew all about the currents in the central channel which had swept unwary children to their deaths in the past. Could Miss Sam have drowned? Was it the voodoo? Perhaps a wild animal had taken her? She had insisted on taking the juju with her and he cursed himself for his cowardice in not keeping it.

He screwed up his eyes and gazed at the opposite shore. The last vestiges of the sunlight crept through the trees and a golden shaft showed up some footprints in relief on the sand. They must be hers. There was hope at least. She had survived, but, where was she? Why had she crossed the river? He could not follow her. The *sowei* had filled the *bondo* with young women and men could not approach it, no matter what disaster had befallen. He felt frantic, but he knew what to do.

Running at top speed through the trees in the half-light, he reached the jeep and wrenched open the door.

# Chapter XII

The jeep screeched to a halt outside the Chief's house just as the servants closed the wooden shutters to keep out the insects. Sahr ran up the stairs and banged on the door. A flustered Tamba came to see who had arrived, walking erratically to the door and fumbling with the catch.

'For God's sake, man. How dare you disturb the Chief so late? Can't it wait until the morning?'

'It's Sam. Miss Sam. She's crossed the river into the forest and disappeared.'

'What? Disappeared? Why didn't you pick her up?'

'I had to wait at the witch doctor's house because of the juju.'

'What juju? Explain yourself, man.'

'I must speak to the Chief. It's urgent. She may die.'

Adanna appeared behind Tamba, a concerned expression on her face.

'Did you say Sam was missing? What's going on?'

'Madam, please help me.' Sahr put his hands over his face, his shoulders heaving and tears dropping on the floor.

Adanna's eye widened with empathy. She put a gentle arm around his shoulders and led Sahr into the house and through into the sitting room where her father sat holding a large glass of palm wine.

Sahr strangled a sob and stood waiting to be greeted.

'Sahr, you are welcome,' said Chief Sesay, regarding the sobbing youth with his head hanging low between the shoulders. 'Whatever is wrong, young man? Is Mr Fergus treating you badly?'

'Thank you, sir. Mr Fergus is a good boss. It's Sam sir. She's disappeared and it's my fault.'

'Sam missing? How is it your fault? I don't understand.'

'Tell us what happened,' said Tamba. Noticing the distressed look that Sahr flashed him, he added, 'Say exactly what happened and leave nothing out.'

'Someone wishes evil to Sam. They left a powerful juju inside her pillowcase to make her die. I told her we should ask the witch doctor to get rid of it. She wouldn't let me take the juju. She kept it with her and now she has disappeared. It's my fault.'

At the mention of juju, Chief Sesay gritted his teeth and the muscle in his jaw flickered. Tamba, aware of the British-educated soldier's low opinion of all things voodoo, tried to steer the conversation away from the subject.

'But where is she now?'

'I saw footprints going into the forest, near the *bondo*. She swam across the river. She had a bad headache this morning caused by the juju, she could die in there.'

'The *bondo*? We can't get her back if she's gone in there, only women may enter. Adanna, can you go?' said Chief Sesay.

143

'Father, how can you ask me that?'

'She can't enter the forest because she is unclean, sir,' said Tamba. 'We need someone else.'

'Can no one free me from this superstitious nonsense? What about Fatimata? She used to be a *sowei* until the rebels came,' said Sesay.

'If you are looking for a culprit for the voodoo, I doubt you need to look much further than Fatou. She's jealous of Sam because of Fergus,' said Adanna.

'What's Fergus got to do with this?' said the Chief, exasperated.

'Nothing really. He doesn't notice Fatou is dying of love for him, but I suspect that Fatou is trying to get rid of Sam because she wants Fergus for herself,' said Adanna.

'Well, in that case she must help us. If she's responsible for the voodoo, she must rescue Sam. I won't hear any excuses.'

'She won't do it,' said Tamba. 'She is also unclean now because of what happened with the rebels and she can't enter the forest. They may kill her.'

The Chief rose to his feet in fury. 'I don't care how bloody unclean she is. She must rescue Sam. And that's an order.'

Tamba flinched. Caught between loyalty to his Chief and the fear of breaking all the taboos surrounding the *bondo*, he vacillated, but not for long. Superstition ruled his life, but the Paramount Chief could not be crossed.

'I'll talk to her,' he said.

'Sahr, take Tamba to the compound and tell Fergus to help you with Fatimata.'

Sahr, who had been mute, lifted his head. 'Mr Fergus and Mr Ned aren't here. They left for Mano to speak to the artisanal miners.'

'When will they be back?'

'Tomorrow, sir.'

'Okay, we must do it without them. Take Tamba and go now. Tamba, report back to me if she refuses. We can't do anything tonight, anyway, as it's too late and it would be dangerous to go into the forest now. There may be leopards hunting in the dark.'

'Auntie Fatou is a stubborn woman,' said Adanna, 'I wish you luck.'

***

The *bondo* floated in the forest, surrounded by a rim of light created by dozens of candles merging into one. It resembled a spaceship hovering in the gloom. It was much larger than she had imagined and the cracks in the walls between the dried-out planks spoke of its age. Light and noise leaked out of these cracks like water out of an old gourd. Loud cackling laughter escaped from the *bondo* too. It sounded as if a coven of witches were partying inside. She staggered and fell as she reached the hut. The door was bolted, but something stopped her from knocking. She sat on a bench under a window, trying to make sense of the sounds coming from within. She shivered and sweated at the same time. A shriek came from inside. Unable to resist, she knelt on the bench and peered through one of the wider cracks in the wood.

The painted girls sat opposite her on a long bench. They were naked, except for the white paint covering their bodies and faces. They were enveloped in a cloak of terror which made Sam feel ill. In the middle of the room stood a table with an old woman at each corner. The women had dressed in traditional robes. They sang in Krio, their voices rich and harmonious.

An older woman took charge, calling a small girl forward. The child whimpered in fear, but, instead of comforting her, the adults laughed and made comments and poked her with their fingers. Nervous laughter floated from the bench. One girl banged on a leather drum with a large well-worn stick and the other girls clapped and stamped in time with the drum. As the noise reached a crescendo, the *sowei* lifted the girl onto the table. The women took the child by the hands and feet and bore down on her limbs so she could not move. She wept with fear.

The drumming made Sam feel dizzy. She couldn't focus her eyes. Was she hallucinating? She rubbed her eyes and pressed her forehead to the cracked plank. The woman in charge of the ceremony reached into a hidden pocket and took out a box cutter, its blade catching the light as she raised it high in the air. All the other women cheered. The girl on the table screamed, her voice becoming ever higher and higher pitched as her terror increased. The woman turned her back to Sam and thrust her hands between the girl's legs. A scream emitted by the child was so piercing Sam's eardrums almost split.

On and on she screamed while all the women laughed and sang. The sound pervaded Sam's fevered body and scarred her for ever. Nothing she ever did could rid her of that memory, although it would become less prominent in time. She would keep it hidden as something she couldn't bear to remember but could never forget. She did not see the wound being sealed with thorns or the child being placed in a back room as she had fallen from the bench in a faint.

\*\*\*

Sahr drove Tamba to the compound where Fatimata worked with Fergus and Ned. The lights blazed on the veranda, illuminating the housekeeper who was lying in the hammock which now almost touched the floor.

'Come on then,' said Tamba, getting out of the jeep.

'No! I won't go near that woman. She's evil. I don't want the bad juju to get me too.'

'Don't be silly, that's not how it works.'

'I don't care. I won't go in.'

Tamba shook his head in resignation. Then he walked to the house, climbed the stairs to the porch and addressed the colossus in the hammock.

'Good evening, Auntie Fatou. How are you?'

'Tamba? What a surprise!' She pulled herself up and out of the hammock with surprising agility by using the porch fence. Proffering her hand, she bowed her head so that her forehead touched his. 'You are welcome to this house, unlike some people,' she said looking around. 'Where is Sam? Did she not come home with Sahr? She's late. The dinner has dried out.'

'Sam's missing, perhaps she is dead.'

Fatimata struggled to contain her emotions. She had never expected the juju to work so fast. In reality, she had not been expecting anything. Voodoo coursed through her blood, but she had only gone to the witch doctor for comfort. She had seen death up close and you didn't kill people with bags of salt and chicken blood.

'But she worked at the terrace today. Didn't you see her?'

'Yes, but we left her waiting for Sahr and when he got there, she had gone.'

'Gone where?'

'It seems as if she crossed the river to the forest where the *bondo* is.'

'Why did she do that?'

'I don't know. She was sweating and had a bad headache today. Maybe she got in the river to cool down.'

'Sounds like malaria.'

'Whatever happened, she got swept across the river. You know what the current is like. She's lucky she didn't drown.'

'The girls are being cleansed. No one may enter the *bondo*. They will send her away.'

'I doubt it. She has bad juju in her pocket. The *bondo* has been defiled by an unclean foreigner. They'll do anything to save it from evil. They will kill her.'

'Where is Sahr? Why didn't he come in?'

'He's afraid because he thinks you who put the curse on Sam. Did you?'

Fatimata could not hide her guilt. She stood up shouting.

'What if I did? She deserves it. That woman tried to steal Mr Fergus from me.'

'Are you mad? Do you imagine an old woman like you would interest Mr Fergus? It is not Sam's fault she's young and attractive.'

Fatou sank back to her chair.

'I didn't believe it would work.'

'Well, it has and now you need to help us. Chief Sesay demands you rescue her before something awful happens.'

'No! I can't go. It'll make it things worse. You know I'm banned and why. I won't do it.'

'But the Chief orders you to go. You don't have a choice.'

'I won't go. You can't make me.'

Fatimata crossed her arms and turned away from Tamba. He would not persuade her. The Chief would have to summon her himself if he wished to force the issue.

'Please Fatou, that young woman will die if you will not help. Only a *sowei* can enter the *bondo*.'

'I will not go.'

Tamba stood up and stumbled down the stairs in the dark yard. Sahr saw his face and started the jeep. They drove back to the Chief's compound to impart the bad news.

*\*\*\**

Ned and Fergus got to their hotel in Mano just in time to eat dinner. The food was a delicious potato leaf stew with goat on a bed of rice. The two men ate in silence, savouring every bite after their long day in the field.

'Is there a telephone in the hotel?' said Ned, when he had finished.

'Yes, but you need to ask reception to dial the number for you.'

'I'm going to call Gemma and tell her about Sam.'

'Good for you. It's always best to make a clean break.'

'I hope I'm making the right decision.'

'Neddy, all decisions are right, it's indecision that is fatal.'

Ned got up from the table and walked over to the reception desk to book his call.

Fergus smoked a cheroot and drank a glass of brandy of dubious origin. A big cloud of moths had invaded the dining room and collided with the cheap chandeliers before taking swallow dives on to the floor and tables. Fergus put a beer mat over his brandy glass to discourage their swimming. He wasn't able to avoid hearing Ned's contribution to the conversation that followed, carried out at full volume due to the poor connection.

*** 

'Gemma? It's me Ned.'

'Hello, sweetheart. I'm so glad you called …'

'I have something important to tell you.'

'Me too! Can I go first? I'm …' The line buzzed and crackled.

'The line is terrible. What did you say?'

'… so, the doctor said … Isn't that wonderful?'

'I don't understand. Can you say it again?'

'Pregnant! I'm … You will be …'

'Pregnant? Is it mine?'

'The doctor says … Sorry what did you say?'

'I didn't say anything. Is the baby mine?'

'Yes …' The line cut off.

Ned dropped the receiver and it swung there, banging into the reception desk. He turned to look at Fergus, who stared at a moth crawling in slimy potato leaf gravy.

'Did you hear that?' said Ned.

'Sorry? I wasn't concentrating.'

'She's pregnant. It's mine.'

'Jesus, Ned, how did that happen? Don't tell me you had a final shag when you saw her in London?'

He saw Ned's face and didn't need an answer.

*** 

When Sam came to, the girls had gone, but the women stood over her. She felt strange. Her skin was tight and dry and she wasn't wearing any clothes. She lay in a tiny cot with a basic foam mattress. Fever raged in her body, but she shivered. She opened her eyes wider and saw she had been painted white. Then she remembered the blood. She tried to scream, but no sound would come out. The women talked among themselves, but she couldn't understand any Krio so she did not understand what they said. She was tired, dog-tired, dead-tired.

Closing her eyes, she tried to pull herself into foetal position, but they had tied her limbs to the frame of the bed, so she lay still, sweat pouring off her body into the damp mattress, trying to become tiny. She did not know what they wanted, or if they were even real. Perhaps she was still on the terrace. Or even at home in the compound.

Even in her confused state, she realised that she had malaria. She had little time to escape and take her medicine before it got a lot worse, but she didn't have the strength of a new born baby and sleep tempted her with oblivion.

The hairs on Ned's arm had brushed hers then and she jumped, but he disappeared. Fergus laughed at her. Why was he so mean? She never understood. Her eyes became heavy and her breath rasped in her chest. Just five minutes sleep and she would try to escape. Five minutes would be enough.

'Is she sleeping?'

'I think so. She has a high fever. It may kill her.'

'What are we to do?'

'She has brought bad juju into the *bondo* and she's not clean. The maximum sanction is required.'

'But are you sure the sanction applies to her? She's not one of us. And she's ill. I doubt she even knows where she is.'

'You know what the traditions say.'

'I'm more worried about what the police will say. If we kill this woman, they will come for us. Being *sowei* will not save us anymore. The world has changed.'

'What's wrong with you? Have you lost your beliefs? This is no time to wilt like old jungle flowers. We must save the forest from outsiders. Whether she knew it or not, she brought a voodoo curse into the *bondo* and there is only one way to lift it.'

'How should we proceed?'

'We must prepare the hut for the sacrifice. Tomorrow night, we will carry out the ceremony.'

'She must die?'

'It's the only solution.'

# Chapter XIII

When Fergus and Ned got back to Fona the next day, Tamba was waiting for them in the sitting room of their house. He plucked at his robes as he perched on the edge of the uncomfortable sofa. His usual bumptious exterior had been replaced by a deflated melancholy. He had the air of someone who had been waiting a long time, but he did not look pleased to see them. His stomach rose and fell as he breathed out an extended sigh. There was no sign of Fatimata.

'Hi Tamba! This is a surprise. Are you seeking refuge from Sam? She's a real devil, isn't she?' said Fergus, taking in his bedraggled state without comment.

Tamba did not smile. He looked at the ground and drew in a deep breath. 'I have bad news,' he said, 'about Sam.'

'What sort of news? Is she hurt?' said Ned.

'She is missing.'

'What do you mean missing? Didn't she come to work yesterday?' said Fergus.

'Oh, yes. She came, but she wasn't well, she had a headache. Do you know what voodoo is?'

'Yes,' said Fergus.

'Not really,' said Ned.

'Voodoo is a mixture of the beliefs of various ethnic groups from Africa. We use it to make sense of events and to influence life in our favour by using a healer or witch doctor to intercede for us with the spirits of our ancestors,' said Tamba.

'I understand all that, but what's this got to do with Sam?' said Fergus.

'Someone put a serious curse on her, trying to kill her or make her disappear.'

'Jesus, Tamba! Are you telling us that Sam is missing because of a spell?' said Ned.

'Steady on there, Neddy,' said Fergus. 'People around here believe powerful spells can make you fall in love or die.'

'Have you searched for her, Tamba?'

'Um, not exactly, but we know where she is.'

'What on earth are you doing here? Why didn't you get her right away?'

'She is in the *bondo* in the sacred forest. It is forbidden for men to enter there.'

'And what is a *bondo*?' said Ned, looking incredulous.

'It's a ceremonial house where they circumcise the girls,' said Fergus, 'to get them ready for marriage.'

Ned winced.

'Circumcise the girls? How do they do that? I thought you could only circumcise boys?' said Ned.

'Jesus, Ned, do I have to give you all the details? They cut out their clitoris, so they won't stray.'

Ned blanched. 'Jesus, don't tell me that Sam …'

'It is unlikely, but there is something else,' said Tamba.

'Something else? Isn't this bad enough?' said Ned

'Sam took bad juju into the *bondo* with her.'

'I don't understand.'

'Someone planted a voodoo fetish on her, a bag full of evil spirits, to make her die. If the *sowei* find it, they will kill her and burn the body to stop the curse contaminating the sacred forest.'

'They'll murder her over a superstition! Do something, Fergus.'

'We will stop them. There must be a way.'

'You can't go there, sir.'

'I understand,' said Fergus.

'What are you talking about, Fergus? We must go there now and save her.'

'No, we can't. I'm sorry, Ned, but they would kill us too. It is their most sacred place.'

'So we let her die then? For God's sake, man!' Ned whipped around and grabbed Tamba by the shoulders. 'Tamba, help us! How do we save her without violating your beliefs?'

'There is one person who can go because she used to be *sowei*, but she has refused.'

'Adanna? Why won't she go?'

'No, not Adanna. Fatimata.'

'Fatimata is a *sowei*? Why isn't she in the *bondo* for the ceremonies?'

'She's not gone since the soldiers came here. She's no longer a *sowei* after what happened.'

'What happened?' said Ned. 'Oh, God, did they rape her?'

'It's not my business to tell you. She will come back soon from the shop. You may ask her, but she will refuse to go.'

'Thank you, Tamba. This can't be easy for you,' said Fergus.

'Mr Fergus, I've become fond of Sam, she's kind and brave. Please save her.' Tamba's bottom lip wobbled and he brushed his eyes with the corner of his robe.

'Okay, don't worry. We'll think of something. How long do we have?'

'If they found the juju, they will kill her at sunset and burn the *bondo* with her inside.'

'Leave it with me. I'll persuade Fatimata as soon as she gets here.'

\*\*\*

Sam woke with the dawn. A chorus of birds sang and tweeted their ownership of the forest like a crowd of chattering children. She tried to shush them, but her lips were dry and her tongue felt like it belonged to somebody else. Her limbs had been tied down and she thrashed around, unable to work out what was wrong. Then she realised her eyes were still shut and she forced them open to find she was bound to a bed made of logs in a tiny bedroom with no window. Light streamed in through the wood's cracks and illuminated her chaffed wrists where the cords that bound her had rubbed her skin raw.

Fear flooded her body. What was going on? She couldn't remember anything about the night before and she felt awful, cold and hot at the same time. Why couldn't she piece together past events? Had she been drugged? She stopped moving and listened for a moment. Someone crept around outside her room. She forced a whimper. The door opened a crack and a white face peered into the gloom.

'Help me,' said Sam, 'please help me.'

The face disappeared. She heard frantic whispering on the other side of the door. It creaked open again and more faces swam into view. Suddenly, the small room filled with girls giggling and poking her.

'Water,' said Sam. 'I need water.'

One girl disappeared and came back with a wooden bowl. They all crowded around and supported her head while one girl poured water into her mouth. She gulped it down. The cool liquid was the best thing she had ever tasted, quenching her thirst and lubricating her throat. She forced out another word, 'Why?' tugging her wrist to show she couldn't get up. One girl, older than the others, came forward. They pushed her towards the bed.

'You bring bad juju to *bondo*.'

'But it's not mine.'

'The *bondo* is now cursed. The *sowei* will burn it.'

'And me?'

'You will die.'

A rising panic broke through her fevered consciousness, followed by a growing realisation. These girls were her only chance of escape. She couldn't let them leave or she would die. Somehow, they must be persuaded to free her.

She shook her head.

'No,' she said, lowering her voice and growling, 'you must save me. My blood will be on your hands if you don't. I'm a witch and I will curse you too.'

The girl stepped back and whispered to the others whose eyes widened.

'Why didn't the *sowei* tell us that?'

'The *sowei* do not understand. They found a juju in my pocket I made for someone, didn't they? I can transfer it to you if I want. If you don't save me ...'

'But they will punish us if we free you.'

'I won't tell them how I escaped. Please, I don't want to curse you, but I will. White women are powerful witches – that's why we are white. It's the power of our spells that does it.'

Even Sam amazed herself with this lie, but it seemed to have an effect. The girls withdrew from the room, but they did not leave the hut. Sam could hear them next door giving water to someone else, the newly circumcised girl.

Resisting the temptation to beg, she listened to another whispered argument. She must have convinced them. Superstitious people, afraid of witches, wouldn't risk a spell from a white witch, would they? They were young, likely to be gullible. The discussion continued. Sam got more nervous as time passed. The girl who spoke English put her head around the door. She wore a triumphant look on her face.

'If you are a witch, why can't you use a spell to escape?'

\*\*\*

When she spotted Fergus and Ned sitting on the porch, Fatimata stopped halfway across the yard and tried to sneak back out of the gate. There was something pathetic about a person in a dress that could have served as a circus tent trying to be inconspicuous in a yard with no cover and a couple of chickens. Fergus stood up and beckoned her to join them. The fact that she seemed surprised that they noticed her made the whole scenario comical, despite the circumstances. She touched her chest and raised her eyebrows in question as if to say, 'Who me?'

'Fatimata, please come here. I need to talk to you.'

'I have forgotten I have to look after my sister today and can't come to work.'

'Please don't lie to me. I need your help and you know what this is about.'

'I can't help you, Mr Fergus.' She had not moved from the centre of the yard. 'You must understand.'

'Fatimata, I still need to talk to you. Please come here.'

Fergus stood up and moved to the steps in one fluid movement. Before she could flee, he was at her side and he had her arm in a vice-like grip. Her eyes filled with tears and her chin quivered.

'I don't want to. Please don't make me.'

'Would you prefer me to let Sam die?'

'You don't understand. I can't do it.'

'You're right. I don't. Please come to the house and talk to me. I need you to explain to me what's going on. You can't escape from your past any more. It's not just your life at stake.'

Her resistance evaporated and she wilted a little, the defiance ebbing away as he manoeuvred her up the porch and into the sitting room. She walked past Ned as if he didn't exist. Ned stood up to follow them in, but Fergus shook his head, shutting the screen door behind them.

Fatimata sat on the sofa which wrapped around her like an arm chair. She wept, big raw ugly sobs which had been locked into her chest for ten years. Fergus handed her a drying up cloth which was hanging over the back of a chair. She wiped her face and blew her nose into it, panting with emotion.

Fergus did not speak. Sitting on an armchair, he pulled it close to the sofa. He waited for the waves to break on the shore and calm into ripples. Reaching out, he took one of her plump hands and patted it, before massaging her palm with his thumb.

Ned had stayed standing out on the porch. When Fatimata cried, he moved to the hammock out of her line of sight. Fergus could still see his agitated breathing through the material. He took a deep breath and spoke to Fatimata in his caramel voice, honed over the many years of seduction.

'Now then, Fatou, what's this all about?'

# Chapter XIV

Eight months into the conflict the rebel forces were approaching Fona. Paramount Chief Joseph Sesay fretted, at his wit's end with worry. It was his responsibility to protect the town from the rebels, but he could not offer any protection to his people, despite all of his hereditary power. Rumours circulated about the horrors that had been perpetrated in villages that had been overrun. The ruthless savagery of these disenfranchised men had resulted in a wave of rape and pillage

They could not offer any resistance to the rebels. Modern weapons had not yet arrived in Fona. A few of the men had ancient rifles for shooting foxes or pigeons, but the Chief had discouraged the ownership of guns in his kingdom. The women of the town begged him for help. They had no place to hide and nowhere to go. The Chief was well aware of what would happen to them when the rebels arrived. He visited Fatimata, the senior *sowei* in the town, to discuss the options.

'No man will marry a woman who gets raped. They'll be ostracised for life,' said Fatimata

'I have never understood why the girls must live with the blame for being raped. Sometimes I despair of our culture. We live in the Stone Age,' said Joseph Sesay.

'You can't save them if they get caught.'

'Can we hide them somewhere?'

'There is shelter in the forest near the *bondo*, but if they come for us, we can't escape.'

'What's the alternative?'

'The girls would rather die than be violated.'

'What are you suggesting?'

'There are poisons we can use. The girls don't have to know. We can feed them a good beef stew.'

'But that's barbaric! Why should they die?' The Chief rubbed his head in anguish, pulling at his tight curls as if he would rip them out. Then a crazed expression appeared on his face. 'That's it! I have a plan. You must help me.'

'If I can. What do you want me to do?'

'We will prepare the beef stew, but not for the girls. I'll feed it to the rebels.'

'But, sir, if I kill the rebels, I can no longer enter the *bondo*. I'll be unclean.'

'Fatou, the rebels are evil, you'll be a heroine.'

'No, I'll be an outcast. Those are the rules.'

'The rules! You may kill the girls, but not the rebels? Will you let the girls die then?'

Fatou avoided his eyes. Chief Sesay understood how proud she was of her status as a *sowei*. He could feel her anguish, but he needed to protect his people. He waited.

'No,' she said, 'I'll help you. It's a small price to pay.'

'God will reward you.'

'But the spirits will banish me. I'll lose my status.'

'You can never lose your status in my eyes. I'll give you the big house in the centre of town. You'll be a woman of property.'

'What's the use of property when I lose my soul?' She turned to him. 'You ask too much of me, Joseph.'

'But you'll do it?'

\*\*\*

The rebels were only hours away. News of their imminent arrival had reached Chief Sesay's compound, which was full of local refugees from the surrounding countryside, crowding into the relative safety of its high walls. Inside the Chief's house, Joseph Sesay was pacing the visitors' room. The tribal elders were packed inside, sitting on anything they could find, muttering in low tones and pulling their robes around them as if for protection. Tamba followed the Chief around the room, wincing as Sesay bumped into chairs and people in his agitation. Finally, the Chief stopped in the middle of the room and held up his hands to still the murmuring elders.

'The rebels arrive tomorrow,' he said. 'We must act now.'

'How will we stop them?'

'We cannot do that. Take the people to hide in the forest. I'll stay here and greet them.'

'But, Joseph, they will kill you.'

'It is of no consequence. My daughter will be a fine Paramount Chief.'

'But, sir ...'

'Tamba, this is not your decision. I need you to help me.'

'Anything.'

'Go to the terrace with thirty men and fill in the excavation. Do not stop until you have finished. Cover

163

the workings with leaves and palm fronds and twigs. Spread them thin so no-one can tell that mining was taking place there. When you have finished, hide in the forest until you are sure it's safe.'

'What are you going to do? Invite them to dinner?'

'That's exactly it. Now get organised.'

'Father, I won't leave you here.' Adanna stepped out of the shadows and clung to him shivering.

'You will, I have Pakuteh here. He will help me.'

'But, father.'

'Do not defy me. You must go. The future of Fona is your responsibility. Take the women into the forest and hide with them.'

Adanna tried to hold on to her father, but Tamba pulled her away.

'You heard your father. Save the women before the rebels get them. You know what will happen if they get captured. It is your duty.'

Adanna nodded and left the house with the rest of the elders. Chief Sesay turned to Pakuteh.

'I need you to lay the ceremonial table with a feast for the rebels. There is a large beef and chicken stew already prepared. Make a big pot of rice and a basket of fried bananas. Place all the food on the table after you have covered it with one of the red table cloths. When you finish, come to find me.'

'Yes, sir.' Pakuteh avoided the Chief's eyes, but he did not question the instructions. If the Chief had gone mad, it was not a good time to challenge him. He turned to go to the kitchen.

'And, Pakuteh, whatever you do, don't eat any stew. I want you to promise me.'

'I promise.' The doubt which crossed his face made the Chief consider telling him again, but he had no time for the recalcitrant young man.

'I'll be back,' he said.

\*\*\*

Pakuteh entered the kitchen where the chicken stew sat on the hob at the back. The rich aroma of the food filled it with savoury temptation. He grabbed the handles of the pot and moved the stew onto the battered wooden table in the centre of the room. Using a large wooden scoop hanging from the ceiling, he covered the bottom of another huge saucepan with a thick layer of rice. He filled the saucepan with water and lit the gas hob underneath it. Then he collected a large bunch of plantains from a dirty corner in the larder and lifted it onto the table. A large spider fell out of the bananas onto the table and made him jump. It launched itself into the air, landing in a hairy heap on the floor and then scampered away, disappearing under the rusty fridge.

Pakuteh hacked individual plantains off the stem and peeled their skin off and slice them length ways. When he had a large pile of sliced bananas, he put a flat pan on the other hob and poured in a bottle of cooking oil. He waited for the oil to heat, before frying the plantains in batches and placing them on a long wooden serving platter. He drained the rice and put it into two bowls decorated with local motifs.

The aroma of the stew had sustained him though this task, but when he finished, his hunger got the better of him. He served himself a bowl of the lukewarm stew and sat down to eat. Spicy and meaty, he had never tasted better. The juice ran down his chin and he rubbed it off with his sleeve. He bolted his food and soon finished it. He washed the bowl in the sink so that there was no evidence of his disobedience and hid it among the plantains. There was plenty left.

He couldn't understand why the Chief was feeding the rebels. It made no sense. He carried all the food out to the table in the ceremonial hall.

Having laid it with bowls and cutlery, he went to find the Chief.

Joseph Sesay was sitting outside the hall in his ceremonial chair, his head in his hands, deep in thought. When he noticed Pakuteh come out, he stood up and gestured to the chair beside him, which belonged to his wife, but was still pristine.

'Ah, Pakuteh, my boy! Sit down. I need to talk to you.'

Pakuteh's face betrayed his alarm. As far as he was aware, the Chief didn't know of his marriage to Adanna, his beloved daughter, as, otherwise, he would not be so amicable. He sat down on the edge of the seat as if ready to flee.

'Shouldn't we be going, sir? They'll be here any minute.'

'I'm not going. Someone has to stay for the plan to work.'

'But they'll kill you.'

'I doubt it. Anyway, that's not what I wanted to talk to you about. There's the small matter of my daughter.'

'Your daughter?'

'I heard about your marriage. You can't keep a secret in this village. And while I don't approve, what's done is done.'

'I love her.'

'I know and that's why I want you to take her away. The longer she stays, the worse it will get for her. They won't ever let her be Chief because I stopped her going to the *bondo*.'

Pakuteh was speechless.

'Where will we go?' he said.

'Anywhere you want.'

Pakuteh was about to protest when the Chief stretched out his arm.

'Put out your hand,' he said.

Trembling, Pakuteh offered his hand palm up and the Chief dropped something heavy and warm into it. Pakuteh gasped.

'Is that what I think it is?' he said.

'The Star of Simbako,' said the Chief. 'The biggest diamond ever found at Fona. I want you to take it and run far from here with Adanna. Never come back.'

'What about you?'

'I've a date with destiny. The gods want their pound of flesh in exchange for your freedom and I will give it to them.'

'But what will I tell Adanna?'

'Tell her I love her. Go now. Quickly.'

*** 

Fona village was empty. The whole population had left, fleeing before the ferocious reputation of the rebel battalion. The sound of wood splintering at the edge of the compound heralded their arrival and destructive mood. A lone chicken pecking the ground was swooped up by one rebel and its neck wrung before it could squawk in protest. The Chief could hear them getting closer and he steeled himself for the coming confrontation. He intended to keep them occupied until the deadly stew had its effect.

The double doors of the ceremonial hall burst open and a tall, muscular man barged through. He had a belt of bullets slung over his body like a deadly sash and his skin shone from the evening drizzle. A newly healed scar was visible on his arm. He scanned the room for something to break. His gaze fell on Chief

Joseph Sesay who was sitting in the shadows in full ceremonial dress with a leopard skin cloak over his shoulders. He sneered.

'Who the fuck are you?' he said.

'Chief Joseph Sesay at your service. And you are?'

'They call me Black Death.'

Despite the awful danger represented by this musclebound thug, Sesay had to fight a smile. Another of the rebels caught his smirk. The butt of a gun hit him in the guts before he could react. He fell to his knees where he was hit again, this time in his face. His world shrank to a pinhole and disappeared.

When Sesay came to, he was tied to a chair in the dining hall. The rebels sat around the table, stuffing themselves with stew and rice making sounds of noisy appreciation.

'Ah, you are back with us,' said Black Death. 'I want the Star of Simbako and you'll tell me how to find it or you'll die.'

'What's that?' said the Chief, through his swollen mouth.

'Where is the Star of Simbako?'

'There's no such thing.'

Black Death gesticulated and one of his men came forward. Swinging his rifle over his shoulder around his body, he slammed it against the Chief's shins, causing the chair to pitch sideways and to tumble on the floor with the Chief still attached.

'What are you waiting for? Pick him up, you fool!' said Black Death.

The man grabbed the chair back and pulled it upright. Sesay slumped over. He was bleeding into his shoes and dark pools crept over the floorboards.

'Where is it?'

'It is a myth. I have never seen such a thing.'

Black Death stood up and approached the Chief. In his hand, he carried a ceremonial cudgel.

'You will tell me.'

\*\*\*

The gate of the compound hung from one hinge and bits of splintered wood covered the ground. Tamba and Adanna pushed their way past it and into the deserted yard which shimmered in the heat.

'Where are the rebels?' said Adanna

'They've disappeared. It makes no sense,' said Tamba.

'It's my father I'm worried about. Why did he stay behind? It thought he was coming with Pakuteh.'

'So did I. He wouldn't tell me the plan. He sent me to fill in the diamond pit.'

'And Pakuteh?'

'He left.'

'What do you mean left? Isn't he coming back?'

'I don't think so. He said he was going to South Africa to work.'

'South Africa? He can't have.'

'Look, let's discuss this later, okay? We must look for the Chief.'

They edged across the yard towards the ceremonial hall, but there was no sign of life anywhere. The door of the hall fell open and the metallic smell of blood hung in the air. The sound of blowflies buzzing became audible. Their presence was an awful clue.

'Oh, God. I can't face going in,' said Adanna.

Tamba shoved the door with his foot and it swung open to reveal a tableau that was almost unbelievable in its horror. There were thirty or forty bodies, most of them still sitting at the table. A few had fallen to the floor. There was an odd white foam emerging from some of their gaping mouths. Adanna gasped. Tamba used his foot to flip over one body. It was rigid with rigor mortis and had both hands clasping its neck as if choking.

Tamba vomited.

'Sorry,' he said.

'For what?' said Adanna. She was scanning the room with panic in her eyes, trying not to breathe the air which was thick with death. Then she emitted a cry and ran around the table to where a brightly coloured body was tied to a chair, the face smeared with dried blood.

'Daddy? Oh, my God, Tamba, it's my father.'

She held out her hand and touched his dear face. It was still warm.

'He's still alive!' she said. 'Help me.'

'He can't be. Look at him.'

'Help me for God's sake.'

Tamba undid the cords lashing Sesay to his chair and laid him on the floor. His robe fell to one side, revealing his crooked, battered shins. Adanna flinched. She pulled the robes back over his legs, grabbed a jacket from the back of a chair and put it under his head. Tenderly stroking his face, she sobbed and a large tear fell onto the Chief's lips. The tip of his tongue poked out and licked the tear.

'Daddy? He's alive! Tamba get the doctor. Quickly.'

# Chapter XV

Fergus' upbringing in Simbako meant everything that had happened so far made perfect sense. Fona relaxed him and he felt at home, despite the local shenanigans which drove Ned mad, but then he had grown up in the English countryside and did not understand how life happened in a town ruled by superstition and black magic. Chief Sesay was a sceptic, but his respect for the tribal elders and the *sowei* meant that he tolerated most of the goings-on as normal.

And then there was Adanna. An enigma wrapped in a cool coating – her calm exterior was as much a mask as any of the examples on the walls of the Chief's house.

What made her so sad?

The biggest surprise was Fatimata. Whoever would have imagined that she was a heroine? The grumpy battleship with her simple prejudices was an avenging angel, who had saved the town from the rebels with her fatal potions.

Despite her protests, Fergus made Fatimata a cup of tea. As he waited for the water to boil, he leaned back against the wooden table in the kitchen and tried to get his thoughts together. The revelation about the poisonous stew had shaken him. Alex never told him about Fona's brush with the civil war. Perhaps he wasn't aware of the town's troubled history. It explained why there were still diamonds in the terraces around the town, even though the nearby terraces had been exploited. How did Alex know these were virgin? Sam seemed to think the one they were given had already been exploited, but she wasn't sure. The sabotage only made sense if diamonds waited to be discovered at the bottom of the terrace.

He was no wiser as to who orchestrated it. Tamba was his main suspect, but he couldn't say why, and now that Tamba cooperated with Sam and even appeared to enjoy working with her, the interference had stopped. This surprised him. He had expected complaints from her about the basic conditions in Fona, but nothing seemed to faze her. It was a measure of the effect she had on everyone. As far as he could see, the only person who was taking everything in her stride was Sam. His initial scorn turned to admiration and something else, something he couldn't admit to himself.

That he might also find Sam attractive hadn't crossed his mind when Ned had laid claim to her. He appreciated the sensibilities of interfering with his fiery friend's desires. The chip on Ned's shoulder sometimes seem to weigh on his good sense. Ned committing himself to Gemma would be a bitter blow for Sam, but maybe she would need comfort. Fergus was good at that. Many women had fallen victim to his charms when looking for solace from a bad romance. They never stayed long, he didn't encourage it, but they adored feeling attractive again and he accepted their affection, giving nothing real away.

He poured water into the teapot and took the tray to the sitting room. Fatimata sat at the table under the fan which rotated drunkenly above her. Dembo, the parrot, sneaked inside and hovered under the table, hoping to get offered a piece of biscuit.

'I can't do it,' she said.

'You must. Sam will die.'

'She is not a good woman. It is of no importance.'

'What is wrong with you? Sam is a special person who gets on with everyone.'

'She wears clothes like a whore and I saw her go into your room. She is not worth saving. God will judge her.'

'God? What kind of Christian are you? You're just a hypocrite.'

'I saw her. She tried to take you from me.'

'You silly woman. Sam has no interest in me. She entered my room to clean the snake bite on my hand. Ned likes her, but they are not a couple.'

'Why does she wear clothes like a whore then?'

'Those belong to her sister. She took the wrong bag. It's a long story.'

Fatimata harrumphed and moved in her chair so that her back faced him.

'Fatou, please, the girl will die. She doesn't deserve to die just because you are jealous.'

'I need a message from the spirits. They have not spoken. I will not go.'

Fergus stood up and walked out to the veranda. He was livid, but he did not want her to see it. What would make her see sense?

'What the fuck is going on?' said Ned. 'Why don't we rescue Sam from the *bondo*?'

'We can't. They will stop us and kill us too. We are dealing with deep cultural roots here.'

173

'Fatimata is a hypocrite. She goes to church. She doesn't even believe in all that voodoo nonsense.'

'I'm working on it. Stay out of it. You can't help.'

Inside the house, Fatimata wolfed down a plate of shortbread. Dembo pulled himself up the curtains with his beak and claws and dropped onto the table. He walked to the plate and put his head to one side, pleading. Fatimata almost smiled, but she stayed where she was with the last biscuit between her fingers halfway to her enormous mouth. Dembo's head followed the biscuit which she waved in front of him, just out of reach. He tried to grab the morsel with his beak, but she lifted it to her mouth again, provoking panic in the parrot who jumped up and down flapping his wings in distress. He squawked in frustration and then, as clear as a bell, said, 'Sam's the boss, Sam's the boss.'

Fergus, who had been smoking outside to compose himself, burst back into the room. 'What did he say?' he said, astonished.

'Sam's the boss, Sam's the boss, Sam's the boss,' said Dembo, desperate for his biscuit.

Fatimata's eyes bulged out of her head in fright. She dropped the biscuit onto the plate and Dembo pounced on it. He bounced off the table and scampered away with it.

'That's not possible,' she said. 'I won't do it. I won't.' She pushed her chair backwards and it creaked ominously. Fergus put out a hand to steady her, but she brushed it away.

Suddenly, a splintering sound filled the room and before anyone could move, there was a loud crack. The ceiling fan crashed onto the table inches from her face, collapsing it onto the floor.

Dembo screeched in terror and fell over himself trying to get away, ending up in a heap of dust and feathers at Fergus' feet.

In the moment of silence that followed, big lumps of plaster fell into Fatimata's lap, but she did not move. She sat petrified like a pillar of salt in the face of the gods.

'What the fuck was that?' said Ned, jumping out of the hammock.

'Fatou's spirits just gave her a sign,' said Fergus.

***

Sam woke with a start. She had been shivering in her sleep and tried to curl up, forgetting she was tied up. One of her hands jerked free and hit the wall giving her a fright. Hardly daring to look, she opened her eyes and peered at her hand. She couldn't see well, but the string had been cut and hung from her wrist. Relief flooded her body. Someone must have sneaked in to her room while she slept and freed her hand. Despite the majority deciding to leave her captive, one girl must have decided that she was a witch after all and was not willing to risk her wrath.

She pulled at the string binding her other arm to the bed. Her fingers felt like bananas on the tight knot. She didn't have any nails to speak of and the string kept slipping through her sweaty digits. Finally, she got a good grip and pulled the knot apart.

She fell back on the mattress, gasping with the effort. Come on, you must get out. They may be back at any minute. She forced herself to sit up. Some white paint had flaked off her body and she looked like a dappled pony. She leant forward and shuffling nearer her knees, she pulled at the knots around her ankles. The skin felt chaffed and sore. She winced as she

175

pulled the string free of her legs, but it was a relief to move again.

She swung her feet onto the floor and searched around for her clothes, spotting her trousers and T-shirt in the corner. The pockets had been opened and her penknife and the cigarette packet with the juju bag had gone. She pulled the trousers on, surprised at how loose they were. The T-shirt was stuck under the leg of the bed and she had to tug hard to free it. She turned it right side out and pushed her arms into the sleeves. Dizzy and shivery, she wanted to go back to sleep, but every moment she spent in the *bondo* increased the danger. She took a deep breath and opened the door to her room.

Sam stepped outside and tried to remember how to get back to the river. Sweat ran down her back and her eyes wouldn't focus.

She saw two fish on the boards in front of her. Cautiously, she tested them with a toe. Flip-flops!

She slipped them on. They were too small and her heels hung over the back, but they were better than nothing. Her clothes were catching the white paint on her skin and she resisted the urge to rub some of it off. She wiped the sweat off her face with her filthy T-shirt and peered into the trees. They were a funny shape, short and round. They had no leaves. Was it winter?

Confused and disorientated, she wobbled her way down the short staircase and stood swaying at the bottom. One tree moved towards her with its branches out. She shrank backwards and tripped over a root. A violent shiver overcame her. She needed to leave, but her legs would not function. Had she been drugged? And then she remembered the mosquito bites. Malaria! If she didn't escape, she would die. She almost wailed. Screwing her eyes up, she tried to spot the path she had used to get to the *bondo*. But the trees were blocking it. She wavered uncertainly. The trees seemed to surround her, their branches closing in as she whimpered. Her legs would not hold her and she crumpled to the ground.

***

The light was fading when Ned and Fergus arrived at the entrance to the forest, bringing their reluctant passenger. Fatimata sat like a stone in the back seat, showing no inclination to get out. She had dressed herself all in white. Underneath the white turban that swathed her head, she had put streaks of white paste on her cheeks. They sat in silence, waiting her out. Long shadows reached out to their car as if trying to pull it in to the gloom. Fatimata sighed, filling the car with resentment. Finally, she pushed the door open and stepped out onto the hard-baked mud. Hesitating, she glanced at Fergus for reassurance.

'The gods have spoken, Fatou. Go get our girl,' he said.

She pulled her robes about her, walked away from the car and entered the forest. Her rolling gait took her into the trees where she hovered for a while as a white blob and then disappeared. It looked as if the Michelin man had gone for a late evening stroll in the woods.

'Will she arrive at the *bondo* in time?' said Ned.

'Of course. Sam will be fine, you'll see.'

'Bloody stupid superstitions.'

***

Many hands were touching her like clumsy moths bumping into a light bulb. They painted her again. The cool liquid on her burning body gave her some relief, but when it dried, it tightened hot on the skin. They

177

pulled her arms away from her body and tied her wrists with string to the struts of the table. She was too weak to struggle. She wasn't even convinced this was really happening. Malaria had taken over her brain and her confusion was absolute.

Suddenly, the women drew back from the table, leaving the head *sowei* standing at her feet. She had the box cutter in her hands. The other women stamped and clapped, shaking the *bondo* to its foundations. They chanted and sang. Sam shut her eyes, letting the sound rattle her bones. The woman with the box cutter held up her hand for silence. The other women came forward again and pressed her to the table. An awful memory pierced her blurred consciousness and she struggled. As her fear increased, she could hear a strange keening noise filling the room. Someone put their hand over her mouth and it stopped. The *sowei* approached the table. Her knees were forced apart and she bit the hand holding her mouth, screaming with fear and fury. The *sowei* took out her knife. The women held Sam down.

***

Fatimata had pushed her way through the forest, cutting corners on the path, increasing her pace as darkness fell. Her heart was thundering. Unused to exertion, she was desperate to rest. She slowed down, gasping for breath. A strange wailing noise floated through the trees. Was she too late?

Picking up the pace again, she almost ran now, losing a shoe, but not stopping to pick it up. The lights of the *bondo* shone through the undergrowth. There was a chilling silence. She burst through the trees into the clearing and ran up the steps. She took a lungful of air.

The door of the *bondo* burst open and slammed against the wall. A piece of bark fell to the floor. The group stood open-mouthed and they backed away from the entrance. The head *sowei* still had the blade in the air. She hardly had time to turn around before she was swept aside by Fatimata's enormous arm. She hit the ground hard and the other women went to her assistance.

'Untie her!' said Fatimata.

'How dare you come to the *bondo*? You're unclean. Leave now!' The head *sowei*, still being supported by her fellows, had recovered her poise.

'I will not. Have you forgotten that I saved all of you when the rebels came?' Fatimata glared at the other women who avoided her eyes. 'Why am I unclean? I am a hero, not an outcast.'

'The gods decide who is permitted, not you. You're defiling our culture.'

'Ha! You call this culture? Murdering an ignorant stranger?'

'She brought a death fetish into the *bondo*.'

'No, she didn't. Not on purpose.' Fatimata sighed. 'I planted it in her room. She doesn't know what it is.'

'If she's ignorant, why were you trying to kill her?'

'Because I'm ignorant too. I was jealous of her. I wanted her out of the way because I thought my boss fancied her and not me.'

The head *sowei* tutted.

'And did he?'

'The only person Mr Fergus fancies is himself.'

'This is all about your hurt feelings?'

'Yes. I'm an idiot. I admit it. But you can't blame Sam for that. You must let her go.'

'What about the *bondo*? Where will we purify the young women?'

'We can burn it to the ground and that will purify it. We don't have to kill the foreigner. The fetish has no power in here.'

'Let us consider it.'

The *sowei* grouped together in a corner of the hut and there was some heated muttering. Fatimata walked up to the end of the table, holding Sam's head. She stretched out a hand to wipe the hair off her face. Jumping backwards, she faced the group again.

'Holy Jesus!' she shouted. 'The girl is burning up. You will kill her anyway. Let me remove her, for God's sake.'

The head *sowei* turned to face Fatimata. She was shaking with anger and her face was a picture of conflicting emotions.

'Take her.'

*** 

Fergus leaned against the car, looking up at the sky. Scattered stars twinkled in the deepening blue. He lit a cigarette to give him something to do and blew the smoke into the clouds of mosquitoes that hung in the warm early evening air. Ned sat in the car his head lowered to the dashboard.

'We're too late,' he said.

'What makes you say that?'

'She's been missing for days. If she has malaria, it will kill her.'

'Don't say that. She'll be alright, she's strong.'

Ned sighed. 'Your glass is always half-full.'

'Hope is what you have when there is nothing else left.'

'You're such a corny idiot.'

They turned towards the forest. As if on cue, a large white shape loomed into view through the trees, staggering under the weight of its burden. Fergus ran towards it. Ned started the jeep and drove to the edge of the trees, overtaking Fergus who waved him on. Fatimata emerged from the gloom. She was carrying a limp body.

Before Ned could leave the car, Fergus had caught up and rushed over to Fatimata.

'Is she alive?' he said.

'Yes, I am,' muttered Sam, who would not speak again for days. 'I'm alive, but why am I floating?'

*** 

Someone had tried to darken the room by pulling flimsy curtains across the window, but rays of light shot across the room and illuminated the whitewash. The doctor finished his examination of Sam as she lay on her back with her lank hair spread over the pillow. She was porcelain white. Beads of sweat stood out on her forehead. A tube was attached to her arm which led back to a bottle of saline hanging on an ancient rusty holder.

Ned and Fergus stood out on the veranda while the doctor examined Sam. Fatimata, who had hardly left Sam's side, had taken the chance to go for a quick shower. Now she was clattering about in the kitchen, 'murdering the pots and pans,' as Ned put it. Fergus blew a long row of cigarette rings into the still air.

'My wife's arriving tomorrow. I need to go to Njahili today,' said Ned.

'Okay. You must take the bus. I need the car in case we have to take Sam to the hospital there,' said Fergus.

'Why don't I take her now?'

'She's too fragile. She won't survive the journey.'

The doctor came out of Sam's room and joined them on the veranda.

'He's right. Moving her would be dangerous and she has everything she needs right here. Fatimata is an excellent nurse.'

'Will she live?' said Ned.

'I can't tell yet,' said the doctor. 'It looks as if she's had full-blown malaria for a few days now. I'm not sure how she's lasted this long. She has the constitution of an elephant.'

'Are you saying she might die?' said Fergus.

'I'm afraid so. It's in the lap of the gods. I'll be back later to check on her. Keep changing the drip. I have left several full bags in the fridge.'

'Thank you, doc.'

'I'm sorry I can't give you a better prognosis. See you then.'

The doctor shook hands with them and got into his car. Fatimata, who hovered at the door, came outside.

'She can't die, Mr Fergus. I won't let her. The witch doctor has made her a very strong fetish. She will live.'

'Thank you, Fatou. Any chance of some lunch?'

'It will be ready soon,' she said and drifted back indoors.

'For God's sake,' said Ned. 'Hasn't she done enough damage with her voodoo? Why didn't you say something?'

'The fetish will have cost her a great deal. It is not only Sam who needs healing. Leave her alone. She's doing her best.'

'I don't understand you. Sometimes I think you are native to Simbako and your freckles are your real colour poking out.'

Fergus laughed. 'You sound bitter, Neddy. You need to see your wife.'

When Ned had left for the bus yard, Fergus went into Sam's bedroom to find Fatimata swaying with fatigue on a chair beside the bed. She glanced up as Fergus came in. Her eyes had a defeated expression and there were tear tracks on her plump cheeks.

'Oh, Mr Fergus. I've killed her. God will punish me.'

Fergus gazed at Sam lying on the bed with her chest rising and falling, a veneer of sweat on her face.

'No, you saved her. He'll reward you.'

She gave him a weak smile.

'Get some rest right now. That's an order. You mustn't wear yourself out.'

'What about Sam?'

'I'm here now.'

To his surprise, she nodded and stood up. The chair creaked in protest or relief. She glided out, her bottom hitting both sides of the doorframe on the way out, making the whole room shudder.

Fergus was left standing beside Sam's bed. Her pale face emphasised her small red lips and green eyes. She was there, but not there. The fire in her eyes had almost gone out. He felt distressed and impotent.

Now he was alone with her, hidden feelings overwhelmed him. He pulled the chair closer to the bed and sat facing her. An odd sensation passed through his chest and he swallowed hard. A tear ran down his cheek which he brushed violently away. He leaned in close to her and whispered in her ear.

'Please don't die, Sam. Please.'

He wept uncontrollably, his head buried in the sheets. He stayed like that for a few minutes until the storm passed. His reaction had shocked him. From where had this surge of emotion come? It was real.

Suddenly, he felt a touch on his fingers like a mouse had run across his hand. He was startled to see Sam with the slightest smile on her lips. She said something in a hoarse voice.

'I didn't hear you. Say it again,' said Fergus.

'Shorts,' said Sam.

# Chapter XVI

Sam did not die, but her recovery took a long time. She lay in her bed sweating, tossing and turning, while her body fought the malaria. Fergus and Fatimata took turns watching her and feeding her. Fatimata kept her clean and changed her linen once day. She treated Sam like a new born. Fatimata stripped and made the bed with the help of Fergus who lifted Sam in the air.

'Thank you, Mr Fergus. It's much easier,' said Fatimata.

'She's so thin,' he said. 'It's shocking.'

'That's the fever. We'll make her fat when she is better. Like a good Fona girl.'

'I hope so.'

They both left the room, carrying the dirty sheets and various items of cutlery and some glasses to the kitchen.

The door was only ajar for a minute, but Sam had a visitor. Dembo the parrot sidled into the room and climbed up the bedframe above Sam's head where he preened himself. When this produced no reaction from Sam who was dozing between her clean sheets, he jumped down onto the pillow and pulled her hair with his beak. She opened her eyes.

'Sam's the boss,' squawked Dembo.

Her eyes opened wide.

'Sam, Sam, Sam.'

She laughed, almost gurgling.

Fergus, who had returned to pick up the rest of the used things, stood in the doorway, open-mouthed in amazement.

'Sam? Are you awake?'

'Dembo,' she said.

'What is that animal doing in here?' said Fatimata, stamping her foot in indignation. 'Get him out now.'

'You get him out. He bites.'

Dembo had retreated to the frame of the bed and lifted his beak ready to strike.

'He's not doing any harm,' said Fergus.

'Dembo,' said Sam.

'My good Lord,' said Fatimata. 'She spoke. It's a miracle. Get the doctor.'

*** 

The doctor took the thermometer out of her mouth. He held it in the light of a sunbeam and smiled.

'Her temperature's going down. She's not out of the woods yet, but she may pull through,' he said.

'Thank goodness for that. She was in such a state when we rescued her that I thought we were too late,' said Fergus.

'Me too,' said the doctor. 'She's as tough as they come. Tell Fatimata to keep her hydrated and to call me if she gets worse.' He zipped up his bag and sighed. 'Can't you chase the parrot out? It really shouldn't be in here.'

He gesticulated at Dembo who was sitting on the iron railing at the foot of Sam's bed scratching the feathers on his head with a long claw. He preened himself in the spotlight of the physician's glare. 'Sam's the boss,' he said and went back to his grooming.

'He's vicious, doc. I've almost lost a finger several times. He doesn't bother us,' said Fergus, reaching out to touch his shiny back and having to leap backwards as Dembo lunged at him. 'I can't imagine when she taught him to say that, but it seems to cheer her up. I'm loath to remove him.'

'Hmm, well, it's irregular, but I don't suppose it'll do any harm. See you tomorrow.'

'Thanks, doc.'

Fatimata appeared at the door with a tray on which were balanced a jug of fresh lemonade and some glasses. 'Would you like a glass of lemonade, doctor?'

'That would be great. Perhaps out on the veranda?'

Fatimata turned around with a swish of her dress and headed back down the passageway with her tray.

'Do you have enough saline?' said the doctor, following her out of the room.

Fergus stood for a minute looking at Sam before he went to join them.

***

Once the fever had reduced, Sam got steadily better. Soon she could sit up in bed leaning against the pillows. Too tired to talk much, she spent a lot of time dozing. Fatimata brought her nutritious soups and boiled eggs which she toyed with but couldn't face eating. Most of her nutrition came from the drip. Fatimata came in to Sam's room one morning and found her on the floor.

'Sam, what are you doing?'

'I need to wash. I tried to get up, but my legs don't work. Please, Fatou, help me. I am filthy.'

'I will help you, but you must get back into bed.'

187

Fatimata produced a large tin bath from one of the sheds at the back of the property and, after washing out all the cobwebs and hairy inhabitants, she put it in Sam's room. Fergus helped her to half-fill it with lukewarm water.

'You must leave now,' said Fatimata.

When Fergus had reluctantly left the room, complaining he was 'missing the best bit', Fatimata helped Sam take off her T-shirt and underwear and lifted her off the bed into the tin bath. Sam leaned back in the water, an expression of bliss on her face.

'Help me stand, Fatou,' she said. She stood on wobbly legs with Fatimata hovering while she soaped her whole body. 'I'm ready to sit down again,' she said. Fatimata took her arm and lowered her back down into the bath.

Dembo, who had been observing these manoeuvres with interest, tried to climb up onto on the edge of the bath, but fell to the floor which made her giggle. His dignity in tatters, he shuffled off to his usual perch on the end of the bed.

'Put your head back,' said Fatimata and she poured water through Sam's filthy hair. She put a dollop of shampoo on her hands and massaged it into Sam's head.

'You've still got paint in your hair,' she said.

'I haven't thanked you,' said Sam. 'For saving my life. I'm so sorry I misjudged you.'

'I'm the one who was judging. It's my fault you nearly died. I'll never forgive myself.'

'Please don't say that. Fergus told me you saved the whole village from the rebels. You are a heroine.'

'Did he tell you what happened?'

'Not exactly, but if you want to tell me, I'd love to hear about it.'

'I will tell you the story when you are better. Let's get you back into bed.'

\*\*\*

'Where is Ned?' said Sam.

She was feeling much better. Well enough to have visitors.

'What's wrong with me?' said Fergus, who had brought her some fresh coconut water. 'I'm here, aren't I?'

'If you don't know by now, I'm not sure I can help.'

'How can you be so mean when I haven't left your side for days?'

'I thought that was pretty mean.'

'You've cut me to the quick.'

'I'm sure you are. Can you answer my question now?'

'Ned's in Njahili with Alex.'

'When will he be back?'

'Um, I'm not sure he will be. His wife is also there.'

'Gemma? But I thought they were getting divorced.'

'There's been a hitch.'

'What sort of hitch?'

'I'm afraid it's the big sort. Gemma's pregnant. And Ned's the father.'

'Oh. I see. Or rather, I don't. I thought he'd left her.'

'Yes, he has, had, but they met in London before he came out to Simbako and they had break up sex.'

'Break up sex?' Sam was crushed.

'I'm sorry. I had no idea. He's an idiot.'

'Can you go now please? I need to be alone. I'm tired.'

'Sam.'

'No, just go. Please.'

She couldn't even cry. It was like she had a hole in her chest full of misery. So much for her dreams. She had fantasised about Ned taking her in his arms and making love to her ever since that first night in the bar. He had been leading her up the garden path and with a pregnant wife in tow. She was the idiot.

Sam did not have time to recover from the news about Ned. Rumours of her recovery had spread and, a few hours later, she received a visit from Adanna.

'Are you better?' said Adanna. 'We were so worried about you. My father is distressed. He blames himself.'

'Why on earth does he do that?'

'You gave him your repellent in the airport.'

'I'd forgotten about that. But I had more repellent in my luggage so tell him not to blame himself. I'm fine now.'

'Thank goodness. Fatimata told me that you were dying.'

'Reports of my death are greatly exaggerated.'

'I can see that. You are too thin. I hope she's feeding you.'

'If she could fatten me up like a foie grass goose using a funnel down my neck, she'd be ecstatic.'

'She's overcompensating for trying to kill you with voodoo.'

'It nearly worked. I was lucky.'

'You look sad though. Is something wrong?'

'Ned has gone to Njahili to be with his wife.'

'Ned? I didn't realise that you liked him. I thought ...'

'What? Tell me.'

'I thought Fergus was more your sort of man. He's handsome and funny. And he really likes you.'

'Oh, God, no. How can you even say that? He doesn't like me.'

'Forgive me, but according to Fatimata, he sat beside your bed for days willing you to live. He hardly ate or slept.'

'Don't be silly. I don't remember that. How ...?' But suddenly she did. She remembered his voice in her ear asking her not to die. She blushed to the roots of her hair.

'What's wrong?' said Adanna. 'Is it the malaria? Shall I call Fatou?'

'No, don't call her. I'm fine. Shocked. Don't tell him that I know.'

'Now why would I do that?'

'Thank you. It's a lot to take in right now.'

'When will you be able to get up?'

'The doctor tells me I can sit on the veranda or lie in the hammock from tomorrow morning.'

'Tamba will be pleased. Fatimata isn't the only person who's been feeling guilty.'

'Will he come and see me? I'd like to talk to him.'

'Yes, I'll tell him. I've got to go now, but I'll be back soon.'

\*\*\*

Fatimata brought Sam some fresh mangoes which she had cut and peeled fresh from the tree. The first of the season, they were small and sweet, with an addictive odour. Dembo had to be shut in his cage with his own supply of fruit to prevent him inflicting sharp pecks with his beak when he didn't agree with his share of the spoils.

'My favourite,' said Sam. 'Thank you, Fatou. I love mangoes.'

'You're welcome.'

Fatimata pulled an old armchair up to the bed and sat down.

'I will tell you about the rebels now,' she said.

Sam was surprised, but she tried not to show it, making a show of rearranging her pillows so she could sit up in the bed facing Fatimata, whose face showed her conflicting emotions.

'I am listening, auntie,' she said.

Her colloquial term for respected local women had the required effect. Fatou's face lit up.

'The Chief came to see me when the rebels were planning to pass through Fona. I shared a small house in Fona with my sisters. I was a *sowei* despite being young for the honour. He told me the rebels were coming and he asked me to make them a stew.'

'A stew? I don't understand.'

'He wanted me to put poison in it.'

'Poison?'

'We couldn't fight back any other way. The rebels were looking for diamonds and they were ruthless. They killed everyone in their path.'

'What about the Simbako army?'

'They were defending the capital. We were alone.'

'But how did you know about poisons?'

'My father was a witch doctor. He taught me about many herbs and potions.'

'What happened?'

'I agreed to help the Chief in return for this house. By killing the soldiers, I broke a sacred rule meaning that I'm now unclean and may not attend the ceremonies at the *bondo*.'

'But you rescued me there.'

'You may thank Dembo for that.'

'Dembo? What's he got to do with it?'

'I was prepared to let you die. I could not defy our culture without a sign from the gods. Fergus tried to make me go, but I refused. Then the fan fell down and Dembo told me that you were the boss.'

Sam blushed. 'What? I can't believe it.'

'Everything happens for a reason.'

'But what happened when the rebels came?'

'Chief Sesay waited alone for them in the ceremonial hall. He intended to delay them long enough for the poison to work.'

'Wow, he must be so brave.'

'It's a pity you didn't know him then. He was so tall and strong and handsome. A real leader.'

'So why is he in a wheelchair?'

'Has no one told you? They tortured him and left him for dead. The feast distracted them and they failed to confirm that he was dead. The stew poisoned them and he survived. Just.'

'Bastards. Serves them right. Where did you bury them?'

'Somewhere they won't be found.'

Fatimata stood up. She had an expression on her face Sam recognised. No more information will be forthcoming.

When Fatimata had gone, Sam sat in bed and tried to digest the day's events. The fortitude shown by Joseph Sesay amazed her. The rebels had broken his body, but not his spirit. A true hero. Without him, the village would have been burned to the ground. She had seen some of those ghost villages on her way to Fona. Blackened walls and trees standing testament to the savagery. Listless people sitting on the side of the road, their faces blank with suffering.

The news about Ned was a body blow though. All of her fond imagining was shown to be just wishful thinking. Had he lied to her? It was unlikely. They were both looking for a distraction after their partners had dumped them. Perhaps it wasn't real at all. Oddly, she was struggling to remember what he looked like. That must be the malaria.

In fact, whenever she wanted to daydream about Ned, Fergus intruded on her thoughts. Big, blonde and handsome, like a human lion, no wonder he was distracting. Ned didn't have that animal magnetism, but he was nice. Fergus was not nice. He had dismissed her out of hand when she arrived. The only time he noticed her was when she wore Hannah's shorts. But now that had been turned on its head. She remembered all too clearly. He had cried for her. She couldn't un-hear it. He may even have saved her. Please don't die. Was it even her he was crying for?

*** 

'How's Sam?' said Alex.

'She'll live. She wants to get back to work.'

'Is that going to be possible?'

'I don't see why not. She's asking to start already.'

'Let's see how she progresses. Can you get the pitting going again? I'd like to be sure that we are digging in the right place.'

'Okay, I'll speak to Tamba to see if we can restart operations. How's Ned?'

'Shell-shocked to be honest. Neither of them has taken this in yet. Gemma vomits a lot and Ned stands around looking helpless.'

'Will they stay together?'

'No idea. I'll tell him you were asking after him.'

'You do that. I'll call you if we find anything.'

***

Fergus drove up to the Chief's compound and parked among the chickens who did their utmost to get run over. Tamba emerged from the house and waved.

'Come in, come in,' he said, gesticulating.

Joseph Sesay was in the formal guest room, looking out of the window. He beamed with pleasure when Fergus came in.

'Good morning, Fergus. How is our patient?'

'Good morning, sir. She's on the mend. I can't keep her in the house much longer.'

'That's great news. We've been so worried about her, especially Adanna.'

'That's why I'm here – about Sam. We'd like to start work on the terrace again, as soon as possible.'

'Tamba can start tomorrow, if that is not too soon. But don't you need a geologist on site?'

'She has taught me a lot about sampling, so I can carry on with it and just show her the results when she is better,' said Tamba.

'Okay, we agree. I'll work with Tamba until Sam is ready to start again,' said Fergus. 'If we turn up any surprises, we can show her what we find.'

Tamba winced, but he said nothing. Fergus noticed the tiny movement but ignored it. Tamba was difficult to fathom at the best of times, but he had been a lot more cooperative since working with Sam.

'Let me know how it goes,' said the Chief.

# Chapter XVII

As Sam recovered, she became frustrated that Fergus had taken over her work on the terrace. This gave her all the incentive she needed to get better as fast as possible. She ate everything Fatimata prepared for her, especially fried food. Batter-covered sweet plantains were her favourite. She was regaining some weight and growing stronger every day.

One morning, she heard Fergus in the hall and called out to him. He came in and sat on her bed, instead of the chair beside it, and the unexpected closeness of his body radiating health and warmth caused her to blush bright red.

'You okay? You're flushed,' he said.

'It's the malaria.'

'Aren't you getting better?'

'Much better. I should go back to work soon.'

'Work? Oh, I'm not sure. Maybe we should ask the doctor.'

'I'm sure he won't object. Perhaps you could ask Tamba and his men to build me a shelter with a chair on the terrace? Then I would come for short bursts until I'm stronger.'

'That's not a bad idea. We are making good progress now. The second row of pits is almost finished.'

'And the results?'

'No diamonds yet, but plenty of indicator minerals. We're in the right place. Tamba's quite the geologist after all the training you gave him.

'He's surprisingly good. Once he got over his reticence, he took to it like a duck to water.'

'I suspect this isn't the first time Tamba's been digging for diamonds. I'd better get going. We'll build you the shelter. Once it's ready, you can come over for an hour one afternoon when it's cooler and see how you go.'

'Brilliant, thank you. Have a nice day.'

He left, but she could still smell him and it made her randy. *How annoying! It's high time I got out of bed and stopped fantasising. Real life awaits.*

Adanna came to visit again and they sat out on the veranda. Fatimata had gone to the market and shut Dembo in his cage to stop him bothering Sam for cashews. Sam swayed in the hammock and Adanna sat on the bench under the window. It had become cooler and the first rains had washed the dust from the leaves of the mango tree. They moved in the breeze, dark green and shiny.

'It's nice to see you looking better. When can you go back to work?' said Adanna.

'Thank you. I'm hoping that I'll spend an hour or two there tomorrow. Fergus is being such a nanny. I'm sure I'm ready, but he is still being cautious,' said Sam.

'What do you expect? The man is crazy about you.'

'Hmm, I'm not convinced.'

'Have you spoken to your parents? They must have worried about you.'

'To tell you the truth, I haven't told them the whole story. They are too far away to help. I hate to worry them for no reason.'

'No reason? You nearly died.'

'That's true, but I was too ill to call them and now I'm better, it seems silly to cause them anxiety. I don't phone them often when I'm away. They understand it's difficult for me from some places.'

'You're a really weird person. If my mother was alive, I'd call her every day.'

'I love my mother. I'd call her a lot more often if the satellite phone was working. It's hard to organise a call via the exchange. It's shut when I go to work and shut when I finish.'

'But doesn't she miss you?'

'We're very British about feelings in my family. My parents are from a generation terrified of showing off. Being too emotional is taboo. You're supposed to keep your feelings to yourself. I suffer from it myself. What about your mother?'

'I never knew her. She died giving birth to me because of her ...' Adanna hesitated and sighed.

'She died giving birth to you? I'm so sorry. I didn't realise that's what you meant.'

'That's okay. You can't miss what you never had. Did you see what they did to the girls in the *bondo*?'

'Yes, I saw it most of it by mistake, but I fainted when they used the box cutter.'

'No wonder. It's a barbaric practice. It resulted in the death of my mother. My father wouldn't let them cut me. He says it's only an outdated custom to keep women from being free to enjoy their sex lives.'

'He says that? Wow, he doesn't appear radical.'

'You mean he looks old and crippled? He isn't. Especially not his mind.'

'I didn't mean that.'

'It's okay. I'm his heir and he wants me to be Chief of this kingdom.'

'He's right. You'll make a great leader.'

'The *sowei* and the tribal elders will not allow it.'

'Is it because you are a woman?'

'No, it's because I am unclean, not cut.'

'But that's ridiculous.'

'I would get it done, but I'm afraid.'

'But you can't. It's too dangerous. Remember what happened to your mother. That procedure should be carried out in a hospital.'

'A hospital? I heard that people die in hospitals.'

'That's a myth. It's caused by people waiting too long before they go to the hospital because they are afraid of going.'

'So?'

'They wait until it's too late to save them and then they die in hospital.'

'Oh. I never thought of it that way.'

'I've had several minor operations. These days you get two days R and R and then you leave.'

'Is it expensive?'

'It's free in Britain, but I guess that you'd have to pay a lot for an operation in Njahili's private hospital. I saw it when we drove through town. It's a brand-new building. Someone has to pay for it.'

'How much is a lot?'

'Oh, I can't guess. About ten thousand dollars? Why do you ask?'

'Just curious. No wonder Fergus kept you here. He didn't want to pay for the hospital.'

Her face crinkled up in a cheeky smile.

After Adanna left, Sam stayed in the hammock reading books and eating fattening snacks most of the day. She was still lounging there when Fergus got home from work. He parked the car in the shade under the tree and jumped out of the car. He had removed his shirt and his chest shone with sweat. Streaks of mud marked where he had wiped his hand across his stomach. He strode across the yard, his flanks gleaming in the sun like a stallion after a run. Sam was mesmerised. She forced a greeting.

'Hi Fergus. How did it go?'

'Good. I think. The bedrock has sloped downwards like you said it might.'

'That's great news. Please don't make me stay at home any more. I'm so much better and I need to supervise the pitting as we get nearer the bottom.'

'We're building the shelter. It should be ready for you to try out tomorrow afternoon for an hour.'

'Fantastic, I can't wait to get back to work.'

'What did you do today?'

Not much but the day had got better. She searched for something neutral to say.

'Um, Adanna came over and we hung out on the veranda.'

'Jaysus, it scares me rigid when you two get together. There's something febrile about it.'

'Don't be silly. We're just catching up on the local gossip.'

'What's the latest on me?'

Sam gulped and flapped her hands.

'Oh, they say you are planning on proposing to Fatimata.'

'Ha! Your sources are drunk.' And with that he leapt up the stairs and disappeared into the house, leaving her ill with lust.

She blamed Ned. If he hadn't got her all worked up for nothing, she wouldn't be drooling over the caveman.

The news about the terrace was illuminating though. She had expected the sides of the pothole to be barren. They had pitted on the thinner end of the terrace and as they progressed the depth to the bedrock would increase, augmenting the likelihood of a bonanza. She needed to get out there and inspect the pit walls in the deeper parts of the terrace.

To her great relief, Fergus allowed her to come to site the next afternoon. He sent Sahr to pick her up in the old jeep. She sat on the steps of the veranda feeding banana to Dembo who had taken quite a shine to her and clicked his purple tongue at her for more. Sahr pulled up in a cloud of dust and came over to see her.

'You are well now?' said Sahr. 'You worried everyone, even the doctor.'

'I'm much better now.'

'I'm so sorry about the voodoo. The fetish contained evil power. I should've realised it would get you.'

Sam did not believe in malevolent forces. The mosquitos that bit her in Fona on her first night in town had caused her malaria, but there was no point saying so.

'Thank you, Sahr. You saved my life by guessing I had gone to the *bondo*, so I think we are even.'

He smiled and helped her into the front seat. Her legs wobbled and she had to pull herself into the car.

'Are you sure you're ready for work?' he said.

'There's only one way to find out. Can you do me a favour?'

'Of course.'

'I must call my parents. Can we stop at the exchange? The satellite phone is rubbish.'

'Sure.'

They up to the telephone exchange and Sahr made her wait in the car while he booked a call and organised a booth for her. He came outside when the connection had been made.

'Your call is through,' he said. 'I think it's your mother.'

A surge of emotion hit her. Despite her phlegmatic attitude, she was still a child where her mother was concerned. She struggled up the steps and entered the booth he pointed out to her, shutting the door behind her.

'Hello?'

'Sam? Is that really you?'

Hannah. Sam panicked. Should she hang up?

Hannah's voice quavered. 'Please don't hang up. I need to talk to you.'

'Okay, I need to talk to you too.'

'Are you alright? You sound funny.'

'Just tired. I've had some long days in the field.'

'I was so worried when you didn't ring. You can't imagine how sorry I am about the whole Simon thing. It's my fault. I should've told you when you got back from Sierramar.'

'You should. It's a little late now. Are you still with him?'

A long silence.

'Yes.'

Sam considered this and realised that she didn't care anymore. Simon was history. Life was too short to waste on him. She sighed.

'Don't feel bad. The discovery that you had both betrayed me hurt me a lot, but you are my sister. That's more important than a failed relationship, even if you are a rubbish sister. I've decided I deserve better than Simon. I won't be going back. You can have him.'

'Thanks a lot.'

'That's not what I meant. Well, it is a bit. Anyway, I'm so over him.'

'Is there someone else?'

'Yes and no.'

'What does that mean?'

'One says yes and I'm not sure about the other one.'

'I've created a monster.' Hannah hesitated. 'I'm such a bitch. You deserve a nicer sister. Forgive me.'

'Give me time. I will.' She changed the subject. 'How are Mummy and Daddy?'

'Both out playing golf. I'll tell them you called. Is there something you wanted to tell them?'

'Um, no, not really. I'll call them another time. Just tell them that it's amazing out here and I'm having lots of fun.'

'I will. Thank you, Sam. I don't deserve you.'

True, but Sam didn't need to rub it in.

'Bye then.'

'Bye.'

Sam hung up. Telling her about the malaria wouldn't help. Her parents would only worry. The mature lack of rancour between herself and Hannah over Simon had surprised her, but having almost died, had made her realise the difference between the permanent and the fly-by-night. Sisters are in the first category. Unfaithful boyfriends on the other hand …

They arrived at the terrace where Fergus waited to greet them. Sam slid off the seat and walked a few uncertain steps. Fergus, who had been watching her, strode over to the car and, without ceremony, swept her up in his arms, knocking her hat off.

'Whoa there, careful, I'm not sure I need to be carried,' said Sam, pink with embarrassment. He smelt of mud and sweat and some pheromone which made hers dance.

'I am,' he said.

Sahr picked up her hat and put it on her head. He saw her flushed face and winked at her.

Oh, God he knows. Everyone knows, except Fergus, and how long would that last. They weren't the most discreet bunch of people she'd ever met.

'Give me my rucksack please, Sahr.'

Rucksack swinging from her free arm, she suffered the indignity of being carried to the terrace where everyone rushed up to greet her and help Fergus accommodate her in a newly assembled chair.

'You're welcome, madam.'

'We missed you.'

'Are you better?'                                '

'Mr Fergus is cross with us.'

'No, I'm not.'

They all nodded. Yes, you are. Their faces accusing. Sam laughed.

'Were you being naughty? I'm sure that's why.'

General merriment resulted with the workers giggling and poking each other, but no-one denied it.

Formalities over Sam sat in her chair while they brought her the results of the day's work. From her position on the terrace, she examined the latest pit. The material in the walls had been disturbed, no longer sorted into strata. Someone had been there before them. She had observed this in other pits. There was only one way of knowing how deep they had been dug before or if they had reached the bedrock where the richest gravels lay. The material they brought her had garnets and diopsides, indicating the likelihood the gravel was, or had been, diamond bearing. A frisson of excitement shivered through her.

'Are you okay?'

Fergus had picked up on the shiver and he put his hand on her shoulder. That didn't help much. His touch made her giddy.

'Better than okay. I'm so happy to be back at work.'

'What do you think?' said Fergus. 'Are we in the right place?'

'Definitely. We need to keep digging.'

'Excellent. Tomorrow's another day.'

With that, he held out his arms. She didn't protest. Hauling herself to her feet, she allowed him to pick her up again and they headed for the vehicle. With the pretext of helping him to carry her, she put her arm around his neck and snuggled up to his chest. Perhaps she would feign weakness for a few days. It had its perks.

Sam's recovery picked up pace though and, before long, she had to walk from the car, being unable to pretend that she needed to be transported. Fergus had been very willing to carry on, but it would be too obvious that she enjoyed it. After all, she claimed to be a tough, liberated geologist. They spent the evenings chatting and listening to music and making notes on the days' labours. His presence was comforting and therapeutic and she never wanted to go to bed.

\*\*\*

After a long day in the sun, Sam sat with Adanna in the shade in Pakuteh's chair, while Fergus had retreated to the shade of Sam's shelter. The women were drinking coconut water to stave off dehydration.

'What was he like?' said Sam.

'Who? Pakuteh?'

'Yes, I mean, what did he look like? Was he handsome?'

'Oh, yes, he had the body of an athlete and the face of an angel.'

The amusement in her voice alerted Sam to the exaggeration.

'No, really, I want to know.'

Adanna leaned back and closed her eyes.

'He was skinny with bony knees. He had bulbous eyes and big lips, not an Adonis by any means, but he had an enormous heart. Everyone else avoided me because I had not been to the *bondo*. Pakuteh didn't care.'

'He sound's nice. You must miss him.'

'I used to. More than a limb. But it's become harder to remember his face.'

'What was so special about him?'

Adanna paused and a laugh rumbled in her chest. She creased up with mirth and giggled until tears ran down her cheeks. Sam stared at her in amazement. She'd never seen Adanna laugh like that before. She was mystified. Finally, the giggling died down and Adanna explained herself.

'He had an enormous thingy. Almost down to his knee.'

And she fell back on the rock, her chest heaving. Sam's mouth fell open in shock. Somehow, she'd never attributed real emotions to Adanna. Hyper-controlled, she was almost alien in her aloofness, yet, here she lay, laughing her heart out.

'Down to his knee? How awful!'

'The first time he showed me, I asked him where he thought it would fit.'

She howled again, joined by Sam.

Fergus heard the two women laughing, a joyous sound. He headed over to the trees to see what the joke was, but suddenly a worker yelped and jumped out of the pit like he had been bitten by a snake.

'Everything okay?' said Fergus, walking over.

Tamba peered down into the hole. A strange expression appeared on his face.

'It's a body,' he said, his tone resigned. He didn't seem at all surprised.

'A body? How on earth?' said Fergus.

'Many people died here during the civil war.' He hesitated. 'This man fought with the rebels.'

'How do you know?'

'I was here when they buried him.'

'What happened?'

'The night that the rebels came to Fona, Chief Sesay sent me to the terrace to fill in the excavations made by local people.'

'Did they find any diamonds here?'

'I believe so. You must ask the Chief. The moon was full, so we worked as fast as possible in case the rebels found us. One man acted as a lookout. A rebel came through the woods and spotted us digging. We couldn't risk him telling the others so the lookout hit him on the head. It killed him instantly. We threw him in the pit and covered him up so the rebels wouldn't find out what happened to him.'

'Did you recognise him?'

Tamba swallowed. 'No, he was a rebel.'

'Maybe he has papers on him.'

'We should wait until tomorrow to remove him. It's too late to do it today.'

'Okay, let's finish up then. Cover the pit with some logs, we don't want a hyena to find the body and take the bones.'

Fergus was intrigued. It was obvious Tamba knew exactly who was in the pit, but he didn't want to say. He doubted the body would still be there in the morning, whoever it was. He avoided local politics in Fona like the plague.

Before Fergus could alert them, Sam and Adanna emerged from the wood to see what had caused the fuss.

'What's going on?' said Sam.

'They have uncovered a body. Tamba says it's a rebel killed during the raid ten years ago,' said Fergus.

'A body?' said Adanna. 'Who is it?' She turned to Tamba, who backed away, unable to look her in the eye.

'Oh, my God, is it be Pakuteh?' said Sam, brain whirring.

Adanna pointed an accusing finger at Tamba. Her expression changed to one of fury.

'You killed him? My poor husband was murdered. You bastard.' Tears coursed down her cheeks and she tried to grab him.

'Your husband? But … No, you don't understand,' said Tamba.

'Oh, yes, I do. You hated him because I loved him and not you. You took advantage of the rebel raid to kill him.'

'We killed him, but by mistake. He was sneaking around in the woods and the lookout hit him from behind. You can ask him yourself, he's over there.' Tamba pointed at a man standing at the edge of the group. He dropped his head when singled out. 'We didn't realise it was Pakuteh.'

'But you let me think he had abandoned me. I have spent a decade thinking he ran away and left me. How could you?' She was beside herself. Fergus had to hold her to prevent her attacking Tamba.

'I'm s-sorry. I planned on telling you, but the assault on your father had distressed you to the edge of reason. It m-might have been too traumatic for you. I meant to tell you later, but as time went on, it seemed better to keep it a secret.'

'A secret?' said Adanna. 'From me? Does my father know?'

'No. I've never told anyone.'

Tears coursed down Adanna's cheeks but she was mute, her slim body trembling with fury and misery. Sam's distress was increased due to the contrast with their laughing fit only minutes before. She put her arms around Adanna, but it was like hugging a fence post. Tamba stood apart, with his fists clenched and his eyes shut tight.

When the storm had receded, Fergus offered to take Adanna to the compound.

Tamba was left to seal off the pit with his team. He cut a lonely figure in the gathering gloom.

# Chapter XVIII

'What did you say?' said Joseph Sesay, blood draining from his face.

'We found Pakuteh's body,' said Tamba.

'Where did you find him?'

Tamba swallowed. 'He's buried in the terrace where Sam is working.'

'But how did he get there? I don't understand.'

'He got killed by mistake. He was spying on us when we filled in the terrace. The lookout hit him from behind thinking he was a rebel.'

'He's been dead a decade? Why didn't you tell me?'

'Because of Adanna. If she thought he had abandoned her, she might come to love me instead.'

'But they were married. She couldn't be with anyone else until she had confirmation he died.'

'No-one told me that. It's hard to accept that she's been miserable for years and it's all my fault. I'll leave the village. I can't stay here.'

The Chief put his hand on Tamba's shaking shoulder. 'You've made a serious mistake, but you're not the only one in the wrong here. There's something I haven't told Adanna either.'

'What more is there, sir?'

'Pakuteh ignored my orders and ate a bowl of the poisoned stew intended for the rebels. He would have been dead by morning anyway. Killing him was a mercy. At least he didn't suffer.'

'But Adanna has had years alone because of me.'

'Tamba, Tamba, Tamba. What shall we do with you?'

'I don't know,' said Tamba and sobbed like a child.

\*\*\*

Joseph Sesay insisted on coming to the terrace for the disinterment of the body of Pakuteh, who was an orphan, his parents having drowned after a ferry coming from Liberia sank on the way up the coast. Pakuteh's brothers had left town after the rebels disappeared and gone to the capital to look for work so, apart from Adanna, no-one remained to mourn him. Fergus picked Sesay up at the compound early the next morning. The Chief waited on the veranda of his house in his wheelchair.

'Good morning, Chief Sesay,' said Fergus.

'Good morning. It's a sad task we have today.'

'Yes, sir, it's a tragedy. I see that Tamba's not here. May I help you into the jeep?'

On receiving a nod of assent, Fergus put one arm under the Chief and one around his back and lifted him out of his chair. He placed the Chief into the front seat with no trouble as the crippled man was as light as a bird, despite appearances. The robes had disguised the fact that his weight had plummeted. Fergus folded up the wheelchair and placed it in the back.

'Okay then,' he said, putting the car in gear and driving away with care not to jolt his frail cargo. The potholes made it difficult to go at more than a snail's pace.

They arrived at the terrace where Tamba and his crew waited to carry Chief Sesay in his wheelchair to the edge of the pit. Sam and Adanna stood beside the pit, the latter looking sad and pale. Work began to free the body from the gravel and sand. It was a painstaking and solemn process. They removed the material with great care so as not to disturb the body and piled it up on the side of the pit. Before too long, they had exposed a skeleton still clad in T-shirt and trousers. The material fell away, rotten from years in the damp gravel. The skull still had hair attached, but the flesh had been eaten by the local micro-fauna. A blue satchel lay on top of the body and they removed it first. Fergus shook the sand from it and took it to Joseph Sesay for inspection.

'Can you check the contents please, Fergus?' he said.

The satchel was still intact, being made of some manmade fibre that did not rot. Fergus tried and failed to open the zips on the pockets which had rusted shut. Sam lent him her penknife to slit them open. He cut through the material of the front pocket and pulled a plastic covered identity card and some old bank notes from the interior. Adanna stepped forward and took the card from him, cleaning it with the edge of her dress. She let out a whimper, dropping it on the ground.

'It's him. It's Pakuteh.'

Her father held out his arms to her and she hid her face in his neck.

Fergus took some rotting clothes out of the main section of the bag and then shook it out.

'There's something in the pocket,' he said. He took the penknife, slit it open and slipped a finger into the hole, feeling around inside the damp pouch. His eyes widened and his hand flew to his mouth.

'Oh, my God,' he said. 'It's here, it's been here all along.'

The Chief raised a finger to his lips and shook his head at Fergus, who put his hand into the pocket and picked out something that he handed to Sesay without revealing it.

'What is it, father?' said Adanna.

'It's your wedding present.'

'My what? You knew? I don't understand.'

'If you will permit me, I don't want to discuss this here. Can we please recover Pakuteh first? I promise to tell you everything later.'

'Okay, father, if that's what you want.'

'Carry on please,' he said to Tamba.

Fergus turned to Sam, who had no idea what he had given to the Chief, and he mouthed something she didn't understand. Life in Simbako was full of unexpected events. What was the wedding present? How did the Chief know that Adanna had married Pakuteh?

*** 

They wrapped Pakuteh's remains in a blanket and brought them back to the Chief's compound in Fona on a makeshift stretcher. The Chief ordered the bones to be placed in a coffin which rested on the table in the ceremonial hall. They sealed the coffin with bitumen to prevent the odour of decay from penetrating the room, but it still seeped out and wrinkled the noses of the mourners. People who had known Pakuteh wanted to touch the body, but they had to settle for touching the coffin and placed offerings around it.

Adanna sat on a chair at one end of the room and received condolences. The news of her marriage to Pakuteh had spread like wildfire and the curious and maudlin lined up to see the widow. She did not raise her head, but kept her eyes fixed on the floor, allowing people to take her limp hand, but making no comment.

Her conflicting emotions about the discovery of the body had disturbed her controlled interior. On one hand, a flood of relief brought on by the knowledge that he had not deserted her, after all. On the other, the sensation that everyone had been lying to her for years hurt so much. Even her father, the rock of her existence, had been in on it. How could he do that to her? Tamba, she understood. He had hoped to break her resistance by pretending Pakuteh had abandoned her. And her father? He protected her because he also imagined Pakuteh had run away with the diamond. She had been a widow for a decade and now she had to go through the mourning again. She felt broken.

As the afternoon came to a close, the number of visitors slowed to a trickle and then stopped as the villagers realised that no food would be offered to the mourners. They returned grumbling to their daily task of making the evening meal and sealing their houses against evil spirits. Adanna sighed and stood up. She approached the coffin and put her hand over the place where his heart would have been.

'Please forgive me, my love. I thought you had deserted me. I should have realised that you would never have left me without a word.'

'It is not your fault,' her father said. He sat in his wheelchair in the doorway of the dining hall. 'I was cruel to you for no good reason, punishing you for being in love.'

'Tamba should have told us what happened. I blame him.'

'It's not Tamba's fault. There is something I never told you.'

'About Pakuteh?'

'Yes, let's go to the sitting room, Tamba should hear this too.'

Adanna followed her father across the yard to the house and Tamba came running out to help push the wheelchair up the makeshift ramp into the back door. They passed through the kitchen to the sitting room and sat down.

'Tamba, sit with us, you need to hear this,' said the Chief.

Tamba came to sit down. Adanna pointed at the chair furthest from her. Tamba cringed like a dog who expected a beating and made himself small in the chair. He glanced at her, pleading with his eyes, but she didn't acknowledge him.

'You remember the day of the raid,' said the Chief addressing Adanna. 'I stayed behind with Pakuteh to prepare the feast for the rebels and I sent you to hide with the women in the woods.'

She nodded.

'Pakuteh prepared the rice and the bananas in the kitchen while I was organising the dining hall. I had given him strict instructions not to eat any of the stew that Fatimata had made, but I had not told him why.'

Adanna gasped.

'He ate the stew?'

'I'm afraid he did. Fatimata told me last year that she had found a bowl hidden behind the bananas in the kitchen when she came back after the feast. Everyone had gone except Pakuteh. Who else would it have been?'

'Why didn't you tell me?'

'I'm not sure,' said the Chief. 'Perhaps I wanted you to retain some hope of seeing him again and I was not a hundred percent sure that Pakuteh had eaten the stew. I'm a fool and I made you so unhappy.'

'It wasn't only your fault,' said Tamba. 'I knew Pakuteh had died, but I didn't tell either of you.'

Adanna looked from one to the other with real distain. She walked out of the room.

'Sweetheart, come back,' said the Chief, but she had gone.

***

Tamba watched Adanna go. Her beauty still filled him with awe, but she held the keys to the kingdom. She would be vulnerable now, searching for comfort. He had no time to lose. The Chief was getting weaker and would not live much longer. He would redeem himself and fulfil his ambitions with one simple move. After taking the Chief a light supper, he went to Adanna's room and knocked on the door.

'Are you there?' he said.

'What do you want, Tamba?'

'I need to speak to you.'

'Haven't you said enough?'

'Please hear me out.'

'You have five minutes.'

Adanna's door flew open. She stood in the middle of the floor.

'What?'

'I come to petition you.'

'Petition me? For what?'

'For your hand.'

'Are you crazy?' Adanna crossed her arms and turned her back on him.

'Hear me out please.'

'I have no intention of marrying you.'

216

'Be reasonable. You're single now. No-one will have you because you are unclean. I have always wanted you and I'm prepared to accept you as you are. We could rule Fona together.'

'How dare you? I wouldn't marry you if you were the last man on earth.'

'With me, you have a chance of being Paramount Chief. Without me, you are nothing.'

'I would rather be nothing than marry you.'

She pointed to the door, eyes blazing.

'You will change your mind.'

'I would rather die.' Tears sprung to her eyes. 'Go now!'

Tamba went to his quarters to ponder the response. Adanna had always been fiery and stubborn. He had planted a seed though and now he would wait for her to weaken as her position did. He knew that he would win her in the end. What other choice did she have? He would enjoy her capitulation.

*** 

Later that evening, the Chief wheeled himself to the door of Adanna's room and knocked on the door.

'Please can I come in? I didn't tell you everything you needed to know.'

'You told me enough.'

'You have every right to hate me right now, but there is something I should give you. Please let me in.'

The door opened a crack, Adanna's sulky face visible in the gloom. Several citronella candles flickered behind her, illuminating her afro which she had freed from its constraints.

'Okay, but you can't stay long.' She sat on a wicker rocking chair in the corner.

The Chief moved his chair right up to her knees which he grasped with his hands. He gazed into her troubled eyes.

'It's been a tough couple of days for you, darling,' he said. 'Now that Pakuteh is at rest, a can of worms has been opened.'

'You're one of the worms,' she said.

'No-one is sorrier than me, but I must tell you something important.'

'What could be more important than finding out I'm a widow and the people who knew kept it a secret from me for years?'

'I don't deny it, but I want to explain what really happened that night.'

'Tell me.'

'When Pakuteh had finished preparing the feast for the rebels, I had a chat with him. I told him that I knew you were married.'

'What did he say?'

'He was astonished. Afraid, even, but I told him that I wanted him to take you away.'

'Why? This is my home.'

'I was worried that you'd spent too much time surrounded by voodoo and superstition. I thought you should leave Fona and see the world.'

'But how? We had nothing except our clothes.'

'I gave him this.' Joseph Sesay took his daughter's hand, which she gave unwillingly and turned it palm up. He dropped the diamond into it with his other hand, its vitreous lustre greasy in the candlelight. Adanna's mouth dropped open and her eyes widened.

'The Star of Simbako? I thought it was gone, lost.'

'Yes, I wanted people to assume that. I've kept it hidden all these years.'

'You gave it to him?'

'To both of you. When he disappeared, I worried that he had run off with it and abandoned you. I thought it might be lost forever, leaving you trapped here. I only found out about the stew when Fatimata told me and I couldn't face telling you. I presumed that Pakuteh had died in the woods or been robbed.'

'Trapped here? But, father, I'm not trapped, I want to be here. I love our people and I want to lead them.'

'But they will not let you.'

'That's your fault too. I'm unclean because of you. Maybe I should take this diamond and abandon you.'

Her father raised his head and looked her straight in the eye. 'Perhaps you should,' he said.

\*\*\*

'Did they identify the body?' said Fatimata. 'Or was it a rebel?'

She was waiting in the doorway when Fergus and Sam arrived back at the house.

'It was Pakuteh,' said Fergus.

'Pakuteh? Oh, my God. Is Adanna alright?'

'Not really,' said Sam.

'But how did he get there?'

'He died on the night of the rebel feast. Tamba and his men were filling in the diamond pit and the lookout mistook him for a rebel soldier and killed him by mistake,' said Fergus. 'Can we discuss this tomorrow please? It's been a long day.'

'Tamba? But why didn't he tell anyone?'

'Dinner, now, please,' said Fergus.

Fatimata crossed herself and returned to the kitchen to serve the food. The noise levels indicated that she was unhappy with the dearth of information offered to her.

'May I go now?' Fatimata had already put on her shawl.

'Of course. I promise to tell you about it tomorrow.'

She sighed and left, slamming the door and threatening to snap the wooden steps with her stomping.

Sam and Fergus ate a subdued dinner together, each alone with their thoughts. Sam had not completely recovered from malaria and she had found the day exhausting.

'Will you have a drink?' said Fergus.

'Oh, I'm not sure. I'm rather tired.'

'Come on. Don't be a spoilsport. Don't make me drink alone. Just one drink.'

'Okay, just one. Can I have a gin and tonic?'

'Only if you wear your shorts.'

'Dream on. Get me that drink. I'm going to sit in the hammock.'

'Yes, madam. I'll be out shortly.'

'Hilarious,' said Sam, but she smiled.

She was swinging in the evening breeze when he came out with the drinks.

'Here you go,' he said, handing her a long glass with a big wedge of lemon in it.

Sam sipped her drink and coughed.

'*Laimh laidir*?' said Fergus, reverting to Gaelic.

'Heavy hand? You could say that. How much gin did you use?' Fergus shrugged and winked. 'Are you trying to get me drunk?'

'You guessed. Well, I thought I'd take advantage of you while you are too weak to fight back.'

'That figures. Please get me some more tonic. This is too strong to be nice.'

By the time Fergus came back, Sam had fallen asleep. He sat for a while sipping his drink and watching her shallow breathing.

When he had finished his drink, he leaned over and slipped his arms underneath her lifting her up and out of the hammock. He pulled his arms to his chest, resting Sam's head on his shoulder. Her fair fell over her face and he could smell the cheap local shampoo she used. He tried not to be excited, but he was fighting a losing battle where she was concerned. The temptation to slip into bed with her was extreme, but he didn't want to break her trust. Leaving her under the mosquito net, he returned to his room.

\*\*\*

Adanna sat in her rocking chair, moving it back and forward on its creaking runners and staring into space. She passed the diamond from hand to hand, rubbing it as if it were Aladdin's lamp. It wasn't shiny, having the yellow film common to alluvial diamonds removable only with hydrofluoric acid. Warm and heavy, it hypnotised her with its unyielding presence. She thought about the mother she had never met. The one who owned the rocking chair. Back and forward she rocked, comforting her baby-self. She could not imagine the pain of childbirth in a woman with a fistula, but it had killed her outright.

For her father, the day of her birth was both the happiest and saddest day of his life. He wanted Adanna to go away before it happened to her too. She wanted to stay and bring modernity to Fona, but the sacrifice was great. Maybe the diamond represented a solution.

Outside, the rain fell again, refilling the water barrels and other mosquito havens with fresh water for larvae. She could smell the wet earth and it made her feel sad.

*\*\*\**

Sam stood outside Fergus' door. The moon shone into the passage that ran along the front of the house from the living and dining area. She had woken with the sensation of his face in her neck. Had she imagined it? She wanted to lie with Fergus and touch the veins on his arms and nuzzle his chest. Desire had permeated her being and she couldn't sleep because her heart pumped hot blood around her body. She hesitated. What if she had imagined it? What about Ned? Did he no longer matter? He had gone back to his wife, after all.

She wrapped her fingers around the door knob and twisted it. The door swung open and she saw his naked body outlined through the mosquito net. His chest rose and fell. He had one hand over his genitals. With his blonde mane and brown skin, he resembled a Greek god. Sam entered the room and shut the door behind her. She walked over to the bed and lifted the net, slipping under it and onto the mattress beside him. She listened to him breathing and she reached out to feel his heart. He opened his eyes and looked into her dilated pupils.

'Sam?'

# Chapter XIX

'Sam's a trooper,' said Alex, to no-one in particular, wiping his mouth with a tattered serviette.

'No kidding,' said Ned. 'The doctor thought she would die.'

William, who was bringing a fresh pot of coffee to the table, held it above the table.

'Is she okay now?' he said.

'Yes, she's fine. Thank goodness.'

William smiled. 'I'm glad. I liked Sam.' He shuffled off to the kitchen with three pairs of eyes following his back.

'Sam's a she?' said Gemma, Ned's wife, who sat away from the table because the smell of breakfast made her nauseous. 'You didn't tell me that.'

'Didn't I? I thought I had,' said Ned.

'No, you hadn't.'

Alex shifted in his seat and dropped his spoon on the floor. He didn't reach down to pick it up.

'What's your plan for today, Gemma?'

'Apart from vomiting you mean?'

The silence hung in the air while Alex searched for something to say. Gemma turned green and she pushed back her chair. 'Excuse me,' she said and ran upstairs.

'Why didn't you tell her about Sam?' said Alex. 'It's not as if …' He saw Ned's expression. 'Oh.'

'It wasn't like that. Nothing happened.'

'But you like her.'

'Doesn't everyone?' Ned threw a resentful glance at the kitchen. 'That's all finished now anyway.'

'I hope so.'

'What did Fergus say?' said Ned.

'Sam's back at work and he gave me some surprising news.'

'Don't tell me. Fergus is sleeping with Sam.'

'What? No. You have it bad. They've found the diamond. The Star of Simbako. In the terrace where Sam is working.'

'I'm sorry. I shouldn't have said that. I apologise. It's just …' Ned swallowed and fiddled with his watch. 'That's incredible news. You must be thrilled.'

'I'm going up to Fona today. I don't suppose you want to send any messages.'

Ned shook his head. 'I'd better check on Gemma.'

Alex poured himself another cup of coffee and admired the view of the bay through the window.

*** 

Joseph Sesay stood by the window, holding himself up with two walking sticks, their lion-head handles knobbly in his arthritic hands. He gazed out over the plains at the thorn trees and smelled the wheaty aroma of new grass. This was his favourite time of the year, one he knew he wouldn't experience again. His injuries from the rebels' beating had never healed properly and now he felt himself weakening and fading. His lungs were filling with fluid and every breath got harder. Fatimata had loaded him with potions and fetishes hidden in his robes, but he knew that death was stalking him. He could sense its black shadow brush by him in the corridor and see the glint of a sickle when the sun set.

Despite this, he appreciated his luck. If it wasn't for Alex, he wouldn't have lived to see any of this. Nor had his position as Paramount Chief, his beautiful wife or his headstrong daughter. He owed a debt of gratitude to the man which could not easily be repaid. By giving Adanna the diamond, he had betrayed that trust, but he was confident that Alex would understand. He wanted to settle his accounts before it was too late. The debt was incalculable.

Joseph Sesay had joined the army to get away from the grind of life in the diamond pits of Simbako. When he and his brother had found the Star of Simbako, he had imagined his troubles to be over, but they had just begun. As the eldest son in his family, he was the natural leader in a group which was traditionally one from whom the Paramount Chief was chosen. The diamond would bring him wealth, a big advantage when it came to taking over the Chiefdom. They had sworn to keep the diamond a secret until it was taken to the safety of Njahili and sold.

Unfortunately, his brother, with a character far removed from that of Joseph, started mouthing off about the diamond and attracting unwanted attention from some of the unsavoury elements in Fona. One night, their family compound was raided and his brother, and several other villagers, died in the ensuing battle. After a period of mourning, Joseph decided to leave Simbako for the British Army, convinced by his uncle who had served for ten years and had been the main influence in Sesay's young life.

Entrusting the diamond to his uncle, Joseph left for England and joined the Royal Anglian Regiment. He was the ideal material for the army, being strong and brave, but he tended to be withdrawn and didn't make friends easily. Alex had befriended him from the first though and they always went on the same patrols and bunked beside each other. He used to crack jokes and sing the latest hits when he was in the barracks, but, when on patrol, he morphed into someone a lot more frightening. His face would darken and assume a brooding stare which made people step out of his way. He became intimidation personified.

Their unit had been stationed in Northern Ireland for six months. Street patrols were a necessary part of their duties. No-one enjoyed the tense walks through the republican areas. A mother of ten had been taken away and murdered by the IRA for helping a wounded soldier on her road. There was no mercy to be found in those grey streets and you could feel the resentment boring into your back as you walked by.

One gloomy Derry afternoon, they were patrolling the Bogside. There had been large communal riot between local Unionists and police on one side and Catholics on the other the preceding night. Two Catholics had died and tension had risen to such a height that police were unable to enter the area to restore order. The army were deployed and Alex and Joseph found themselves struggling to separate the opposing sides who were keen on continuing the trouble.

Their platoon commander sent them to remove one of the main ringleaders from a side road where he had fled. They made their way along either side of the road, covering each other in case of attack. The man they sought was hiding behind a car and lashed out at Joseph with a crowbar as he went by, sending him to the ground. He stood over Joseph with a gun and cocked it. Joseph stared up at the barrel of the gun and knew he was going to die. The man laughed.

Just then Alex lunged through the air and knocked the gun sideways. It went off and the bullet ricocheted off a wall, planting itself in a car door.

Alex pinned the man to the pavement and put him in an arm lock. Joseph lay on the ground too shaken to move.

'Don't just lie there like a courtesan. We need to get out of here,' said Alex, hauling his captive to his feet.

Joseph laughed. 'And there I was, all laid out and waiting for trouble,' he said.

'You are trouble. Come on.'

# Chapter XX

Fergus left the house early. Sam slept, her right arm flung over her face as if in shame, but her slow breathing indicated a deep relaxation. She muttered in her dream but did not flinch when he brushed her hair with his fingertips. He couldn't help smiling as he remembered their mutual need searing the sheets. The feel of her skin and the strength of her embrace had percolated through his defences and her desire had invaded his being like sugar in his bloodstream.

His reaction to her passionate yielding wasn't the usual one of conquest and abandon that had clouded his relationships with other women. A warm sensation like belonging had infiltrated his senses, both alien and frightening. He hadn't felt like that since his mother had died, following which he had blocked out all memory of her by building a brick wall around his heart.

He shook himself. This was just a fling. No different to any other. He shut the door, allowing it to bang against the frame. That should wake her up. If she returned to her own room by the time Fatimata got to the house, they could avoid another tanker-sized tantrum and some burnt food. Maybe Sam would experience remorse or regret and blame him for giving her that gin and tonic. He could cope with that. Perhaps they wouldn't have to talk about it, but just skate around the truth like dancers avoiding a rough patch in the ice.

Descending the steps with one bound, he swept the leaves off the windscreen of the car and got in. He pushed the key into the starter motor and revved the engine. The tape recorder spun into life. Sam always had the volume up at ear-splitting levels and this was no exception. He lunged for the volume control as 'Dazed and Confused' filled the car. Led Zeppelin? Even her taste in music amused him. He was in trouble.

'Hello? Who's speaking?'

'Alex, it's me, Fergus.'

'Good morning. How is the patient?'

'Patient is not how I would describe her. She is back at work now.'

'Already? Christ, she must be made of steel. Have you made any progress?'

'I have extraordinary news. Maybe you should sit down.'

'You've found the Star of Simbako?'

'Buried in the terrace where we are working in the rucksack of a young man called Pakuteh.'

'Did he steal the diamond?'

'No, the Chief gave it to him before the rebels arrived at Fona as a wedding present.'

'That's some present.'

'He married Adanna in secret, at least he thought so. The Chief found out.'

'That's amazing. Where is the diamond now?'

'The Chief has it.'

'Have you broached the subject with him?'

'No, I thought you would like to do that yourself.'

\*\*\*

The bed was too big without Fergus in it. Sam sprawled like a starfish on the tumbled sheets, staring at the cracks in the ceiling. Where had he gone? She had expected to wake up next to him and have an awkward conversation before sloping off to her room to luxuriate in the afterglow of their lovemaking. Instead, she lay alone in a silent house, wondering if she had done something wrong.

Since she had been the one to cross the thin line they had been struggling to maintain, she couldn't blame him. Fergus had not put up a fight, but merely opened his arms and enveloped her. She had expected him to be like Simon in bed, but he was quite different. He'd displayed a tenderness and abandon that took her by surprise and demolished her reserve. Her tiredness had disappeared as their twin desires fought and melted into each other.

So why had he left? He was not the sort of man to need reassurance, but she had expected at least some bashful giggling and touching and discussion of what had happened. She stood up on wobbly legs and grabbed her T-shirt and knickers from the end of the bed where they had wound themselves around the metal struts. Pulling the T-shirt over her head, she ran her fingers through her hair which had a nest-like quality with several intractable knots.

She slipped on her underwear and listened for any sounds in the house. Dembo was squawking in the back yard, but she couldn't hear anyone.

The door creaked as she opened it and peeped out into the passageway. The coast was clear. She left Fergus' room and tried walk nonchalantly to her own. Once inside, she leant against the door for a moment before getting back into her bed and pulling the covers up to her neck. The sun shone high in the sky and warm shadows filled the room. She should have a shower. The water would bring her back to reality and she could comb the knots out of her hair. The tangles in her life might prove trickier to get rid of.

She gave herself one more minute to remember the passion of the night before and then she heaved herself out of bed again, throwing off her clothes and wrapping a towel around her chest. She had put weight back on, but she was still skinny compared to the plump geologist that had arrived in Simbako. Her mother's cakes filled a void in more ways than one. It was amazing what a dice with death could do to your figure. She squeezed her hips and stomach in wonder.

Then she heard Fatimata's elephantine tread crossing the living room.

'Where is everyone?' said Fatou.

'I'm here. I don't know where Fergus is.'

'Do you need breakfast?'

'Yes, please,' said Sam. 'I'm just getting in the shower. I'll be ready in fifteen minutes.'

When Fergus returned, she was sitting at the table, demolishing a plate of scrambled eggs with hot buttered toast. Such was her enjoyment that she forgot to be embarrassed.

'Hi Fergus. Where've you been?'

Fergus did not reciprocate with one of his big smiles, but the tension left his body bit by bit when she did not refer to what had happened between them.

'I phoned Alex. The satellite phone is on the blink again so I drove to the telephone exchange.'

'Is he still in Njahili?'

'Yes, as a matter of fact he's coming here for a visit to pay his respects to the Chief and so on.'

'Great, when's he coming? I hoped we might find something first.'

'Don't worry about that. He's not expecting miracles.'

'Do you want eggs, Mr Fergus?' said Fatimata, who had been waiting for a break in the conversation.

'Yes, please. Can I have three and lots of toast?'

Fatimata beamed. 'Give me five minutes. There's fresh tea in the pot.'

After breakfast, Sam went to see Dembo in his cage behind the house. She gave him the last cashews from her stash without bothering to tease him. He sidled up to the edge of the cage and made a half-hearted attempt to peck her fingers. The car's horn sounded and she sighed. Patience really was not one of Fergus virtues.

He turned the car around, gunning the engine until she got in. The music played at full blast.

'We don't have to talk about it,' she said.

'What?'

She reached over and reduced the volume. 'Don't worry. I'm not one of those girls,' she said.

Sam was not the most experienced campaigner in love, but she wasn't dumb either. She had met men like Fergus before. If you were interested, you pretended that nothing was further from your mind than romance. Like Simon really. Fergus had been rigid in his seat, but now he visibly relaxed.

'Let's go for it today,' said Sam. 'We must be close. I'd love to have something to show Alex when he gets here.'

'Me too,' he said.

Their mutual drive inspired the team who laboured with extra vigour under the hot sun. By the end of the afternoon, a decent pile of bottom gravel sat on the plastic sheeting, ready for panning. They carried it down to the river and sorted the gravel with the sieves, throwing out the larger pebbles and fine sand and reducing the material to common diamond size. The pile was divided into two parts. They poured first through the medium-sized sieves and separated the gravel further until a layer of small rounded stones remained.

At one stage, Sam rested on the chair in the shade, watching as the material reduced from a cubic meter to a bucket's worth of gravel. She made notes and drew profiles of the pit walls. This part of the terrace had not been disturbed before and clear layers of pebble gravel and sand stood out in the cutting.

Looking up, she saw Fergus standing with his back to her. She had not caught his eye all day and he had not even hazarded a wink in her direction. She sank lower over her notebook and feigned concentration. Was it only a one-night stand? How disappointing.

They spread the remaining material over plastic sheets in the sunlight which now came from low on the horizon. The obvious waste was picked out first and the gravel rinsed and spread again. Sam had not seen rough diamonds before. Squinting in the low light, she waited for something to catch her eye. The search seemed hopeless. They all seemed the same to an amateur. She leaned close to the gravel, trying to focus on each pebble.

Then she spotted a small dark stone with an odd shape. She picked it up, put it on her palm and turned it around under her hand lens. The stone was oblong with smooth sides and some obvious faces.

'What's that?' said Fergus.

'Um, I'm not sure,' she said, handing the stone to Tamba whose eyes widened. 'Do you know what this is?'

'A diamond,' he said. 'Not the best quality, but a good size, nearly half a carat, I think.'

'Let me see,' said Fergus, who almost grabbed it. He examined the stone without enthusiasm. 'This is a diamond?' he said. 'Are you sure?'

'Yes, Mr Fergus, I'm certain.'

'How exciting,' said Sam. 'Alex will be pleased.'

'I'm not convinced he'll find this of any interest,' said Fergus, still turning the stone around in his fingers and looking as if he was about to throw it away. 'Isn't it the wrong colour?'

'Not all diamonds are clear,' said Sam. 'The most valuable are pink, green and even blue. You can't tell in this light. The colour is not the only quality that determines value. The shape, clarity and the number of flaws are also vital.'

'Still looks like crap,' said Fergus.

'Beauty is in the eye of the beholder. Where there is one diamond, we should find more,' said Sam.

'This is a good terrace for diamonds,' said Tamba. No-one asked him how he knew.

The discovery of the diamond intensified the search of the washed material. Half an hour later, just as the sun sank below the horizon, one man pointed out a small crystal square. Sam would not have recognised it as a diamond, but as soon as she examined the stone, she experienced the thrill of finding something manufactured deep in the mantle and shot to the surface too fast to carbonise.

'That is a classic type two diamond,' said Tamba. 'It's worth a lot more than the brown one you found.'

'It's a lot smaller,' said Fergus. 'But even I can see that this is a diamond.'

They packed up the tools and covered the pit, leaving a guard to make sure no-one returned to dig in the night. Sam put the two diamonds into an empty film canister and zipped the container into an inner pocket of her rucksack.

'We should enlarge this pit and follow the gravel down the slope,' said Sam.

'You're the geologist. What you say goes,' said Fergus. 'Tamba, take the boys home to rest. We have a full day ahead of us tomorrow.'

The team left for their homes and Sam and Fergus returned to the car.

'Home James and don't spare the horses,' she said.

Fergus snorted. Then to Sam's surprise, he put his hand on her thigh and stretched across to look into her face. He took it tenderly in his hands and kissed her softly. So softly she thought she might faint.

'I've been dying to do that all day,' he said and started the car.

# Chapter XXI

Alex's car was parked in the yard under the tree. Its driver sat on the veranda with what appeared to be a large gin and tonic in his hand. Sam licked her lips.

'Hello, folks. The sun is over the yardarm. Shall I tell Fatimata to make you one too?'

'Yes, please,' said Fergus.

'Me too,' said Sam.

'Should you be drinking, young lady? You were dicing with death only recently.'

'She frightened the bejazus out of us,' said Fergus.

'I'm fine now,' said Sam. 'And I want a drink.'

'Two gin and tonics please, Fatou, one light, one heavy. How did it go today?'

'Not bad,' said Fergus, after Fatimata had gone inside. 'We found two diamonds.'

'You found diamonds? Where are they?'

Sam reached into her rucksack and rustled around. Alex leaned forward, craning his neck.

'I can't find them,' she said and winked at Fergus.

'You must. How could you lose them? Fergus, do something.'

Fergus laughed. 'Don't tease. Give him the diamonds.'

She passed Alex the film canister. He popped off the lid and tipped the diamonds into his hand. He rolled them around. 'Nice,' he said. 'I wasn't expecting these. It's a bonus.'

'Some parts of the terrace have been worked already, but not all,' said Sam. 'I'm hopeful that we have not yet reached the deepest part of the gravels.'

'Where did you get these?'

'In the pit where they found Pakuteh. It's in the middle of the terrace, but the bedrock slopes into the riverbank.'

'I learned about Pakuteh from Fergus. How awful for poor Adanna. That girl has no luck. Do you think there may be more diamonds there?'

'Definitely.'

'Dinner is ready.' Fatimata loomed in the doorway.

'Okay, let's eat.'

No-one spoke during dinner. Fatimata had excelled herself with the arrival of the big boss, cooking a tasty stew with potato leaves and piles of fluffy rice. Bananas baked in brown sugar followed, causing groans of approval. Afterwards, they sat drinking coffee on the balcony.

'Do you mind if Fergus and I discuss business?' said Alex.

'Not at all,' said Sam, not moving.

Alex squirmed in his chair. Fergus shrugged at him. Sam got the hint.

'I've got to go to my room and tidy up my notes,' she said standing up. Both men relaxed. 'See you later.'

As soon as she was gone, Alex turned to Fergus. 'Tell me about the diamond.'

\*\*\*

Sam sat on the chair in her room and sulked for a bit. The fact that Alex might want a private chat with Fergus had not escaped her, but she still felt left out. They were making headway now, but Alex did not appear interested in the terrace. He couldn't wait for her to leave so that he could talk to Fergus, but about what? Were they discussing the Star of Simbako? That seemed obvious. But would the Chief be prepared to part with it?

This appeared unlikely, especially since it was now bound up with Adanna and Pakuteh and the history of the village. How much was it worth? She had not got a good look at it, but Fergus' eyes had nearly fallen out of their sockets when he'd found it in the pocket of Pakuteh's satchel. It must have been twenty-five carats or more.

How irritating that she could not listen to their conversation. Hopefully, they would deem her worthy of an explanation in the morning.

Speculation over, her thoughts soon strayed to the kiss. Was Fergus some sort of magician? He was arrogant and grumpy and said inappropriate things. Not her sort of man at all, in theory anyway. That was the problem. Bad boys were always so appealing, especially ones that made you explode with passion on the strength of one long soft kiss. Was he toying with her? It didn't seem so, but there was something she didn't understand. Now she had to go to bed alone, with her blood boiling and her curiosity unassuaged. Bugger.

She was none the wiser the next morning. Sahr arrived to take her to the terrace and Fergus stayed with Alex.

'See you later?' she said.

'Perhaps, I'm taking Alex to talk to Chief Sesay. Let's see how it goes. Sahr will collect you if we are busy.'

'Okay, bye then.' But they did not answer, having already turned away to resume their conversation.

Normally, she enjoyed a day to herself with Tamba and the crew, but this was irritating. She had no choice, but to get into the car and be driven off by Sahr, who was his usual sunny self.

'Good morning, Sam. Mr Fergus not coming with us?'

'Not today. We can misbehave.'

Sahr smiled, but his eyes flickered from side to side as if he was unsure of the correct answer to that statement. 'Let's go then,' he said.

They stopped in town to buy some fresh bread, tins of tuna and big bottles of fizzy orange to supplement the lunch brought by the crew. Sam bought a large bag of homemade banana chips which were her favourite.

They arrived at site to find that the crew were raring to start and had already marked out the new pit borders. Their energy was infectious and Sam soon forgot that she was sulking and got down to making notes and suggestions. They were enlarging the previous day's pit along the line of the inclining bedrock. The material was fresh and well-sorted into precise layers, some of which contained rounded pebbles of a similar size and others which were more haphazard with a sandier matrix and fewer stones. The layers thickened towards the land edge of the terrace as the slope steepened.

They stopped for lunch and the extra provisions disappeared at lightning speed. Sam shared her banana chips with Tamba.

'Did you find it here?' she said.

'Find what?'

She laughed. 'Come on. You know exactly what I mean.'

He shrugged. 'Not here. At Mano.'

'So how come the Chief had it?'

'He dug it up in his artisanal pit. When he was younger, he used to go there and dig for diamonds.'

'So how did he become Chief?'

'His uncle didn't have any children. He died soon after Joseph came back to Fona from the British army. Chief Sesay was elected by the village elders and kept the diamond hidden all these years. I confess I thought it was long gone.'

Tamba stared at the ground and did not raise his head. He sighed.

'Let's get back to work,' said Sam.

\*\*\*

Fergus and Alex drove into the compound, creating a cloud of dust. They sat in the car waiting for it to abate and Adanna appeared on the veranda. She beckoned them in and they got out and crossed the yard. There was an odour of coffee and fat insects bombed across the compound, buzzing and chirping. A vulture sat on the roof, inspecting them with a practiced eye.

'I hate those things,' said Alex.

'They're the rubbish collectors of Africa,' said Fergus. 'Someone has to do it.'

They climbed up the stairs into the visitor's room where they hesitated. Adanna opened the door, carrying a tray of fruit juice.

'Come in. My father's waiting.' She ushered them into the family room.

'Thank God,' said Fergus. 'Those chairs outside are murder.'

The family room was claustrophobic in both heat and smell. All of the windows were shut and a single lightbulb hung on a ratty-looking wire. The Chief sat on a wide chair which all but engulfed his frail frame. He did not attempt to get up. The change in his appearance was shocking. Joseph Sesay looked as if someone had vacuumed out his insides. His shallow breathing rasped into the ears of his discomforted guests.

'Welcome,' he said. 'Apologies for my appearance. I have been unwell.'

'Not at all, Chief Sesay. I hope you will recover quickly,' said Fergus.

'I'm glad to see you,' said Alex. 'It's been too long.'

'My house will always be open to any of my brothers-in-arms,' said the Chief and held out his frail arms to embrace Alex. The two men hugged for several seconds and, when they release each other, both had tears staining their cheeks. Fergus was startled. He had not been aware of any link between the two men that predated their work in Simbako.

'My dear friend,' said Alex, still holding the Chief's hand and patting it with the other.

'You saved my life,' said Joseph. 'I wouldn't be here without you. What can I do for you?'

*** 

The team set to work with renewed vigour and, under Sam's instruction, removed all of the material, except the bottom gravel. This they transferred to the plastic sheet at the surface. The gravel was wet and the pebbles glinted in the sunlight. Sam felt a frisson of excitement.

'Careful now. There's no hurry,' she said as they edged their way down to the river with their heavy cargo.

Once they had laid the plastic sheeting down, the process of washing and sieving the gravel began. Sam took photographs of the work to distract herself from the pounding of her heart. They spread the reduced material onto the plastic. The rest of the team sat on the bank. Tamba and Sam searched, separating the barren gravel with their fingertips. Time stood still as they moved the small pebbles aside.

They both noticed it at the same time. A clear stone of about half a carat was sitting half-hidden in the middle of the plastic. Tamba reached over and picked it up.

'Lovely,' he said.

'Wow! You can understand why they drive people to war,' said Sam.

Then she realised there were two more, like bits of glass from a windscreen, lying side by side. Carefully, she removed them from the gravel and put them in her film canister. Tamba handed her the other one and she snapped the lid on tight. They kept searching and turned up one more darker diamond of a decent size.

'This must be the bottom of the slope,' said Sam. 'We should follow this gravel tomorrow.'

'Okay. I'll tell the Chief what we've found. Will you bring the diamonds for him to see?'

'I expect Alex will do that. I'll come to work as usual.'

'You're the one who found them. You're a great geologist.'

'Thank you, Tamba, but we found them together. We're a good team.'

He shook her hand and turned to direct the men to store the tools and cover the pit. Sam waited for them to finish and then walked to the car where Sahr was waiting.

'Good day, Sam?' he said.

'Not bad.'

***

The Chief sat motionless and his shallow breathing made a painful, dry sound in his throat.

Alex waited. He brushed a large horsefly off his arm and swatted it to the ground with his hat, squashing it to the floorboard with a wet crunch. The bloodstain sank into the dry wood and he watched, fascinated, as it crept along the cracks. A cough alerted him to the fact that Chief Sesay was ready to speak.

'Alex, I must apologise to you. I've broken the terms of our agreement.'

'How so?'

'I no longer have the Star of Simbako,' he said. 'It's now the property of my daughter, Adanna. If you wish to purchase it, you must speak to her.'

Alex thought for a moment.

'Will she sell it?'

'She has plans for the money. A modernisation of Fona, starting with sewers and electricity.'

'I'll pay top dollar if she sells it to me.'

'I know I can trust you to be fair. How will you calculate the market price?'

'I'll take it to the diamond exchange in Njahili and get it cleaned. They will set up an auction. That way I can bid on the diamond and win it fair and square. Adanna can come with me and witness the whole procedure.'

'An auction might raise the price you have to pay.'

'If the price goes too high, I'll retire from the auction. I want that stone.'

'You're an honourable man, but you must deal with my daughter. She won't listen to me anymore.'

'Is Adanna here today?'

'She's in her room, but I don't know if she'll speak to you.'

'Please can you ask her? I'll meet her at any time that suits.'

'I'll try. She's been in mourning for her husband and she doesn't come out often.'

'Sorry to hear about Pakuteh. She must be shocked.'

'We all were. Sorry, Alex. This matter is out of my hands and I can't help you with it.'

'I understand.'

'I will find out if she'll speak to you and let you know.'

'Thank you, Joseph, and don't fret, nothing will ever break the bond we have.'

Alex stood up to go.

'Come alone,' said the Chief.

Fergus was waiting for Alex in the car. His stormy countenance spoke volumes about his thoughts on being made to leave the room like a child while the adults were speaking.

'Any luck?' he said.

'Maybe. Adanna is in charge now.'

'Will she speak to you?'

'I don't know yet. Let's go home.'

*** 

By the time Sam got home that evening, Alex and Fergus were having their second drink on the veranda.

She had stopped off in town to have a celebratory soft drink with Tamba and Sahr and was now stifling burps.

'Hi Sam. Good day at the office?'

'Not bad.'

'Not good?' said Fergus.

'I wouldn't say that. Give me a gin and tonic and I'll show you.'

'Fatou, get the geologist a drink please.'

'I'll be back in a minute,' said Sam and she slipped through the front door. She went to her room and peeled off her dirty clothes.

After a quick rinse under the shower, she took her hair out of its bun and brushed it. As she had hoped, it had soft waves in it after being confined all day. She put on her denim shirt and clean khaki trousers and examined her reflection in the mirror. Almost glamorous, she thought.

Both men looked up as she returned. Fergus stared at her as if he hadn't seen her before.

'Is my drink ready?' she said.

'It's on the table,' said Alex. 'Did you find anything today?'

Sam gave him the canister which he shook.

'That sounds good,' he said.

After dinner, Sam put on her Walkman and lay in the hammock while the two men examined the booty. Their surprise at the day's haul had been all the praise she needed.

'The diamonds you have found will cover all our expenses,' said Alex. 'That's good work.'

'Thank you,' said Sam. 'I followed the clues.'

A car pulled into the yard with its headlights on. They covered their eyes to protect them from the glare. Sam got out of the hammock and leant over the railing. Sahr opened the door and half got out of the car.

'Mr Simmonds, Adanna will see you now.'

'Now? Okay, give me a minute.' He walked across to the car. 'I'll be back,' he said.

'Do you want me to come?' said Fergus.

'No, it's not necessary. I'll fill you in later.'

Sahr drove off as suddenly as he had arrived.

Fergus came over and stood beside Sam at the railings. She could sense him close to her, close enough to make the hairs on her arms stand on end, and she suddenly became awkward and unsure. Turning around to say something witty, she felt herself pulled into his arms. He peered down into her eyes and she drowned in his gaze.

'Did anyone ever tell you that you're as beautiful as a pint of Guinness?' he said. He had a strange look on his face.

'Um, no, I don't think so.'

'Are you some sort of witch, Sam Harris? You have me befuddled.'

She searched for an answer but was paralysed by anticipation.

'How long do you think he'll be gone?' said Fergus.

'Long enough, I hope,' said Sam.

*** 

Alex knocked at the door of Chief Sesay's house in the compound. It opened almost immediately and Adanna stood there, regal and sombre in a loose, dark robe.

'Please come in,' she said.

'Thank you for seeing me,' said Alex. 'Please accept my deepest condolences.'

'That's nice of you. Finding Pakuteh has been very shocking.'

'I can't imagine how awful that was. I'm so sorry.'

'Won't you sit down?'

Alex perched on the edge of a chair with his elbows on his knees.

'Did your father tell you why I wanted to see you?'

'He did.'

'Look, I know it's very early to talk about these things as you are so recently widowed …'

'It's been ten years. I think I always knew he must be dead. He would have come back for me otherwise.'

'Still, it's difficult for you, finally knowing for sure.'

Adanna stood up and crossed the room. She turned to face him.

'My father told me that you want to discuss the Star of Simbako.'

Straight to the point.

'May I see it?'

'Of course.' She stood in front of him, reached into a deep pocket on the side of her robe and found the stone. The smell of karité butter and rose oil wafted past his face. He put out his palm and she dropped the stone into it.

'Wow!' For a moment that was all Alex could articulate. He held the diamond between his fingers and stared at it. The oily hue did not disguise its near perfect interior. He could see a couple of flaws, but they were at strategic places in the stone and would not decrease the overall value by much. He estimated a weight of about twenty-five carats. Once they cleaned the stone, the valuation could be made in a matter of minutes.

'What do you think?' she said.

'It's amazing. I can't believe it has been found again after being buried for so long.'

'Blame Sam. She's not a girl who gives up easily.'

'I've been told.' Alex chuckled. 'She's a gem too.'

'How much is it worth, the stone?'

'I'm not sure. If you can bear to part with it, I would like to get it assessed by experts in Njahili to ensure that you get a fair price.'

'The stone is cursed. I'll be happy to sell it and send it far from Fona. We need clean water and telephones here, not lumps of carbon.'

Alex smiled. He had never heard anyone call a fabulous diamond a lump of carbon before.

'Would you like to come to Njahili and supervise the valuation? It's important a representative of the village is present at the assessment. I presume your father will not come.'

'He's not well enough. Anyway, the diamond is mine to do with as I wish. He has given me his blessing.'

Alex did not show his surprise at her dismissive tone. It was unlike the woman he had grown to admire. Something had changed her. He did not wish to interfere in local politics or family feuds so he did not comment. 'Okay. When can you travel?'

'As soon as possible. Can we go tomorrow?'

'If you wish. We can leave at mid-morning if that suits you?'

'I'll be ready.'

# Chapter XXII

Fatimata was getting ready to go to church when she noticed Adanna through the window of her house.

'Good morning,' she said. 'What are you doing here?'

'Good morning, Auntie Fatou. I need to talk to you.'

'Come in and have some coffee. We can talk in the kitchen.'

'Will you be late for church?'

'Don't worry about me. I'll say an extra prayer later. It must be important for you to visit at this hour.'

They sat in the small kitchen which smelt of spices. It was lined with shelves of mysterious bottles containing the potions bequeathed to Fatimata by her father, the witch doctor.

'How can I help you?'

'Fatou, my father is ill and may be dying. I want to be Paramount Chief.'

'But, my child, that is not possible.'

'Because I am unclean. But what if that were to change?'

'Don't even consider the possibility. It's too dangerous. You are not young enough to use the *bondo*. The *sowei* will not attend you.'

'I can use the hospital in Njahili.'

'Hospital? You'll die. Please don't risk it.'

'The hospital is modern and Sam told me people do not die there.'

'How does she know this? Sam's a clever person, but she's not from here.'

'I'm willing to try, but first I must be sure you will support me.'

'For Paramount Chief? Of course. If you are clean, no one would oppose you. But what about your father?'

'He doesn't need to find out. I'm going to Njahili with Mr Simmonds to sell a diamond for funds to help the kingdom. I'll have the procedure done while I am there.'

'Are you sure about this? It's a big step and you can't go back.'

'Fatou, what future do I have otherwise? I've decided to go ahead.'

\*\*\*

Alex Simmons packed his bag and took it outside to the veranda. Sam and Fergus were still at the breakfast table and he joined them for a cup of coffee before his trip to Njahili.

'I'd like you to finish mining the pothole before you come to town,' he said. 'Don't forget to leave a record of the production with the Chief so that we can square the accounts after I get the diamonds valued and sold. I left you a sheet to fill out. I have already noted the diamonds retrieved from the terrace before today.'

'Can you leave the weighing scale here please? We'll bring it with us too.'

'Sure. And well done on the exploration. The work has paid for itself.'

'I'll make some sections of the terrace based on the pitting we have already done and narrow down the area that we should mine,' said Sam.

'Great. Ah, here is Adanna. We'd better leave right away.'

Adanna dropped her bag beside the car and came to the veranda to say goodbye. Sam gave her a big hug.

'Can you please drop in and see my father while I am gone? He has been asking to see you.'

'Of course. Is he any better?'

'No, unfortunately his lungs are badly congested. Fatou has been trying to ease his breathing, but his lungs are weakening. He needs some relief. The last few days have taken their toll on him.'

'Good luck in Njahili. I hope the valuation goes well,' said Fergus.

'Thank you. I'll be back soon and everything will be okay.'

Alex and Adanna got into the car and drove off.

'What did she mean?' said Sam.

'By what?'

'That everything will be okay.'

'I guess she was referring to the money for Fona.'

Sam had her doubts, but she needed to concentrate on the final phase of exploration. She got to work drawing sections of the terrace from north to south and east to west using her notes and those taken by Tamba. She tutted at his terrible drawing, but he had recorded the important data so she extrapolated from that. The bedrock sloped into the northern sector of the gravels where they had found the diamonds. She traced contours onto the map, showing the depth of the bedrock and selected the best area for them to continue digging.

'Any progress?' said Fergus.

'It'll be straightforward to mine the last part of the pothole. I don't think we have reached the deepest part yet, so we may yet find more diamonds.'

'Fantastic. We'll start again tomorrow. Do you have any plans for today?'

'Do you fancy taking another trip to the diamond fields? I was hoping to recce the geology of the diggings.'

'You have a one-track mind Miss Harris. So do I, but it's a different recording.'

'Take me to the mines and I may dance to your tune later.'

'Okay, it's a deal.' He squeezed her shoulder. 'Shall we go?'

'Give me a minute to put this stuff away and get my gear.'

'Yes, *Bwana.*'

***

Sam couldn't wait to explore the diggings. She had vivid memories of their first visit to the site and the extraordinary panorama that lay below them. This sort of experience was a rare opportunity for any geologist. She would not miss it. When they reached Mano, they took a winding side road which meandered down the hillside until they reached the flats. They left the car and entered the diggings, walking along the tops of the waste heaps.

Many of the pits were deserted, but they soon reached one where a whole family appeared to be working. A noisy pump was sucking water from the

252

bottom. The men were excavating gravel and filling hessian sacks. Ragged, skinny children heaved the sacks up the slope and emptied them beside a group of women who sieved the material through ancient, holey sifters.

The children surrounded her, chirping in their high voices, asking for money and touching her white skin. They had open sores and snotty noses. Sam's romantic notions of Africa had long faded, but the extreme poverty was gruelling to see close up. She gave them some sweets she had bought in Fona. They examined them with suspicion until Sam showed them how to unwrap them and popped one into her mouth. Soon all of them were sucking enthusiastically with big smiles. Amongst them was an albino child with sunburn on his face and arms. Some of his burns were deep and weeping.

'Poor little mite,' said Fergus. 'Albinos don't survive for long here. They get skin cancer.'

'That's awful. Why don't they cover him up?'

'Many people believe albinos are the Devil's work. Gangs kill them to steal body parts for voodoo.'

Sam gasped. The boy stepped back in fright at her reaction and she tried to reassure him by smiling. Then she remembered that she had an old long-sleeved T-shirt in her rucksack. She took it out and offered it to him. He shrunk back from her, but she crouched down and held the garment out again. He grabbed it and moved away to put it on. The sleeves hung over his hands. The women laughed at him, but he modelled it, strutting along the top of the waste heaps. They called him back to work. They washed and sieved the material from the pit, but they had no luck finding any diamonds.

Sam examined the walls of the pit to see if she could help by recommending where to dig. The material was not fresh, being a mixture of sand and gravels of all shapes and sizes. She wondered how often the same material had been washed. The ragged sieves they were using meant that a diamond could easily slip through no matter how many times they processed the material.

'The chances of them finding anything here are slim,' she said. 'They should look for fresh material somewhere else.'

'I doubt there are any spots left. Every inch of this place belongs to someone and violent fights erupt if anyone trespasses,' said Fergus.

'I'm surprised they haven't invaded the terraces at Fona.'

'That is tribal land. The locals would chase off any invader before they could start digging.'

They stayed a while longer, watching the vain attempts at finding a stone - back and heart-breaking work. As they turned to leave, the albino boy offered Sam his hand to shake. She looked into his burned face and gave him a wink. Taking off her hat, she placed it on his head. He beamed tying the string tightly under his chin. His long white eyelashes stood out against his pink cheeks. Fergus shook his head.

'You can't help everyone, Sam.'

'No, but I could help him.'

He shrugged. 'Okay, Florence, let's go home.'

\*\*\*

The new hospital sat on the hillside on a side road off the main highway into Njahili.

'Can we stop at the hospital please?' said Adanna.

'Are you feeling alright?' said Alex.

'Oh, yes, I'm fine. I just want to check if they have a particular medicine for my father. He has run out.'

'Do you want me to come?'

'No, thank you, I shouldn't take long. Do you mind waiting a few minutes?'

'I hate hospitals. I'm happy to smoke a cigarette in the car park. Take as long as you want.'

Adanna pushed her way through the new chrome doors of the hospital. In front of her, the imposing reception desk was staffed by five formidable looking women. She chose the woman with the least terrifying expression and approached her.

'Good afternoon, auntie.'

'Good afternoon, madam, how can I help you?'

'I wish to talk to someone about an operation.'

'Is the matter urgent?'

'Yes, it is.'

'What sort of operation?'

Adanna blushed and gazed at the floor. She searched for the right words but found the hard stare of the receptionist intimidating. She wrung her hands and looked imploringly at the woman whose expression changed to one of sympathy.

'I think Dr Kamara is free. I will ask him if he can see you. Please wait in the reception area.'

The woman whispered something to her companion who winced. Then she disappeared behind some swinging doors. A few minutes later, she reappeared and signalled to Adanna to follow her.

'He's in room twenty-two at the end of the passage. Good luck.'

Adanna walked along the shiny linoleum floor, sliding her shoes over its smooth surface. She knocked at the door.

'Come in.' A man's voice, soft and rich.

'Good afternoon, Dr Kamara. I am Adanna Sesay from Fona.'

'My backyard. What can I do for you, young lady?'

'I need an urgent operation.'

'Please don't be shy. Patients often come to me with this issue. Do you suffer from a fistula, or are you incontinent?'

'No, neither.'

'When were you cleaned?'

'Oh, no, I haven't been yet. My father wouldn't allow the *sowei* to operate on me.'

'He's a wise man. So why are you here?'

'I want to be circumcised, so I can be Paramount Chief. My friend told me the procedure is safer to do in hospital.'

'We can't help you here.'

'I have money.'

'My dear, it's a barbarous practice which the government are about to make illegal. I can't help you.'

'Please, you must. I ...' Adanna broke into piteous tears. She wept silently, but the tears soaked the front of her dress.

'Now, now. Don't cry.'

'But I have to do this. There's no alternative. The only way I can change our kingdom is from the inside. If I don't become Chief, they will elect someone who doesn't permit change.'

'It's a big sacrifice.'

'One I am prepared to make.'

The doctor peered into her face and sighed.

'I understand your position. My family is from Mano. A female Paramount Chief would be an excellent change. Perhaps we can do something. Wait here.'

The doctor left Adanna with a box of tissues. After a few minutes, he returned with another doctor.

'This is Dr Mohammed. He's an expert in this field. Talk to him and see if he can provide an answer for your dilemma.'

Thirty minutes later, Adanna emerged from the hospital, a radiant smile on her face. She found Alex on his third cigarette.

'I'm so sorry to have kept you waiting,' she said.

'Not at all. But where is the medicine?'

'Oh, they ran out and had to ask for a new order. I must pick it up on Wednesday.'

'Good, well, that gives us two days to get the valuation and sell the diamond. Let's go to the office. You can use Sam's room.'

\*\*\*

Sam was quiet on the way home. Fergus drove with studied concentration, avoiding the worst of the potholes and they were soon back at the compound. He stopped the car and turned to her.

'Are you okay?'

'I don't know what I was expecting. I'm a little drained, that's all.'

'It's a tough life for people in Simbako. At least finding a diamond gives them a chance of a better life.'

'The odds are horrible. I feel like a fraud.'

'We all do what we can. Many families in Fona are better off because of us.'

'I suppose so.'

'Come on. Let's get something to eat. I'm starving.'

They raided the fridge and heated some leftovers on the stove. Fergus mixed the last of the gin with some old tonic and they sat down to eat.

'Cheers,' said Fergus.

'Cheers. Thank you. I'm better now.'

'That's all right. Mano is a depressing place up close.'

'How long did you live in Simbako?'

'Until I was ten, when …'

'When what?'

'My mother died of malaria. We left for England soon after.'

'I'm so sorry. I didn't know.'

'It was a long time ago.'

'Do you remember her?'

Fergus sighed. He shut his eyes as if trying to see into the past. He opened them again, but he was looking right through Sam as if she wasn't there anymore.

'She was beautiful and funny. Every day was an adventure. I remember the time we found a snake in the garden. She wouldn't let the gardener kill it and trapped the snake in a bucket. We took it to the riverbank and released it. The funny thing is it tried to bite her. She thought the whole episode was hilarious.'

'She sounds wonderful.'

'My father never recovered from her death. He sent me to boarding school so he could drink in peace.'

'That must have been ghastly for you. I'm so lucky to have both parents alive. I'm ashamed that I complain about them sometimes.'

Fergus pulled his chair closer to her. His eyes were shining.

'She was like you, Sam. I thought I would never find someone who came close to matching her, but then I met you. You confuse and beguile me in equal measure. I don't understand my feelings for you.'

Sam felt as if she would faint under his scrutiny. She searched his eyes and read pain and bewilderment. This was not her usual experience of love, but she sensed its intensity penetrate her being.

'I'm not sure what to say,' she said.

'Say nothing. There are no words for this.'

They stood up and he embraced her. His heart hammered in his chest, or was it hers? He cupped her face in his hands and kissed her. Her passion almost overwhelmed her and she pressed her body against him, but then he drew back from her.

'Let's take it slow tonight,' he said. 'We have all the time in the world.'

# Chapter XXIII

Fatimata bent over Chief Sesay and put her hand on his chest.

'You won't find anything in there, Fatou. I'm a heartless old bastard.' He laughed and his chest rattled like a viper.

'You're a good man, but you're dying. Why did you let your daughter go to Njahili? She should be here by your side.'

'She has her own destiny. I'm too old to tell her what to do. I trust Alex to pay the best price for the stone. She'll spend the money wisely.'

'Fona needs electricity.'

'Oh, I don't intend for her to spend the money here. I hope that she'll travel and see the world first.'

'She hasn't told you.'

'Told me what?'

'Joseph, your daughter intends to go to the hospital in Njahili to be cleaned.'

The Chief was struck by a fit of coughing. Fatimata helped him to sit up further on his cushions. 'Did she tell you about this? What the hell is wrong with you? Why didn't you stop her?'

'She's always wanted to be Chief. I couldn't stop her. You say that she has her destiny. This is the one she has chosen.'

'No, I won't allow it. This is not what I wanted. We have to stop her. Tell Sam to come and visit me please.'

'But Joseph …'

'Don't but me, woman. How could you let this happen? I didn't want that for my daughter.'

'We may be too late.'

'Bring Sam to me now.'

***

The traffic in Njahili ground to a halt. Alex drummed his fingers on the dashboard and whistled tunelessly. Adanna stared straight ahead, her profile serious. They pulled into the parking space outside the diamond trading building, only for a jobsworth to approach their vehicle, trying to make them leave again.

'Only bona fide buyers and sellers may park here,' he said, flapping his hands. 'You must leave.'

Alex ignored him, got out of the car and gave him a couple of dollars. He led Adanna into the hallway.

'Ah, you are buying a diamond for your engagement. You should have told me.'

Adanna laughed.

'It's not that funny,' said Alex.

'Sorry. I didn't mean to be rude.'

'I'm only kidding. Relax. Today is just the beginning. First, we have to get the diamond cleaned.'

'How do we do that?'

'They boil the diamond in acid.'

'Really?'

'Yes, hydrofluoric and nitric. Dangerous, but effective. You won't recognise the diamond when

261

they've finished. Cleaning will reveal whether any flaws are hiding under the dirt.'

They descended the stairs to the basement and entered a grimy office inhabited by a dwarf who was sitting on a beanbag stuffed on top of an antique, spindle-back chair. His legs stuck out in front of him and he had pince-nez glasses balanced on the end of his short nose. He leered at Adanna for a good ten seconds.

'Good morning, Alex. I see you've brought your niece with you today.'

Alex ignored the jibe.

'Good morning, Nelson. May I present Adanna Sesay, the daughter of Chief Joseph Sesay, Paramount Chief of Fona.'

The dwarf's eyes widened and he blushed.

'My apologies, madam. To what do I owe this honour?'

'We'd like you to clean a diamond for us and organise an auction. It's an urgent matter. Can you schedule the process for today?'

'It depends. Show me.'

Adanna reached into her bag and deposited the diamond on the table in front of Nelson. His mouth fell open and he poked at it.

'The Star of Simbako? I thought that was a myth.'

'It's quite real. Can you help us?' said Alex.

'Absolutely. Come tomorrow morning and I'll have it ready.'

'I presume you'll advise the traders about the auction?'

'They'll be here.'

Nelson took out some electric scales and placed the diamond on the plate. The digital scale showed twenty-four point six carats. He whistled in admiration and took out some forms which he filled in triplicate. 'Please check the weight and provenance. I need you to sign here and here. Then we will register the diamond with the state and royalties will be due.'

'I understand.' Alex picked up the pen.

'Not you,' said Nelson.

Alex handed the pen to Adanna who read the papers and signed at the bottom.

'Is that all?' she said.

'For now. The most important part happens tomorrow.'

***

When Sam and Fergus came home from the project that evening, Fatimata was waiting for them. They were both in high spirits, having found another five good-sized diamonds in the pit. The sight of Fatimata sitting at the table with her arms folded and a grim expression on her face took the wind out of their sails. Fergus rolled his eyes at Sam who shrugged.

'Good evening, Auntie Fatou,' said Fergus.

'Good evening, Mr Fergus and Miss Sam.'

'Are we late?' said Sam.

'No, dinner is ready in five minutes, but I've bad news.'

'What has happened?' said Fergus.

'The Chief is dying.'

'But I thought he was getting better,' said Sam.

'No, he's fighting, but he will die. I've done my best, but his body is too weak.'

'That's terrible. Should we call in and check on him?' said Fergus.

'He wants to see Sam.'

'Me? Why?'

'I don't know. You should go in the morning when he is stronger.'

'I'll go first thing tomorrow.'

'What about me?' said Fergus.

'He didn't ask for you.'

She stood up and disappeared into the kitchen where the clanking of pots and pans indicated her disinterest in continuing the conversation.

'What about Adanna? We should call her before he gets worse,' said Sam.

'I'll go to the telephone exchange right now.'

'Aren't they closed?'

'Damn, I forgot. I'll drop you off at the compound in the morning and go straight there.'

'What about the sat-phone?'

'Alex took it to Njahili to get fixed.'

Fatimata came out with the dinner which she placed on the table without ceremony.

'I must go now,' she said. 'I want to talk to the doctor.'

'Can I take you?'

'No, Sahr is coming now. Leave the plates in the kitchen. I'll wash them tomorrow.'

Just then, the lights of the jeep appeared at the gate. Fatimata waddled down the stairs to the car and struggled in.

Sahr gave them a wave and drove away.

'We should fill out the register. I want to take the sheet to the Chief tomorrow so he can sign it. Otherwise, they'll be seen as illegal and the state can confiscate them,' said Sam.

'That's true. If he dies, we can sell the diamonds to benefit the community. I'll get the scales.'

They tipped the diamonds out onto the table and weighed them one by one, noting their size and colour on the sheet. Then they put them in the film canister with the others. Neither spoke much. When they had finished, Fergus took Sam's hand, led her into his bedroom and closed the door.

***

The diamond exchange was still closed when Alex and Adanna arrived early the next morning. They went to a local hotel for coffee and returned to find that all the parking spaces were full.

'I see the word is out,' said Alex.

'What word?'

'The auction for your diamond.'

They parked the car down the street outside a local shop. The owner's son promised to look after it for a small tip and they walked back to the exchange. The place was buzzing with expectation as they entered the hall and descended to the basement. Several people in linen suits hung around outside Nelson's office. They parted to let Adanna and Alex enter.

'Ah, there you are,' he said. 'The process was a great success. The Star of Simbako is looking fantastic. Would you like to see?'

'Yes, please,' said Adanna.

Nelson spun around on his bean bag and opened a small safe in the wall. He stretched his arm into the back and pulled out a black felt bag with a gold string which he handed to Adanna. She took it from him and pulled the string. The bag opened and she let the diamond fall into her hand. She gasped.

'Wow!' said Alex. 'That's extraordinary.'

The diamond had lost the oily lustre and was now transparent, like a large, rounded, crystal of quartz. Adanna picked up the gem up and held it to the light. The stone was almost flawless.

'Now it really is a star,' she said.

'Probably worth more than one,' said Alex. 'I hope I can afford it.'

'Are you going to buy the diamond? But why are we doing an auction? I'll sell it to you with no other bidders,' said Adanna.

'I promised your father that I would pay the correct price. This way, if I'm the top bidder, I can keep my word to him. It'll be worth more when I have it cut and polished. I'll take my profit that way.'

'Thank you, Alex. You honour him.'

'The auction room awaits,' said Nelson.

'I'm ready,' said Adanna.

*** 

The next morning, Fergus dropped Sam off at the compound and went to use the telephone. She climbed the stairs of the Chief's house and knocked on the door. It was opened by Tamba who was red-eyed with grief.

'Come in. He's waiting for you.'

Tamba led Sam to the back of the house and pointed to a door on the left.

'He's in there.'

'Aren't you coming?'

'He wants to see you alone.'

Sam walked to the door and stood outside. It was open and she could see a bed against the wall. The Chief was propped up on some pillows. He gazed out of the window. Light poured in and hit the foot of the bed. The room reeked of Vicks and the fetishes hung around the bed. Sam coughed and the Chief turned his head.

'Is that you, Sam?' he said.

'Yes, it's me. Can I come in?'

'Of course. Sit on the bed so I can see you.'

266

Sam walked around the bed and sat facing the Chief. His face had hollowed out and his skin was grey. He choked on a breath.

'Fatimata told me that you wanted to me to visit.'

'I need your help.'

'My help? With what?'

'Adanna. She travelled to Fona with Alex.'

'To sell the diamond. Yes, Fergus told me. But what's that got to do with me?'

'She's planning to get mutilated in the hospital. You've got to stop her.'

'But how do you know? She didn't tell me anything.'

'You've been busy with Fergus and Alex. She discussed the risk with Fatimata.'

'But why would she do this?'

'She wants to be Chief after me. They will not accept her if she is not clean.'

'Did Alex know what she is planning?'

'I don't think so. He wouldn't agree to help her if he did.'

'Fergus has gone to phone him, but we can call again and warn him before it's too late.'

'Please find her and bring her to me. I need to talk to her and change her mind.'

'We'll do our best. I have a favour to ask you too.'

'Anything.'

'I need you to sign the registry sheet for the diamonds that certifies their origin in Fona so Alex can sell them for the good of the community.'

'Tell him I said he should first take out all the expenses and give you a bonus.'

'I'm not sure he'll believe me on that second thing but thank you.'

'No need to thank me. You've helped heal old wounds and I'm grateful you came.'

She pushed the sheet in front of him flattened on a book. He signed without checking the figures.

'Get Tamba to stamp it with the community seal.'

'I will.'

'Come closer, child.'

Sam leaned close, steeling herself against the smell of decay. The Chief lifted his hand and put it on her head.

'Bless you. Go find my daughter. Tell her to come home.'

Sam kissed him on the forehead. 'Get better soon,' she said.

Tamba was waiting outside and gave her a hug.

'Chief Sesay can't last more than a couple of days. Please hurry.'

Fergus was waiting for her outside, the engine running.

'Get in,' he said. 'We're going to Njahili.'

*** 

Alex was hungover. He was wearing dark glasses in the house to mitigate the pain caused by the sun shining through the windows. William had made breakfast and the odour was overpowering. He stifled a retch.

'Aren't you going to eat anything?' Alex said.

'No, thank you. I'm not hungry this morning. Maybe the rich food we had last night took away my appetite,' said Adanna.

After the auction they had gone to the bank where Adanna had opened an account in the name of Fona Chiefdom. Alex had arranged a transfer of the sale amount minus the government royalty, which they deducted at the diamond exchange, to the account.

'I need ten thousand dollars in cash,' said Adanna. 'I'll give you a cheque.'

'Ten thousand? It's dangerous to carry that much around with you.'

'I'll get a taxi and deliver the money tomorrow. I'm staying with my family for a couple of days.'

They had then gone to a restaurant to celebrate the sale. As usual, he had drunk too much and was now regretting it. He sat at the table and poured himself a cup of black coffee. Alex wanted to ask what the money was for, not that it was any of his business, but he resisted. Adanna was not the sort of person who invited questioning.

'Okay, I'm planning on travelling back to Fona on Saturday morning after I have finished my business in town. Does that suit you?'

'That should be perfect.'

'What about the hospital? Don't you have to pick up your father's medicine?'

'I'll do that first.'

'Are you sure you don't want me to drive you?'

'I'm sure.'

Alex had a large amount of money in cash stored in the basement of the house, a habit he had developed to ward off sudden changes in government or outbreaks of civil war. He put ten thousand dollars in a duffel bag and dropped it on a chair beside Adanna.

'There you go, be careful.'

Adanna patted the bag and carried it upstairs where she added a nightgown, a washbag and some clean clothes. She had changed into jeans and a tunic when she got to Njahili and there was no reason to believe anything other than she was a young woman off on a short visit. Alex relaxed. William went out onto the street and returned with a taxi which waited outside the gate.

'See you soon then,' said Alex.

Adanna had a strange look on her face as she left as if expecting something wonderful to happen. Perhaps she had a secret boyfriend in her life, after all. Inscrutable didn't get close to describing that young woman. Alex retreated inside for another cup of coffee.

*** 

The roads were in a terrible condition after all the rain and progress was slow. Sam changed the tape in the cassette player to break the monotony. They stopped for lunch in a small town a couple of hours from Njahili. Sam ate rice and eggs and Fergus chose a meat stew.

'What meat is that?' said Sam.

'Bushmeat, I expect,' said Fergus.

'Bushmeat?'

'Better not to ask. Could be anything, but it won't be monkey this far from the forest.'

'I'll stick with the eggs.'

'Wise.'

Sam finished her food and watched as Fergus cleaned his plate. He had cut the meat into neat cubes and now he was eating them one by one with the concentration of Dembo when presented with some cashews. She had been fighting a dilemma for several days. Fergus had all the hallmarks of a serial dumper. He got nervous if she showed any inclination to be with him. If he initiated contact, she could reciprocate, but she had to play it cool most of the time as he preferred it when she pretended she wasn't interested. Not the best basis for a relationship.

They might not get another chance to chat privately with Alex and Adanna around though, so it was now or never. She leaned forward and put her hand on his arm.

'What will you do next?' she said.

'Next?' He wiped his mouth with a napkin, pulling his arm away from her grasp. This wasn't the reaction she had hoped for.

'After Simbako, I mean.'

'Oh, I'm sure Alex will have some scheme going to keep me busy.'

'And if not?'

'Home, I guess. Why do you ask?'

Sam panicked. There was no good answer to that one that didn't involve opening herself up to rejection. Why were men so difficult? Why couldn't she just tell him that she wanted to be with him without being rejected out of hand as a defence mechanism? Why was talking to Fergus annoyingly like looking in a mirror when it came to commitment? She had probably lost Simon due to her habit of running off to foreign parts every time things got tricky.

'Um, no reason. Just wondering.'

But she saw from his expression that she had triggered the fright, fight or flight mechanism. He glanced at the door. Checking his escape route.

'I don't expect Alex will need you much longer,' he said. 'I'm leaving soon myself.'

She wanted to slap him, but instead she grunted in assent. Suddenly, a telephone rang in the background.

'Listen. They have a phone. Let's ring Alex.'

'Okay, you call him. I'll finish my lunch. Tell him we are about two hours away, roads permitting. I've got the telephone number written here.' He handed her a scrap of paper.

Sam asked the owner if she could use the phone to call Njahili.

'That will be one dollar, madam. I'll add it to the bill.'

He showed her into a back room.

'You make a local call from here. Just dial the number without the code in front.'

'Thank you.' Sam fiddled with the piece of paper given to her by Fergus and made out the numbers scrawled across it. Holding the receiver between her ear and shoulder, she dialled.

'Hello?'

'Alex, it's me Sam.'

'How are you? Where are you?'

'I'm not sure. We're in a small town about two hours from Njahili. We tried to call you from Fona, but the line is down. I'm afraid we have bad news. The Chief is dying.'

'That's terrible. We should go back at once.'

'He asked me to bring Adanna.'

'Oh, but she's gone.'

'Gone? Gone where?'

'I think she went to visit a friend. Oh, and to the hospital.'

'The hospital? What for?' A cold sweat crept up her back.

'She said she had to collect medicine for her father.'

'But … Okay, we'll see you later.'

Sam hung up. The Chief was right. They would be too late. She was panicking and her lunch invaded her throat. The toilet was beside the phone booth. She only just made it to the bowl before being sick.

Afterwards, she stood holding on to the basin and looking at her reflection in horror. As if the debacle with Fergus wasn't bad enough. This was turning into a nightmare. She cleaned up and came back outside. Fergus was standing in the doorway ready to leave.

'Are you okay? You look like hell.' He put his hand on her shoulder. 'I've paid the bill. We should leave.'

Sam began to cry. 'It's all my fault,' she said.

'What's happened? Is the Chief dead?'

Sam forced herself to speak. 'No, Adanna may be in danger. I may have done something terrible.'

# Chapter XXIV

Adanna stood outside the hospital and gazed up at the gleaming structure. The coming operation petrified her, but nothing would impede her ambitions. As if she would share power with someone like Tamba. No-one understood her. Now she had the means to escape from the destiny enforced on her by her father and to forge her own path. Fona would be hers now.

She approached the reception desk again.

'I have an appointment for surgery at midday with Dr Mohammed. I wish to pay now.'

'Of course, madam. What is your name?'

'Adanna Sesay.'

The receptionist opened a filing cabinet positioned behind the desk. After shuffling through the papers, she found the right one and brought it to Adanna.

'You need to sign here and here and date it at the bottom. How will you be paying?'

'Cash. Dollars.'

The woman's right eyebrow rose almost as far as her wig line.

'Cash? Okay, can you follow me, please?'

They stepped into a side room where Adanna emptied the money onto the table.

'Please can you wait here while I fetch the accountant from the back office,' she said.

Adanna sat on the faux leather chair, picking her nails. Her heart rose to her mouth. Waves of panic overwhelmed her. She stood up, intending to leave. At that moment, the receptionist returned with another woman.

'This is the accountant. She'll check the amount. It's nine thousand five hundred dollars in total please.'

Adanna remained standing when they entered, ready to flee at the least opportunity.

'Are you okay, dear?' said the receptionist.

Adanna shook herself. 'Yes, I thought I'd forgotten something, but I didn't.'

'Have you got the cash?' said the accountant.

Once the money had been double-checked and the papers signed, the receptionist led Adanna through to an antechamber where she had her blood taken and her vital signs noted.

'Wait here, dear. You will go straight to the operating theatre because there was a cancellation this morning. I hope you haven't eaten anything today.'

'No, not since last night.'

'Perfect. Wait here.'

Adanna became faint with anticipation and fear. Despite the reassurances from Dr Mohammed, she could not rid herself of her suspicious fear of hospitals. Sam had told her hospitals were safe though and she trusted Sam so she pushed the fear out of her mind. The door opened and Dr Mohammed filled the frame.

'Good morning, my dear. All ready for the big day? My companion, Dr Bemba, will now send you to sleep and when you wake up, it will all be over.'

The young anaesthetist made Adanna lie down on the trolley and covered her with a sheet.

'Just a sharp prick,' she said.

Adanna felt the anaesthetic burn its way through her hand, but before she had time to be alarmed, she had the sensation she was falling into a dark pit. She tried to grab the sides, terrified that Pakuteh lay at the bottom.

'There, there. Let go now and rest. Everything will be fine.'

The anaesthetist held her arms down. She had seen this irrational terror often in first timers at the hospital. Soon Adanna slept though and they wheeled her into the theatre where Dr Mohammed was having his gloves pulled on.

'Ready, everyone? This has to be perfect. Okay, let's go.'

***

Sam had stopped gabbling, but she still sat on the edge of her seat willing the car forward. Fergus had not known how to deal with the torrent of emotion and decided that his best option was to drive to the hospital as fast as he could. The roads fought him, however, wrenching the steering wheel from his hands whenever he tried to speed up. The shock absorbers were getting an unwanted workout due to the uneven pavement too.

'We'll be there soon.'

'Please hurry. Maybe we can stop her.'

'I don't understand why you feel that you are involved in this. Adanna is an adult and she can make her own decisions. We don't have to agree with them, but it's hardly your fault she planned to do this.'

'But I told her.'

'You told her what.'

'That hospitals were safe. About the big new hospital outside Njahili.'

'So?'

'She didn't do this before because she feared infection or death. Once she realised that modern hospitals didn't kill you, there was no stopping her.'

'But she would have known about it eventually. Perhaps by going now while she is still young, it has saved her from worse trauma.'

'You don't know that.'

'Neither do you. Be reasonable, Sam. The world doesn't revolve around you, no matter what you think.'

'And is that what you believe? That I imagine the world revolves around me?'

'Just a bit. But has it put me off?'

Sam sulked for a while and put on some Led Zeppelin to cover the silence. Soon they drew up to the hospital. Fergus parked the car and turned to Sam.

'Do you want me to come?'

'Can I go in first?'

'I'll have a cigarette.'

Sam leant over and kissed him without thinking and, when he didn't resist, she kissed him again for good luck.

'Get out of the car, Sam.'

She walked across the car park and entered the double doors to reception.

'Hello, have you got patient called Adanna Sesay here today?'

'Are you a relative?'

'Not exactly.'

'Then you can't see her.'

'But her father is dying and I came to give her a message.' It wasn't hard to force out a few tears in her emotional state.

'I'll see what I can do.'

Five minutes later, Sam walked into a private room in the East Wing of the hospital. It was painted in hospital magnolia with cheap furnishings and chrome beds. Adanna lay on the second of two beds beside a window looking out over the main road.

'Sam, you came. I'm so glad.'

'You were expecting me?'

'No, well yes, I thought my father would send you. Fatimata is not good at secrets.'

'I don't understand why you did this to yourself.'

'I didn't.'

'What do you mean?'

'Dr Mohammed is a genius. He has hidden the evidence. It looks like I had it done, but I still have my clitoris, it's hidden beside the urethra. I have the best of both worlds.'

'Really? That's amazing. You had me so worried. I blamed myself for you coming here.'

'Well, that was your fault, but it brought me to Dr Mohammed so the result is brilliant.'

Fergus knocked on the door. He came in with his fingers in his ears. 'Whatever you did, please don't tell me the details. Hospitals make me faint. Are you alright? That's the only thing that matters.'

'Yes, I am fine. I can leave hospital tomorrow.'

'Have you told her?' said Fergus. Sam looked blank. 'About her father.'

'Oh, God, I forgot.'

'You forgot what?'

'I'm really sorry. Your father is dying. He sent us here to get you and bring you home.'

Adanna did not reply, but fat tears rolled down her cheeks.

'We need to see Alex first this evening, but, if you wish, we can leave tomorrow when you are discharged.'

Adanna nodded.

'Your father isn't in any pain. I promise. His body is just slowing down.'

'He wanted to die without me because he couldn't bear to leave if I was at his side.'

'We may get to Fona in time,' said Fergus.

***

'You're here. Thank goodness. Did you find Adanna?' said Alex.

'Yes, she's in the hospital,' said Fergus.

'What's she doing there?'

'Um, just a minor procedure. She was too embarrassed to tell you about it,' said Sam.

'Ah, well, glad she's alright. William has made dinner. Get washed up and we'll eat.'

Dinner was delicious, but Sam struggled to do it justice. Her jumbled emotions killed her appetite. The whole affair with Adanna had confused and upset her. It may have ended well, but she felt guilty for being the instigator, even so. Alex was still hungover and didn't seem to notice. He was thrilled with the haul of diamonds from the terrace.

'I'll take them to Nelson tomorrow. Everyone will do well out of this, including you, Sam.'

'Thank you. It surprised me they had missed the best bit of the pothole. I guess Pakuteh stopped them working just before they hit it.'

She excused herself and went to the bathroom.

'I've got to go back to Britain,' said Fergus.

'Right away? Can't it wait? What about the ceremony? Aren't you coming to Fona?'

'No, I can't. Something's come up.'

Fergus avoided Alex's inquiring look.

'Sam? It's Sam, isn't it? That woman amazes me. I can understand Ned falling for her, but I thought you were an eternal bachelor.'

'I am. At least, that's what I thought. I'm panicking, Alex, I need to leave now and think about this.'

'What about Sam? Does she know you intend to leave?'

'I'll tell her this evening.'

'You're an idiot.'

'I'm aware of my failings and I don't want to hurt her, but I'm not ready.'

'Not ready? Are you sixteen? I married at twenty-one.'

'And you got divorced at twenty-six.'

'Touché. But you are thirty-five and it's not like you haven't played the field. Do you imagine there are many women like Sam wandering around the planet? You may never get the same chance at happiness.'

'I'm sorry. It will be tough on her, but I can't commit right now. I hope she isn't too heartbroken. It's not like we had a lot of time together.'

'You've been through near death situations with her. That forms bonds that are not easily broken. My friendship with Joseph was built the same way.'

'If it was meant to happen, I'd find a way. I just don't want to hurt her.'

'I don't think that's a realistic expectation. But she can deal with it. Can you?'

Their conversation was cut short when Sam reappeared. They chatted for a little longer and then Alex stood up.

'I'm going to bed. See you two in the morning.'

'Night, Alex,' said Fergus.

'Diamond dreams,' said Sam.

They were left sitting together at the table after William cleared away. Fergus poured them each a glass of whisky and water.

'Cheers,' he said.

'Cheers.'

'I've got something to tell you.'

'That sounds ominous.'

'I have to leave for England. There's a matter I have to attend to.'

'You won't be coming back to Fona with us?'

'No. I'm sorry. I wanted to spend more time with you.'

'Is that it then?' Despite the heat, a cold shiver went up her spine.

'Is what it?'

'Will I see you again? Or was it all a mirage?'

'You know I care about you.'

'I thought I did.'

'I can't explain now. You must trust me. Give me your number and I'll call you at home.'

'Alex's got it. Ask him for it.' Sam stood up abruptly and stuck out her hand. 'It's been a pleasure working with you,' she said.

'Sam!'

'Don't Sam me. Call me when you grow up.'

She ran upstairs and just got to her room before she lost control, throwing herself on the bed and shoving her head into the pillow to scream abuse and misery. She should have known. Simon, mark II. It was her fault for allowing lust to overcome judgement. She punched the pillow and bit her lip. Why was she surprised? Einstein defined insanity as doing the same thing over and over and expecting different results. She switched out the light and got under her mosquito net.

\*\*\*

Fergus had gone when she came downstairs in the morning.

'He went to the diamond exchange to register the diamonds and leave them for auction,' said Alex. 'Afterwards, he's going straight to the airport. He told me to say goodbye.'

'Do you know why he had to leave?' said Sam.

'Some woman, I expect. He's quite the lad.'

'Yes, he is.'

She forced herself to eat breakfast. Alex avoided her eyes and fiddled with his toast. Finally, he said. 'You've done a great job at Fona and I've deposited a bonus in your account along with your salary.' He paused, but Sam stared at her plate and said nothing.

'However, I came here for the Star of Simbako and mining the terraces was only secondary. Your success with the first terrace meant that I intended to continue, but the death of my dear friend, Joseph, will put a stop to that. Adanna told me she will not allow any more mining by outside parties at Fona.'

'Oh, I see.'

'I'm afraid it's the end of the line for this project.'

'That's a pity. I enjoyed working with you.'

'Before you go home, I'd like you to come with me to bury the Chief and support Adanna in her bid to succeed him. You can pick up all your stuff while you are there. I'll organise a plane ticket home for you this morning, business class.' Despite her efforts to focus on the wall, he caught her eye, sympathy on his face. 'I'm sorry. You did a hell of a job. I'll keep you in mind for the next caper.'

Sam nodded. 'When are we leaving for Fona?'

\*\*\*

'Hallo?'

'Hi, darling. Daddy and I were just talking about you. Aren't you due home for a break soon?'

'Yes, I'll be home in a few days. Alex has just gone to buy me a ticket.'

'That's nice. How's it going out there?'

'It's been amazing. Unfortunately, the project has finished. It's too complicated to go into on the phone. I'll tell you when I get home.'

'I'm sorry to hear that. You must be disappointed. But there is good news. Hang on a minute. I'll hand you Daddy.'

There was a delay on the line. No doubt her mother was relaying the news.

'Hello, sweetheart. Sorry to hear about the job. We're looking forward to hearing all about it and seeing your photos.'

'That's alright. There's plenty of work around.'

'That's the spirit. Before you go, I wanted to check something with you.'

'What?'

'The bank called this morning. They wanted to confirm that you're expecting a transfer from Simbako. The thing is, it's for twenty-five thousand dollars.'

Sam gasped. Alex owed her twelve and a half for her ten-week shift.

'Wow! Alex said he'd paid me a bonus, but I wasn't expecting that. How amazing.'

'I'm sure you deserved it. Well done, darling.'

'Thank you, Daddy. It's a long story, but I promise to fill you in when I get home.'

'Look after yourself.'

'I will. See you both soon.'

Sam put down the phone. Twenty-five thousand dollars? How much is that in sterling? The day had brightened.

Despite herself, she trusted Fergus. Whatever had happened, this was one story that hadn't ended. She was convinced of it. Perhaps he just needed time to digest his feelings for her. The manner of their parting had devastated her because he had seemed so distant. But she understood his reluctance to change the habits of a lifetime. A man like him was worth waiting for.

When Alex came back from the travel agents, she gave him a big hug.

'Thank you,' she said. 'My father told me about the bonus.'

He was embarrassed. 'I meant that to be a surprise.'

'It is. The best surprise I've ever got.'

He beamed. 'Let's go to Fona.'

# Chapter XXV

Adanna was waiting for them in the reception of the hospital. Her face was pale and she was unsteady on her feet, but her expression radiated triumph and happiness. Alex helped her into the back seat where she curled up like a cat. Sam folded up a jacket and put it under Adanna's head.

'Everything okay?' he said.

'Perfect. Thank you.'

Despite stops for toilet breaks and lunch, they made good time to Fona and pulled into the compound in late afternoon. Fatimata was waiting on the veranda. She had dressed in white. It was as if a cloud had landed. There was an anguished cry from the back of the car. Adanna jumped out and ran to the house.

'Is he gone?'

'Yes, this morning at dawn. I'm so sorry.'

Adanna sat on the steps with her head in her hands. Sam came and sat beside her. She put an arm around her shoulders. 'He is gone,' said Adanna. 'My father is dead.'

'He was a good man and brave. I owed him my life,' said Alex.

Fatimata had brought mourning outfits to the house for everyone. Adanna helped Sam to put on her red robe and headdress.

'Today you will be part of the family,' she said.

'Your father was kind and treated me with respect,' said Sam. 'I'll never forget him.'

***

After the funeral, Fatimata and the *sowei* gathered to discuss the election of the new Paramount Chief. They held the highest authority in the village besides the tribal elders who had the final say. They were entitled to put forward their own candidate. Women held equal rank as far as being Paramount Chief was concerned and, though rare, they sometimes held the position.

'I think we should recommend Adanna,' said Fatimata.

'What are you saying? She can't be Chief.'

'And why not?'

'Fatou, you know why not.'

'You are wrong. She has been cleaned and is now worthy of our vote.'

'When did this happen? Why were we not involved?'

'She went to the hospital in Njahili.'

'The hospital? Is she mad?'

'The new hospital and she is quite sane. She is waiting outside if you wish to verify the operation.'

'Call her in. I don't believe it.'

'Me neither. No-one survives hospital.'

Fatimata opened the door. Adanna was standing outside in loose robes tied at the middle. She moved to the centre of the room and undid the belt. The robes slid down her shoulder and she stood naked on the floor. The stitches stood out on her healing flesh. She turned so they could all see her. One woman knelt at her feet.

'Open your legs,' she hissed.

'Please be careful. It's still painful,' said Adanna.

The woman peered at the wound and poked the stitches. Adanna flinched, but she did not complain.

The *sowei* stood up and addressed the group. 'She is clean.'

Adanna pulled the sides of the robe back across her body and tied the belt in place.

'Aunties, you know me. You knew my father. I will carry on the work he started. We have money now. Money for water and sewage pipes. Money for electricity. We can bring Fona into this century. Please recommend me as your candidate. I learned honesty from my father, who was in the British army where it is prized. I promise to spend the money fairly.'

'What about the *bondo*?'

'Soon it will not be our choice. The government plans to legislate for a ban on cleaning of young girls. We must move with the times. How many of you have difficulty urinating? Have any of your relatives died during childbirth? Are you suffering with fistulas? Why is this a good thing? We must move into the future and protect our children. I was cleaned in solidarity with the past, your past, but I want our girls to have a future free from pain.'

There was a sullen silence. Fatimata ushered Adanna out of the room. 'Be strong. I'll persuade them. It is your time.'

*** 

They held the Coronation Ceremony in the Paramount Chief's compound. All the plastic and rubbish had been swept away and random benches placed in a semicircle in front of a platform made of old shipping pallets and covered in a tarpaulin. The throne had been removed from the ceremonial hut and placed on the platform. The whole village thronged the compound, sitting or standing depending on their seniority, waiting for the coronation. Sam and Alex sat to one side of the crowd, taking photographs and shaking hands with the locals.

There was the sound of a trumpet from the village band and the crowd parted to let a group of women enter in single file and stand in line below the platform. Sam felt a cold chill as she recognised the *sowei* women from the *bondo*. She screwed her eyes shut to push away the memories of the screaming and hung her head, considering running away. Alex noticed her discomfort.

'Are you okay?'

'Um, yes, those women in white, the *sowei*, they were about to kill me when Fatimata arrived.'

'I think you're safe now. They won't touch you here.' He reached out and squeezed her hand. She forced out a smile. Then the women sang and, despite herself, she raised her head again to listen to the rousing music. A local band did their best to keep up.

Their song silenced the crowd and a hush descended. A procession entered the compound main gate and approached the platform. Adanna sat in a sedan chair at its centre, an object of such an advanced age that its material was hanging from the sides and threatening to trip its bearers. They tottered under the weight of the chair and set it down on the ground with a thud, sweat soaking their ceremonial robes.

The dignitaries from the procession spread out onto the platform, sitting on either side of the throne. When they were all settled, Adanna stepped down from the sedan in a purple gown with blue stars and stood in front of the throne, turning to face the crowd. The tribal elders approached Adanna and one of them spoke.

'Do you, Adanna Sesay, accept the will of the people and agree to be our next Paramount Chief?'

'I do,' she said. To Sam, it sounded like a marriage vow. Until death do us part.

The elders put a lion's mane headdress on Adanna's bare head with tresses made of claws. They presented her with a staff for one hand and a club for the other. The crowd roared its appreciation as Adanna stood in full regalia to acknowledge them.

'She looks even more dangerous now,' said Alex. 'I wouldn't like to get in her way.'

Sam felt proud for her friend, who had risked all to get what she wanted. It was hard to comprehend her sacrifice, but easy to appreciate it.

Tamba lurked on the left of the dais. He was smiling, but only just. He saw Sam and Alex and waved.

'Poor old Tamba,' said Alex. 'No chance of Chiefdom for him now.'

'I thought he wanted Adanna,' said Sam.

'Only to get power.'

Was that why Fergus wanted her? To get power over her? Did he leave because she was too free?

'I think there was more to it,' she said.

*** 

After the ceremony, Sam and Alex went back to the house to take off their robes and put on their everyday clothes. Alex poured himself a drink and sat on the veranda with his feet up. Sam packed her bag, pausing to hold up Hannah's shorts and gaze at their tarty glory.

'You girls have a lot to answer for,' she said, before folding them up and putting them in her bag. If it wasn't for those shorts … Well, who knows what might have happened. She glanced out of the window and was surprised to see Adanna approaching the house.

Sam ran downstairs to welcome her friend.

'Chief Sesay, you are welcome. Come in.'

'Honestly, Sam, could you be any more formal? Call me Adanna please.'

'What is it like to be Chief? Are you excited?'

'More than you can ever imagine. I have a mountain of ideas for this place.'

'Alex tells me you'll be doing your own mining here now.'

'That's true. I am sorry if you'll lose your job, but I'm determined that we must take charge of our destiny in Fona. Mining is part of it. I've asked Tamba to train the other young men and women in the methods you have taught him.'

'Tamba? Is that wise?'

'Keep your friends close and your enemies closer, my father used to say. Anyway, perhaps if he has an important job, he won't bother me. It's high time he got married.'

'And you? Are you planning on it?'

'Not really. You?'

'Hard to say. If I don't meet the right person, I won't. But how will I know?'

'What about Fergus? I presumed something was going on there.'

'It was, is, I'm not sure. Perhaps he panicked.'

'He'll be back. If a man ever looks at me the way he used to look at you, I might change my mind if I were you.'

'I'll keep you posted.'

'So where should we start the mining operation?'

'The terrace across the river from where we were working looks fantastic. You should send Tamba there.'

Adanna laughed, her whole body shaking with mirth.

'We won't be mining that terrace in a hurry.'

'Why not? I've had a look at the geology and it's the most prospective of them all.'

'Where do you think we buried the rebel bodies?

<<<< 0 >>>>

Thank you for reading my book. If you enjoyed it, won't you please take a moment to leave me a review at your favourite retailer?

# Other Books in the Sam Harris Series

## Fool's Gold - Book 1

A drunk historian, a dodgy entrepreneur and a lost Inca Treasure - Has rookie geologist Sam Harris bitten off more than she can chew?

Newly-qualified geologist, Sam Harris, is a woman in a man's world - overlooked, underpaid, but resilient and passionate. Desperate for her first job and nursing a broken heart, she accepts an offer from notorious entrepreneur, Mike Morton, to search for gold deposits in the remote rainforests of Sierramar. With the help of nutty local heiress, Gloria Sanchez, she soon settles into life in Calderon, the capital. But when she accidentally uncovers a long-lost clue to a treasure buried deep within the jungle, her journey really begins.

Teaming up with geologist, Wilson Ortega, historian, Alfredo Vargas, and the mysterious, Don Moises, they venture through the jungle, where she lurches between excitement and insecurity. Yet there is a far graver threat looming though when Mike and Gloria discover that one of the members of the expedition is plotting to seize the fortune for himself and is willing to do anything to get it. Can Sam survive and find the treasure or will her first adventure be her last?

The first book in the Sam Harris Series sets the scene for the career of an unwilling heroine, whose bravery and resourcefulness are needed to navigate a series of adventures set in remote sites in Africa and South America. Based on the real-life adventures of the author, the settings and characters are given an authenticity that will connect with readers who enjoy adventure fiction and mysteries set in remote settings with realistic scenarios.

Set in the late 1980's, themes such as women working in formerly male domains and what constitutes a normal existence are examined and developed in the context of Sam's constant ability to find herself in the middle of an adventure or mystery. Sam's home life provides a contrast to her adventures and feeds her need to escape.

You can download this book free at your favourite retailer or buy it in paperback. Please go to the website for links. (www.PJSkinner.com)

## Hitler's Finger - Book 2

The second book in the Sam Harris Series sees the return of our heroine Sam Harris to Sierramar to help her friend Gloria track down her boyfriend, the historian, Alfredo Vargas. Alfredo, and journalist, Saul Rosen, have disappeared while searching for a group of fugitive Nazi war criminals. Sam and Gloria join forces to find them and are soon caught up in a dangerous mystery. A man is murdered, and a sinister stranger follows their every move. Even the government is involved. Can they find Alfredo before he disappears for good?

The basis for the book is the presence of Nazi war criminals in South America which was often ignored by locals who had fascist sympathies during World War II. Themes such as the tacit acceptance of fascism and local collaboration with fugitives from justice are examined and developed in the context of Sam's constant ability to find herself in the middle of an adventure or mystery. Sam's home life provides a contrast to her adventures and feeds her need to escape.

Her continuing attachment to an unsuitable boyfriend is about to be tested to the limit.

You can buy this book at your favourite retailer in digital format or in paperback. Please go to the website for links. (www.PJSkinner.com)

## The Pink Elephants (Book 4)

Sam gets a call in the middle of the night that takes her to the Masaibu project in Lumbono, Africa. The project is collapsing under the weight of corruption and chicanery engendered by management, both in country and back on the main company board. Sam has to navigate murky waters to get it back on course, not helped by interference from people who want her to fail. When poachers invade the elephant sanctuary next door, her problems multiply. Can Sam protect the elephants and save the project or will she have to choose?

The fourth book in the Sam Harris Series presents Sam with her sternest test yet as she goes to Africa to fix a failing project. The day to day problems encountered by Sam in her work are typical of any project manager in the Congo which has been rent apart by warring factions, leaving the local population frightened and rootless. Elephants with pink tusks do exist, but not in the area where the project is based. They are being slaughtered by poachers in Gabon for the Chinese market and will soon be extinct, so I have put the guns in the hands of those responsible for the massacre of these defenceless animals

# Connect with the Author

**Digging Deeper** - Book 6 in the Sam Harris series - is in the works for a 1st September launch. Sam is kidnapped by rebels while working in the diamond fields of West Africa. Can she survive the ordeal or will this adventure be her last?

If you would like updates on the latest in the Sam Harris Series or to contact the author with your questions please use the following links to join my newsletter for updates and special offers:

Website: www.pjskinner.com
Facebook: www.facebook.com/PJSkinnerAuthor
Twitter: www.twitter.com/PJSkinnerAuthor

# About the Author

PJ Skinner is the author of the Sam Harris Series of adventure mystery novels. A geologist who has spent thirty years roaming the planet and collecting tall tales and real-life experiences, she now writes fact-based novels from the relative safety of London. She still travels worldwide, collecting material for the series and having her own adventures.

The author is working on the fourth book in the Sam Harris Series, *The Pink Elephants*, about gold exploration in West Africa, which will be published at the end of 2018. She is also researching two other new books, one of which, Rebel Green, is being written using her background knowledge of a childhood spent in Ireland.

The Sam Harris Series will appeal to lovers of adventure and mystery. It has a unique viewpoint provided by Sam, a female interloper in a male world, as she struggles with alien cultures and failed relationships.

Made in the USA
Middletown, DE
03 August 2021

45319797R00182